F

"Belinda Acosta's DAMAS, DRAMAS, AND ANA RUIZ delivers all its title promises and more: It's a book about damas of all ages, from teenage girls to the struggling mothers of those teenage girls; it's packed with drama so you don't want to stop reading; it's a novel that deeply and honestly tells the story of Ana Ruiz, her own coming of age as a woman and as a mother. Belinda Acosta is up to all of the challenges of such a rich panorama of characters and events. She's sassy, she's smart, she makes it look easy! But it takes a lot of hard work and a pile of talent to write such an engaging, touching book. A wonderful quinceañera of a novel!"

—Julia Alvarez, author of *Once Upon a Quinceañera: Coming of Age in the USA* and *Return to Sender*

DAMAS, DRAMAS, AND ANA RUIZ

A Quinceañera Club Novel

BELINDA ACOSTA

GRAND CENTRAL
PUBLISHING

NEW YORK   BOSTON

Copyright © 2009 by jacob packaged goods LLC
All rights reserved. Except as permitted under the U.S. Copyright
Act of 1976, no part of this publication may be reproduced,
distributed, or transmitted in any form or by any means,
or stored in a database or retrieval system, without
the prior written permission of the publisher.

Grand Central Publishing
Hachette Book Group
237 Park Avenue
New York, NY 10017

Visit our Web site at www.HachetteBookGroup.com.

Printed in the United States of America

First Edition: August 2009
10 9 8 7 6 5 4 3 2 1

Grand Central Publishing is a division of Hachette Book Group, Inc.

The Grand Central Publishing name and logo is
a trademark of Hachette Book Group, Inc.

Library of Congress Cataloging-in-Publication Data
Acosta, Belinda.
Damas, dramas, and Ana Ruiz / Belinda Acosta.—1st ed.
p. cm.
Summary: "The first book in a new series that explores the
relationship between mothers and daughters and revolves
around one of the most important days in a young girl's life: her
quinceañera"—Provided by publisher.
ISBN 978-0-446-54051-3
1. Mexican American teenage girls—Fiction. 2. Mothers and
daughters—Fiction. 3. Mexican Americans—Fiction.
4. Quinceañera (Social custom)—Fiction.
5. Domestic fiction. I. Title.
PS3551.C57D36 2009
813'.54—dc22
2008044700

Book design and text composition by Greta D. Sibley
Cover design by Brigid Pearson
Cover photo by Herman Estevez

To my mother,
Geneva Acosta,
who deserves more credit
than she's ever received;
and to my father,
Eugene S. Acosta,
who continues to wait
for a miracle.

ACKNOWLEDGMENTS

Mil gracias to my sistah scribes for keeping me upright when I felt most like crashing: Maribel Sosa, Pat Alderete, Liliana Valenzuela, and Amelia Montes. My deep appreciation to Rosalind Bell, who graciously lent me a few days of respite at Casa Azul in San Antonio, Texas, and to Sandra Cisneros and the staff of the Macondo Foundation who greeted me warmly, then left me the hell alone to work. A bit of kitty crack to Max and Marie for providing amusement.

For sharing their San Antonio with me, un abrazo and mil gracias to: Elaine Ayala, JoAnn Carreon Reyes, George Ozuna, and every person throughout San Anto heard and overheard.

My heartfelt thanks to Isabel Guerrero for inviting me to her daughter's quinceañera mass. Thanks to Silvia Reveles, who sees and hears young people every day, and shared her observations. I thank my lucky stars Stuart Bernstein agreed to be my agent, and that Grand Central Publishing Editor Selina McLemore read the manuscript closely and offered her thorough, thoughtful notes. Props to Ellen Jacob for bringing everyone to the table. And finally, to my brother in all things writing related, Vicente Lozano, who struggles with words, understands what the work requires, and does it anyway.

—Belinda Acosta
October 3, 2008

DAMAS,
DRAMAS,
AND
ANA RUIZ

≫ PROLOGUE ≪

Don't let anyone tell you that being a woman is like—cómo se dice?—a piece of the cake. Mira, take a look around. All these niñitas dressed up like Barbie dolls outside of Our Lady of Guadalupe Church, their toes scrunched into pointy high heels, hair pulled into tidy buns, bangs springing over their foreheads or hanging in gaunt strands alongside their girlish faces. The smell of hairspray and designer perfume, starched shirts and polished shoes mingle in the air. The matching boys are tucked into tuxedos looking like they want to be someplace else. They do! The Spurs game starts in thirty minutes. The limo driver, allá, is looking at his watch for the same reason. And then there's pobrecita Ana Ruiz. That poor woman! All she wanted was to have a small quinceañera, a nice way to celebrate her niña Carmen con cariño. She wanted Carmen's fifteenth birthday to be special and lovely. Instead, there she is, the one in the lilac dress, her wavy hair going flat and her feet screaming from running around in heels, taking care of one disaster after the next. Today, she looks older than her thirty-eight years, weary from months of worry. The few streaks of gray she has, she got this month alone! Still, everything about Ana is

soft—her hands, her laugh, the color of her amber skin.
She has a small patch of dark skin below her ear that some
women get when they have babies. But because Ana is
what you would call pretty, you don't even notice. She's a
good-looking woman; thin, but with meat in all the right
places, as the men might say. For the women who need
to be the center of attention when they walk into a room,
Ana is the last one they worry about. They think, *She's
like a sugar cube*—easy to melt with the heat they make
with the sway of their nalgas or the heave of their chichis.
But oh no! Ana is the one that surprises them. With those
bésame mucho lips, the whispery hollows of her cheeks, the
way her neck curves like poured water, and finally, that
look from her smoky black eyes—that alone will make
some men walk into walls while the women, who thought
they were the main dish at the party, will cluck to themselves and think, *Her? Quién es esa?*

You can tell right away that Ana Ruiz is respectable.
She's no spring kitten, but she's way too young to cover it
up in housedresses. But right now, Ana doesn't care what
she looks like. She's wondering how this wonderful day
turned to this. All she wanted was a little tradition, a nice
way to mark this time in Carmen's life and maybe get back
to the way things were before Esteban left.

Carmen is officially becoming a woman today, in a time
when becoming a woman happens in a flurry like a million
cascarones broken over your head. Just this week, she was
figuring out the best way to brush her hair to make the
tiara sit just so. Pero, no one knows where the tiara is now
and Carmen doesn't even care. Today means nothing and
everything to Carmen who, right now, only really wants
to know, *When will this pinche day be over?*

Ana is standing near the door of the church. No one would be surprised if she snapped in two from all this drama! But no, like always, there she is: like a blade of grass in a hurricane. You can smash her down but she will never break. She's the one they call a strong woman, though she never understood why. She would say she only did what she had to do and that if patience and hard work are what it takes to be a strong woman, then okay, call her what you want. But right now, she feels spent. She feels like she might lose it. Her son, Diego, didn't come home last night, and Carmen has been barfing since midnight. The band that showed up is not the nice mariachi Ana thought was coming but three boys, one with tattoos on his arms and silver rings poked aquí y allá on his face and ears. And did I tell you about the cake? The cake is late. There was talk that there might not even be a cake, and well, you can't have a quinceañera without a cake, can you? Well, the cake finally comes, right after Ana made some calls and that girl they call Bianca tore her dress (accidentally on purpose, if you ask me). One of the boys in the court showed up with a black eye. And just when it seemed like the ground should open up and swallow this whole mess, then, *then* there comes la señora with the cake. Four stories tall, all pink and sparkly. Bien pretty, but late. And because she's late she shows up in shorts and chanclas. No "discúlpeme." No "perdóname." Instead, she laughs como la loca, saying she's on Mexican time. "Mexican time"? Ay, por favor! La señora toda sin vergüenza in those chanclas and that thing stuck in her ear like she works in the secret service.

One of the boys in the band goes to help la señora with the cake, and then so does the boy in the tuxedo with the black eye. They're all talking, no one is listening, and everyone wants to be in charge. So of course you know what's going to happen, right? La señora with the chanclas and the boy with the black eye he can hardly see out of, they look like they're going to crash. I see the whole thing before everyone else. I see the whole picture. I can tell you why Ana is wrung out. I can tell you why Carmen is sick. I can tell you why Ana and Carmen have been fighting. I can tell you where Diego is. I can tell you why the cake is late and why that boy has a black eye. And I can tell you if, and when, that cake is going to fall.

Pero, let me go back to the beginning. The very beginning, because híjole! I love a good quinceañera story. And I got to tell you this one.

ONE

Ana was finishing her coffee when she saw the full-
page ad in the morning paper:

*Everything you need for the ultimate
teen birthday party!*

"Take a look at this, mi'ja." Ana slid the paper toward
Carmen, who was stuffing her backpack for school. Carmen glanced at the paper, then up at her mother, then back
to her backpack. It didn't matter if Ana asked Carmen for
the time or if she wanted a new car; the look was always
the same: a sour mix of annoyance with y qué? It was a look
Ana had come to expect but would not ever get used to. It
was a look Carmen had since her beloved 'apá moved out
of their house a month earlier. They called it a separation,
something temporary to work things out. Carmen didn't
care what they called it. She didn't like it. She didn't like it
at all, and it was all on Ana where she put the blame. To
say Carmen was angry was to put it softly. That girl was
as furious as a blister, as mean as a sunburn, as popping
mad as water sprinkled on hot oil. Carmen Ruiz was as
angry as a fourteen-year-old daddy's girl can be without
her hair catching fire. And even though the girl with the

sweet round face and her mother's eyes could be so, so—
órale, let's just say it, cabrona!—Ana wanted her daughter
back. She wanted things to go back to the way things were
between them, and she had a plan.

"Let's go to this," Ana said.

"Why?"

"To check it out. I've been thinking—it would be nice
to have a quinceañera for you."

"Why would you think that?" Carmen snapped. But Ana
goes on like she didn't hear the sting in her daughter's voice.

"It's a nice tradition. I've been hearing a lot of girls are
having them these days."

"Did you have one?" Carmen asked.

"Well, no," Ana said, "but that doesn't mean you can't
have one."

Carmen was wishing her mother would have said,
"Yes," so she could have said, *Well, then what makes
you think I'd be interested in that old-fashioned thing?* or
what she was really dying to say, *What makes you think I
want to be like you?*

"It says the expo is this Sunday," Ana said. "Maybe we
could have a nice breakfast somewhere and then go. You
know, just you and me." Carmen kept digging in her backpack. She wasn't looking for anything; she just didn't want
her mother to have all her attention.

It's been a month already, Ana thought. Longer if you
counted all the hushed talk behind their bedroom door,
and the long nights when pobrecita Ana would cry into
her pillow after Esteban left in the middle of the night.
Maybe it wasn't the best way, but they waited till the lat-
est possible time to announce the separation to their kids.
So, when Carmen and Diego finally learned what had happened, they felt as if the house they grew up in had fallen

on top of them. With Esteban gone, Ana was left to poke through the remains and put things right again. Diego, the oldest, was sad and brave. He did his best to help around the house and look after his mother and sister, but Carmen—ay, Carmen!—that one wasn't making it easy. She was so sure that the reason her father left was all her mother's fault. Carmen clung to her anger and held it so tight it left a mark on everything she said or did.

Ana noticed the time and gulped down the last of her coffee. She pulled on her navy linen blazer and inspected herself in the mirror as she tied a rose-colored scarf around her neck, which looked good against her amber skin. It was going to be a busy day at work, and she liked this outfit because it was comfortable but professional, and if she were to take the time to notice, Ana would have to agree that she looked bien pretty, too.

"Dieguito! Vámonos, mi'jo!" she called.

"He's gone," Carmen said. Ana felt panicked.

"What do you mean, 'he's gone'?"

"He's gone. You know, to school? That place you send us to during the day?"

"I didn't hear him leave."

"Yeah, well, se fue," Carmen said. "Bianca is coming for me, so you can go." (Hear how she talks to her mother? Híjole!)

Ana hated it when Diego wasn't around. Her son had a way of sweetening Carmen's bitterness. It wasn't what he said or did; it was something about his quiet way. He wasn't angry like Carmen. Ana was thankful for that, only she wasn't sure *what* he was feeling these days. Because of this, Ana said he took after his father, but really Diego took after Ana—serene on the outside but twisted with worry on the inside. Oh, Diego was suffering like Carmen, all right; he just didn't make a show of it. Diego was the cool water to calm the pot that was always on the edge of boiling over when Carmen and Ana were together. Mornings in the Ruiz house used to be so nice. They were always hectic, the way they are when everyone is scrambling to get out the door to school and work. But Ana loved it. It used to be a calming start to her day, being with her babies—her corazones—before sending them out into the world. Ay, Ana would take a bullet for those kids, even that ungrateful girl who decided that Ana was to blame for everything gone wrong in her world.

"Okay, mi'ja." Ana stood up and gave Carmen un abrazo, but Carmen did not hug her back. Ana swallowed the lump in her throat and tried to ignore the stab in her heart. She wanted to take her daughter by the shoulders and wail, "Do you think this is fun for me!" But no. Instead, she calmly pulled the car keys from her purse and left for work. By the time she reached her car, the tears had swollen in her eyes and had spilled down her cheeks. When she got into her car she looked into her rearview mirror and patted dry her mascara with a smashed tissue from the bottom of her purse.

To call Bianca de la Torre Ana's niece was not enough. That girl was a cotton-candy tornado. Just as Ana was pulling out of her driveway, Bianca screeched up in her bubblegum-pink VW Bug (the girl was all about the pink). Although she was what most would call a girly-girl, Bianca could handle a car like los NASCAR drivers. She barely missed the bumper of Ana's car, a clunker they called La 'Onda, because the silver *H* in the grill had been knocked out, so it smiled at the other cars like a jack-the-lantern. Bianca brought her Bug to rest partly on the curb, the street, on the drive, and over the trash can left on the curb from the night before. Ana angrily pushed open her car door and pounded down the driveway toward her niece. Bianca was sixteen, two years older than Carmen. She was lean and curvy like most of the girls in the family, but unlike the rest of them, she was blond with sea-green eyes, something that used to bother her when she was a little girl. As a teenager, she came to accept her "güera" label. So, when some tonto said, "Hey, how come you don't look Mexican?" Bianca replied, "We come in all flavors, menso!" turning on her heel to leave the baboso, her ponytail snapping like a whip.

Bianca smiled as she popped up through her car's sunroof, her honey-blond locks pulled tightly from her long face into a high ponytail. Ana groaned when she saw her trash can wedged under Bianca's Bug.

"Hola, Tía!" Bianca called out over the blare of her car stereo. She pushed her white-framed sunglasses to the top of her head. Ana thought Bianca's eyeliner was a little too thick, ending in dramatic wisps at the edges.

"Bianca!"

"Mande?"

"Look at my trash can!"

"Cómo?"

"Bianca! Turn down the da—"

As soon as Ana got to the part that would make the neighbors gasp, Bianca had turned off the music and popped up through the sunroof again.

"Ay, Tía!" Bianca said playfully, shaking her head side to side, her chongo bobbing like a spring. Ana went to pull her trash can out from under Bianca's bumper.

"It's okay, Tía. I'm sure it didn't hurt my car." Ana threw Bianca a look that could have frozen the sun. "Can't you just buy another one?"

Bianca wasn't trying to be smart. She honestly thought that that was the way to solve this and any other problem.

"That's not the point, Bianca!"

After two hard tugs, Ana freed the trash can. She thought about hauling it back to the house, but now she was really late for work. She pushed the trash can to the curb where it fell with a thud and turned back to her niece.

When Bianca saw Ana's eyes, she knew her aunt was not in the mood for tonterías.

"I'm sorry, Tía. If there's something wrong with the trash can, I'll buy you a new one, okay?"

Ana knew it wouldn't be her but Bianca's father who would buy the new trash can. The last thing Ana wanted was to give her older brother, Marcos, a chance to lecture her on how Esteban moving out was a bad idea, on how a good man is hard to find ("especially the way you are"), and on how she could save herself a world of struggle by forgiving her husband and letting bygones be bygones already.

"It's fine, mi'ja. Just move your car. I'm late for work."

Ana pulled out of the driveway and drove her car alongside her niece's so the driver-side windows were next to each other. Bianca pulled her sunglasses down over her eyes. She hated to see how tired and sad her tía looked at the beginning of the day.

"Have a good day at school—and be careful!" Ana said.

When Ana pulled away, Bianca zipped her Bug back and forth and charged into the driveway, honking the horn in time with the music she'd turned back on full blast.

Carmen would have heard the whole thing except she was reading the ad for the quinceañera fair.

Everything you need for the ultimate teen birthday party!

The curly letters were as bright and bouncy as Bianca. Carmen tore the ad from the paper, stuffed it into her backpack, and ran out to meet her cousin.

≋ TWO ≋

"What's that?" Bianca asked, as she backed out of the driveway. Carmen looked at her jeans, checked the top button on her fitted white blouse, felt for the chandelier earrings she'd decided to wear, and ran her hand through her hair, pulling a long wisp of espresso-brown hair behind her ear. She'd just gotten what she called a "posh bob"—short in the back with a long wedge of bangs that swung to the front. The cut was qué cute with her round face, but she was still self-conscious about how it looked; she hadn't got the hang of how to use the hot iron to get her wavy hair to behave like she wanted.

"Do I have a moco or something?" Carmen asked, pulling down the visor to inspect herself in the mirror beneath. Two pink lights blinked on when the visor was opened.

"No." Bianca waved a white-tipped nail toward Carmen's feet. "That."

"My backpack? What about it?"

"It's not made by me, for one thing. Pick one." Bianca motioned toward the backseat, and when Carmen turned to look, she saw it was covered in layers of bags, round ones and square ones, some with big geometric patterns in sharp colors, others in Mexican oilcloth, bursting with tropical flowers set against bloodshot reds and neon blues. The only black to be found was in the trim around the seams and zippers.

"Dang, Bianca! What's all this?"

"I made them, like I told you I was going to. Take one."

"For real? Dang, girl, don't you ever sleep—oooh!" Carmen grabbed a bag patterned with pumpkin and raspberry checks, a large white calavera with a garland of bright roses around its forehead. Bianca smiled. This was the bag she'd made especial for Carmen.

"You're my model. Once everyone sees them, the orders will come in. So don't leave it in your locker."

"This calavera looks painted."

"It's silk-screened."

Bianca bit her bottom lip all nervous as Carmen carefully inspected the bag.

"So?"

"Dang, B. This is *sweet*!"

Bianca was relieved. Carmen happily moved the stuff from her old backpack to her new bag, stopping when she pulled out the ad for the quinceañera fair.

"You won't believe what my mom asked me this morning. She wants me to go to this quinceañera fair."

"Shut. Up!"

"Can you believe it?"

"Where? When is it?"

Carmen rolled her eyes. Of course Bianca would be excited about a quinceañera fair. She was sorry she brought it up.

"Sunday," Carmen said. "Hey, does this thing have a place for your cell?"

"Pos, yeah. What time Sunday?"

Carmen shrugged, putting all her attention on the little zippers and pockets on her bag. Bianca peeked over her sunglasses at Carmen.

"You're going, right?"

"Oh, hell no!"

(Ay, por fa'! You would think Bianca had told Carmen to shave off her eyebrows or something.)

Bianca screeched to a stop.

"You should go."

To be all dramatic, Carmen crumpled the ad in her fist.

"You should totally go!" Bianca said. A car behind them honked, and Bianca surged forward as Carmen looked at the ad again.

"She just wants us to go so she can act like everything is normal."

Bianca remembered the look on Ana's face. She knew everything was far from normal in the Ruiz house. Her tía Ana's house was where she'd gone to birthday parties and Easter egg hunts, where she had helped set up a family altar for Día de los Muertos and then dressed up as a princess for Halloween. It was the place she had gone to slumber parties as a little girl and woke to the warm, sweet aroma of her tía's famous buñuelos the next morning. Ana had always warned Bianca and Carmen about making a mess, but the girls always managed to get cinnamon and sugar all over their faces and hands, and one time in their hair. But Ana always seemed to forget the next time around. Bianca remembered the long, matching pink T-shirts the two of them wore as nightgowns (Carmen wasn't anti-pink back then), the two of them giggling like changuitos till they fell asleep. The next morning, they were the first ones up (after Ana), ready for the first, sweet crunch of a warm buñuelo. Bianca remembered how it flaked onto their plates, sugar sparkling on their cheeks as they licked their fingers and drank ice-cold glasses of milk. Bianca decided Ana was the closest thing she had to a real mother. She would never say that out loud because it would cause drama between Bianca and her father, between Bianca and Ana, and probably between Bianca and Carmen (even though Carmen was anti-Ana lately). Bianca didn't like to think about the woman who used to be her mother. She pushed her sunglasses firmly over her eyes. She wanted to be excited about her new bolsas and how popular they would be. She wanted to think about having a quinceañera, even if it wasn't her own.

"Quinceañeras are nice, or they should be," Bianca said, remembering her quinceañera that wasn't, as Bianca said to Carmen and to Carmen only, "the year my mother lost it."

"Come on, Carma. It will be fun! We could dress up and have a party with cool music . . ."

"*You* would have fun dressing up and having a party. I would have to bring the music since you don't know what's good unless I tell you," Carmen teased.

"Shut up—"

On the stereo, Piñata Protest took off into their punk version of "La Cucaracha." She turned it up to drown out Bianca, like that was going to stop her.

"Come on, Carmen! I bet Mari and Amelia would be on your court. And what's her name, Alicia was a quince last month. She'd be on your court. For the rest, you can get the Valley girls . . ." The Valley girls were a string of cousins from Laredo to Harlingen, and every South Texas town that had a Dairy Queen in between.

"They'll do it. They always want a reason to come up here."

"The Valley girls hate us!" Carmen reminded her cousin.

"Only the twins from Laredo, and they hate *you*—you think that's going to stop them from being damas?" The ideas were flooding in, and Bianca gasped.

"Oh! You know what you should do? Get Sonia on the court—" Bianca screeched to another stop. "Ay! Diego! Was I supposed to give him a ride, too?"

"No, he walked over to get a ride with Rafa so he could see Sonia."

"When's he going to make a move or something? See? That's why you should have a quinceañera. So you can get Dieguito with Sonia already."

Bianca pulled into the school parking lot, her pink Bug prowling like Pac-Man, up and down the rows. Bianca was leaning forward, concentrating on finding a parking space— or so Carmen thought, until Bianca blurted, "Tomás could be your escort!"

"Tomás? You mean Louis?"

"Louis? Who's Louis?"

"Tomás, Louis—it doesn't matter. I'm so over high school boys, B."

"What about your mom, then?"

"She can't be my escort."

"Very funny. I mean if your mom is bringing it up, she must want you to have a quinceañera."

"Bianca." Carmen ejected the CD from the stereo, all serious-like. She wanted to make sure her cousin heard every word she had to say. "I don't want a quinceañera. It's not right with things the way they are."

"Well, just go to the fair with your mom, then. I think she would like it."

"I don't care what she likes!" Carmen yelled, as Bianca pulled into a spot under a pecan tree. "Did she think about what me or Diego would like when she kicked my dad out? She wants to act like everything is normal, and it's not." Her eyes frosted with anger.

"Your mom isn't like that."

"You don't know what my mom is like! When your mom . . ." Carmen could not finish. She didn't know what to say—or if she should say anything—about Bianca's mother. Things were already crazy-upside-down at home. She didn't need to make it that way with Bianca. "You just don't know."

"I know you have a mom who's trying," Bianca said flatly.

The CD stuck out from the player like a bratty kid's tongue and Carmen yanked it out.

"Isn't this mine?"

Carmen felt bad yelling at Bianca, but lately it was getting harder and harder for Bianca to hear her, or for Carmen to be heard by her cousin. She couldn't decide which. A heavy silence filled the car. Carmen opened her car door to let it out and to breathe in the clean October morning. Bianca began to gloss her lips and check her eye makeup while Carmen dug inside the glove compartment.

"It's not there."

"Huh?"

"It's not in there," Bianca said a little louder than she needed to. She wanted to be heard, too. "The case. You're looking for the case, aren't you? There isn't one. I got it on my iPod now. Take it, if you want." Carmen wrapped the naked CD in the quinceañera ad and stuffed it in her bag. She climbed out of the car and pulled her new bag over her head so it slung over her shoulder and across her chest. The cut and shape of it followed the line of her body, with the fullest part of it cupping her hip.

"So?" Carmen asked.

"It looks good," Bianca was happy to say.

"What about me?"

"You always look good. How does it feel?"

"'Stá bien. It feels good, B."

"For real?"

"For real."

"Ándale!" Bianca said. "Go on. My first class isn't for an hour."

Bianca watched Carmen walk into the crowd of kids. She had barely reached the front steps when she saw a couple of girls admiring her bag. Bianca sighed a small, sad sigh, not because she wasn't happy but because she knew before "the year her mother lost it," she would have been pleased, too.

⧼ THREE ⧽

Ana was making good time on the I-10, almost at the I-35, where she would take it straight into downtown San Antonio and right onto the university. An old Stevie Wonder tape played on her cassette deck (Ana was—how did her Diego say it?—todo "old school"). The bad feelings from the morning were fading and Ana was almost smiling, listening to Stevie sing "Isn't She Lovely?" happy as a jingle bell. (How could she not feel better, listening to Stevie sing con cariño y felicidad?) Ana loved this song for a lot of reasons, but mostly because it reminded her of Carmen (sí, her Carmen). Ana taught her the song when she was muy chiquita. Back then, Carmen would sometimes burst out singing it, her arms thrown out así, twinkling like the brightest star in the sky. And to Ana and Esteban, she was. Esteban learned the song because he knew how much Ana liked it, and Ana loved hearing him sing it to put their girl to sleep.

"Ella muy bella . . . Ella es won'erful . . ."

His English wasn't so good back then. But that was many, many years ago, before Esteban did what he did and Ana was forced to see her marriage in a new way; forced to see she was not the same woman she was when she married Esteban at eighteen and, the worst of all, was forced to be the mother of the angriest teenage girl to walk the state of Texas.

Ana ran her hands to the top of the steering wheel and saw the mark her wedding ring left behind. She had taken it to a jeweler Esteban knew for repair the week before. It was a humble two-ring set—the very best Esteban could afford when they were young, handmade by a silversmith in Mexico, with one tiny diamond. Esteban always promised to buy her a better ring "en este lado," pero Ana said no. This ring was the most precious thing she had, outside of her children. Years of wear had tarnished its shine, but it was only after she accidentally dropped it into the garbage disposal that she finally took it off. It was a mean coincidence that her wedding ring got mangled around the time she and Esteban split up. Or maybe it was an omen. Ana didn't want to think that, even though the truth was right there, plain to see.

When Ana's cell phone rang she came back to the present. It was her new assistant, Cynthia, speaking in that high-pitched voice she used when she was nervous.

"Mrs. Ruiz? The dean wants to know . . ."

Before she could finish the sentence, Ana remembered that she was supposed to get to work early to prepare for the dean's faculty meeting.

"I got the meeting room set up, like you told me, but all the other stuff—I told the dean I would find out, but I don't know what he's talking about," Cynthia said.

"Is Mocte there?"

"What's a 'Mocte'?"

"Mocte is me!" Ana heard him say on the other end of the phone. Mocte was the work-study student who had worked for Ana the last two semesters.

"He'll help you find what you need," she told Cynthia. "I'll be there in ten."

She stepped on the gas and prayed that the traffic cops had already gone for their breakfast tacos.

When Ana got to her building, her heart was pounding in her ears. Cynthia jumped up as Ana walked into the office, rattling off a list of things she did, the things she didn't do, the things she thought she should do, and the things she wished she had done. Ana listened, patient like always, relieved that Cynthia had everything under control. She'd done everything the dean wanted and more. To be sure, Ana went to the meeting room, and when she entered, the dean said todo showy, "Ah, my fantastic executive associate, Ana Ruiz."

"Is everything set in here?"

"Everything is great, Ana."

When she got back to her office, she plopped into a chair near the door. Cynthia brought her a glass of water.

"Oh, thank you, Cynthia." Ana drank the water and fished in her pocket for the aspirin she'd forgotten to take at home. "Thank you for everything. What else did I miss?"

"Just a few messages. They're on your desk. Beatriz Sánchez-Milligan from the president's office just called to say she was walking Carlos Montalvo over."

Ana pressed the glass to her forehead. The thrumming of her heartbeat was now in her eye, making everything she saw tremble with each beat.

"Who?"

"The new artist in residence, miss," Mocte said from the workroom, where he was sorting files.

"Is that today?" Ana asked

"Yes, miss. That's why I'm working today, 'member?"

Carlos Montalvo was a Mexican artist doing his first residency at a U.S. university at Texas State University in San Antonio. Ana's dean was proud of this and wanted everything about his visit to be perfect. He had plans for this Montalvo.

"Do you think it would be okay to show him my sketches, miss?" Mocte was standing in the door of the workroom, dressed in his best work shirt, which was buttoned at the neck. A "¡Vivan Los Zapatistas!" T-shirt peeked from the gap where his shirt splayed open from his neck. The shirt matched his taupe pants, both spotless and planchado bien sharp.

"Well, he just got here, and his class is supposed to be for upperclassmen," Ana reminded him. Mocte nodded and silently returned to his work. When Ana rose to go to her office, she stopped at the workroom.

"But I'll see what I can do," she whispered to Mocte.

"Thanks, miss. You *rawk*."

Ana smiled, as she walked down the short hall to her office, wondering what her Carmen would think if she heard this young man talking to her with appreciation. Mocte was an art student. Before that, he'd been a crack baby, a ward of the state, a foster child, a huffer, a onetime street hustler, a born-again Christian, a Chicano activist, and a telemarketer. Somehow, he'd survived all of that— or maybe because of all that—to become, how she called him, a talented visual artist. He had lived on the Southside with his tía since he was seventeen. Ana could see Mocte was a good boy and a good artist. She didn't want him to fall in the cracks again.

Ana was reading her calendar when she heard Beatriz's voice in the outer office.

"Buenas, I'm Beatriz Sánchez-Milligan here with Mr. Montalvo for the dean."

Before Ana could return, she heard Mocte speaking longer than she'd ever heard him speak in the year she'd known him.

"Oh, sir, it's such an honor, sir. I know your work, sir. Since I was a boy . . ." And then, because he was nervous, excited, or both, Mocte began speaking in a language no one understood. Cynthia was silent, and when Ana reached the outer office she saw why. Carlos Montalvo was tall and lean and solid like a pillar of buffed mahogany. His skin was—how do you say?—ebullient (yes, ebullient) against the snowy, short-sleeved guayabera he wore with gunmetal black, straight-legged jeans, which were pulled over polished boots. His close-cropped black hair was flecked with gray, making his skull look like it was carved from a block of stone. To say it plain, the man was fine! As if to drive the obvious to home base, a corona appeared around him. Ana rubbed her eyes. She wondered if a migraine was coming on. When she opened her eyes again, she saw that the wreath of light around him was caused by the glare of the sun bouncing off a window facing her building, behind him. Well, that explained that— but not how this incredible angel of a man came to be.

"And you are . . . ?" Beatriz asked Cynthia, who was standing with her mouth open but no sound coming out.

"That's Cynthia," Mocte said. "I'm Moctezuma Valdez. But I'm called Mocte."

"Wonderful!" Beatriz said, punching every syllable, looking at Mocte and Cynthia with worry. "Perhaps some water? Por favor?"

"Oh, yes. Thank you," Cynthia said, trying to sit in her chair as it rolled away from her.

"Oh, we can do better than that," Ana said, entering the room. "Con mucho gusto, Señor Montalvo. Soy Ana Ruiz."

"Por supuesto! We spoke on the phone," Montalvo said. His voice was—cómo se dice?—exquisite, like whiskey. Todo seductive. And those eyes! Montalvo's coffee-black eyes, his smile, even the whites of his eyes gleamed. *No. Oh no*, Ana thought. *No one is this handsome.* But she was wrong. Carlos Montalvo was that handsome. He was bite-your-lip handsome, movie-star handsome, cold water—sssssss—on a hot comal handsome.

For a second, Ana wondered what would be found if a few more of the buttons on his guayabera were undone. Would there be hair, or more of the same smooth skin arching and curving over muscle and bone? These thoughts came to Ana in a blink, and it shocked her. But who would be surprised? For as long as it had been since Ana had been touched by her man—any man—and because she was too shy to take care of herself, even in the privacy of her own bedroom (lástima, lástima!), thinking about what Montalvo had going on underneath that layer of pale cotton—híjole! Ana needed to sit down, too. Instead, and without missing the beat, she put out her hand to shake Montalvo's. He held her hand delicately and a little too long, Ana thought. So, when he began to bend down to kiss her on the cheek (as was his way) she pulled away like she didn't notice.

"We have juice, we have soda, tea, Topo Chico . . ."

"Eso! Topo Chico!" Beatriz exclaimed. "You were asking for that earlier! Didn't I tell you we would find you one?"

As Ana poured him a glass, she explained that the dean was expecting him at the faculty meeting.

"No rush. I'll be happy to take you there," Ana said, passing the glass of mineral water to Montalvo.

"Gracias, you are too kind," he said. As he sipped, Beatriz explained how San Antonio was really northern Mexico in many people's eyes, so of course they would have Topo Chico, and any other Mexican food or drink he might want. Beatriz talked big about San Antonio and the university, the art faculty and staff, and the dean so much that Ana knew something was up. As Beatriz went on and on, Ana allowed herself a couple of sideways looks at Montalvo. Yes, he was make-you-go-numb handsome (as Cynthia proved). The one time Montalvo caught her looking at him, he smiled as if, it seemed to Ana, he knew what she was thinking! Ana almost choked. She turned away and coughed into her wrist.

"The president is so very pleased to have you with us this semester," Beatriz said. "He's sorry he was away today, but he looks forward to having you come to his home this weekend." Beatriz looked at her watch. "Perhaps we should escort Señor Montalvo to the meeting now?"

"Por favor, if it is acceptable, can this young man show me the way?" Montalvo asked. "I would like to know more about the language he was speaking. Was that Raramuri?"

"You know it, sir?"

"I know only a few phrases, but what I know is beautiful. I would like to know how you came to learn this language."

Ana looked at Beatriz, who nodded, and Mocte led Beatriz and Montalvo to the meeting, chattering the entire time. As soon as they were gone, Ana turned to Cynthia.

"Oh my God!" Cynthia blurted like she had just come up for air. "I mean, he seems nice," she said, her face going red. Ana shook her head and decided to go back to her office. She'd had enough excitement for the day.

"Unless it's my kids or God, take a message, okay?" Ana said over her shoulder.

The morning was nearly over, the crisis at home on hold, the fire at work put out. She turned on her computer and was soothed by its faint hum. She leaned back in her chair as her computer continued booting up and closed her eyes. She would have fallen asleep, but the sound of her door snapping shut surprised her. There was Beatriz, the straps of her sling-back pumps looped over her finger. After she was sure the door was closed, she quickly padded to Ana's desk and leaned over it to speak into her comadre's face.

"Is he a *babe* or what?"

"You had to take off your shoes to tell me that?"

"They're new and they're killing me."

"They're nice. Where did you get them?"

"Forget the shoes! Did you see him?"

"Who?"

"Ay, por favor!" Beatriz said, dropping her pumps onto the floor. "That little cupcake out there almost hyperventilated."

"Cynthia. She's new."

"I thought I was going to have to give her the Heimlich."

"Mouth-to-mouth."

"That, too!"

"I'm sure Señor Montalvo would have offered," Ana smirked.

The thought of Montalvo putting his buttery soft lips on someone's mouth made Beatriz shudder.

"Oh, my God!" Beatriz began to fan herself with a small calculator that sat near the edge of Ana's desk.

"Oh, stop!"

"Don't tell me you didn't notice?" Beatriz asked.

"I noticed. I just don't care," Ana said, going through the pink While You Were Out notes on her desk. Beatriz took off her blazer and tossed it over an empty guest chair and then plopped into another chair behind her, extending her legs and twirling her ankles. No matter how far Beatriz had climbed up the university system, no matter how far she'd come, that crazy girl that Ana had first met when they were students at Our Lady of the Lake High School could reappear just like that when the two of them were alone.

"He's not married, from what I can tell. And he *likes* you," Beatriz said. "You're all he talked about on the way over here. He said he couldn't wait to meet you. 'Ana this, Ana that.' He said you were one of the reasons he decided to take this position."

"Por favor! I only talked to him on the phone about travel and places to live. Nada más, mujer."

"Well, look. Your dean wants to keep him here, and the president wants to keep him here. If you have any way of making that happen, that will put a lot of feathers in your sombrero, 'manita." Beatriz sat back, resting her hands on the pouf of her panza. Beatriz was only a couple of years older than Ana, and everything about her was large—her voice, the way she walked, the way she knew how to talk to los big wigs, and how she knew how to go into a meeting and get things done. Only four feet, eleven and three-quarter inches, to those who didn't know her Beatriz was just someone's mother, someone's aunt, someone's older sister. But cross her and you would learn that she was one shot of tequila and one shot of Irish whiskey, just as her two last names implied.

"Oye, comadre, I was wondering," Ana said, to change the subject. "There's a quinceañera fair on Sunday. You want to go with us?"

"No! Carmen is going to be fifteen already?"

"Six—five months from now," Ana said, flipping through her desk calendar and realizing she didn't have as much time to plan as she thought.

"Ah! I remember when she was just a baby!" Beatriz cooed.

"Yeah, my little baby is almost a full-grown witch," Ana said.

Beatriz sat up in her chair. "Is she still being difficult?"

"Difficult? Difficult would be pleasant."

"And a quinceañera will make things better?"

"It couldn't hurt. It's a nice tradition. You had one."

"I told you about it, didn't I?"

"Yes."

"And you still want to have one?"

"Yes."

"I told you how my uncle got drunk and sang 'Volver' all night? How my brother Rudy lost his pants, and my abuelita knocked over the cake?"

"Yes, yes, yes!" Ana laughed. She knew that if she let Beatriz go on, she would add another kooky incident to her already crazy story. "It doesn't have to be a wild pachanga, just a church ceremony and a small party at the house. I want her to feel—I want to feel—I want us to do something special together, that's all."

Beatriz could see Ana's eyes go glassy, but before the tears dropped, Ana turned away to arrange some files on the credenza behind her desk. Ay, mujer! There was no need to turn away. Beatriz and Ana had seen each other laugh, cry, give birth, get married, worry over sick children, lose their tempers, collapse with exhaustion, and fill with pride; they shared 1,001 other moments, large and small, that would brand them as friends, sisters, y comadres forever. Ana was there for Beatriz when her mother and then her beloved papi died within months of each other, only a few years ago (en paz descansen). Beatriz was the one who encouraged Ana, told her she could do whatever she set her mind to, especially when Ana was the least convinced. But lately, Ana felt nothing but helpless. She knew Beatriz was being patient and compassionate with her during this hard time in her life, but it had gone on for too long. She was tired of being the one who always brought heartache to the table. All of this Beatriz saw in the slump of Ana's shoulders, the dim light in her eyes, the dull sound in her voice. She decided to lighten the mood.

"Well, mi comadre," Beatriz announced. "If you want to have a good quinceañera, the first thing you got to do is get the music. And for that, you need Steve Jordan."

Ana laughed out loud as she wiped her nose with a tissue and spun back around in her chair to look at her friend. Steve Jordan was a—cómo se dice?—local legend, a San Antonio accordion king who could be as surly as Bob Dylan, as outrageous as George Clinton (pero no diaper), as electric as Elvis (without the pelvis), and stoic como el Johnny Cash. Beatriz was todo crazy about him.

"I don't think Carmen would go for him, even if he did play quinceañeras," Ana said. "Does he play quinceañeras? You think Carmen would like that?"

"Don't ask me, mujer. I have boys. I forgot what it's like to be around girls, especially hormone-fired ones," Beatriz joked. Ana could only manage a stale smile.

"Are things really that bad, 'manita?"

Ana nodded.

"Y Diego? How's he doing with the divorce?"

"The separation," Ana corrected. It bothered Ana that Beatriz kept calling the separation a divorce. "He's like he always is. Quiet, like his dad, but he doesn't hate me like Carmen does."

"Ay, no, she doesn't hate you, 'manita."

"You should hear how she talks to me. If I talked to my mother like that when I was her age, I'd be in the ground right now."

"Maybe her father should talk to her."

Ana scoffed. "I can't get him to talk to a marriage counselor. You think he's going to want to talk to his angry little princesa?"

"Well, yes," Beatriz said. She knew a daddy's girl when she saw one, having been one herself. "You shouldn't have to deal with the kids all on your own." Ana knew this was the truth, but she'd had enough.

"Oye, mujer. I have some calls to return," Ana said, the sound of her heartbeat pounding in her ears again.

"Do you have time for a drink after work?" Beatriz asked, knowing that Ana didn't want to talk about her personal business at the office.

"I'm supposed to meet Esteban," Ana said without looking at her calendar. She didn't need to. She'd been looking forward to it all weekend. Beatriz sat up, slipped her pumps back on, and stood to put on her blazer. Even her silence was big, and it filled Ana's office.

"What?" Ana asked. "Qué pasó?"

Beatriz loved Ana, but she knew she was the only one who could tell her what she needed to hear. It might hurt her, it might break her heart, but Beatriz knew that Ana needed a push, and she would have to be the one to do it.

"'Manita, I—"

"What?"

"I think you need to know you did everything you could possibly do before you give up. The thing is, if Esteban is not willing to do any of the work también, what does that say to you?"

Ana looked at Beatriz blankly while her heart writhed like a dying dog.

"I'm not trying to discourage you, 'manita. But it's like that song: You can't make his heart beat something it won't."

Ana stood up and the two women had a long abrazo. Beatriz could tell how tender her friend was, how she was working hard not to crumble.

"Bueno pues, do I look back to business?" Beatriz asked, tugging at the bottom of her sleeves and at the hem of her blazer.

"Sí, bien *charp*," Ana said, trying to sound perky.

"What are you doing for lunch?"

"I don't know. I'll probably get something from the vending machine. Y tú?"

"I have a noon conference call, and back-to-back meetings after that," Beatriz said, as Cynthia politely tapped on the door.

"Pase!" Beatriz called out, like it was her office.

"Excuse me, ma'am, but Raquel from your office is holding?"

"Yes, yes—tell her I'm on my way."

Beatriz slowly closed the door to Ana's office as she left. She stopped in front of Cynthia's desk and dug into her pockets until she found the twenty-dollar bill she always kept stashed on her.

"Cynthia, right? Would you do me a favor? When you come back from your lunch would you bring Mrs. Ruiz a salad from the cart on the plaza? She likes balsamic dressing."

"Sure," Cynthia chirped.

"And in the afternoon, bring her a paleta from the woman who sells them across the street. Ask her for 'la bandera.' She'll know what you mean."

Beatriz saw Mocte in the workroom. "There should be enough money to cover all of you. Buen provecho."

When Beatriz was out of sight Mocte purred, "Eso— she *rawks*."

FOUR

Diego was taller than most of the other boys his age. From the time he started at high school, the man they called Coach made it a point to find Diego and get him to try out for the basketball team. Diego wasn't interested, not even a little bit, but the red-faced man who smelled like cigar smoke and Ben Gay wouldn't take no for an answer.

"So you're a football man, eh? We can use you over there, too."

Even though Diego was Texas born and bred, basketball and most other sports bored him. He liked to read and play music, and now, though he told no one, he was writing songs, something that would have made the basketball coach scoff before complaining about healthy boys like Diego wasting their God-given talents on that "fruity stuff."

"C'mon, boy! Team sports will make you a man and, let's face it, make you popular with the young ladies. You walk around here with a letter jacket and it's like being king of the chicas," Coach would say. The first year Coach asked him about joining the team, Diego said he had a bad knee. The next year, he said soccer was his game. The third year, he said he had an after-school job. (This wasn't exactly a lie. His father, Esteban, got him a job on his worksite, pulling nails from boards and other cositas, but only for a few days.) Finally, in his senior year, Coach got the message when he took a wrong turn and found himself in what he called the "arty-farty" wing of the school. When he passed the music room and saw Diego playing a flute, Coach choked like a mosca flew into his mouth. He shook his head and decided Diego wasn't interested in sports or girls after all, and blocked him out of his mind—which, since there was so little there to begin with, didn't take much work.

Had Coach taken the time to find out who Diego was, he would have discovered that Diego was just messing around with the flute when he happened to see him. He played brass instruments—trombone, trumpet, sax—could hold his own on the piano and had begun learning the guitar. (Why? For a girl—why else?) He could have worn a letter jacket, since he was a senior and in the marching band, but even he knew that that would make him a target for the circle of boys who liked to make it their business to torment good boys like Diego. But Diego was no pushover. If it came down to it, he would surprise himself. Diego could throw chingazos if he had to. Instead, Diego was smart to lay low. He didn't want any trouble. He only wanted to play his music and learn the guitar, thanks to Sonia.

Sonia Castañeda—the thought of her made Diego dizzy. She was—oh, how would he say it? To Diego she was light through sheer curtains, the smell of rain, the sweet music of new birds, the sun rising in the morning, a full moon in fall, the rhyme of mango y chili . . . pero no, those words weren't right either. He'd scribbled all of them in the notebook he kept hidden under his bed, the way other boys his age hid girlie magazines (chiflados!). It frustrated him that he could not find the words to say how he felt about this girl who, years before, was just his friend Rafa's little sister. What happened between last year and this Diego didn't know, but deeply, in the quietest place where God talks to you, Diego thought that he must be in love. He liked how it felt, this strange and glorious thing. It was a welcome distraction, now that things were so—how would he say?—messed up at home. He didn't want to let go of this distraction, because it was the only thing that was solid, that kept him from punching a hole in the wall—or worse, his sister.

Carmen made him angrier than his parents' separation, but he had no words to calm her. Now that he was the man of the house, as his father, his mother, and everyone (except Carmen) told him, he wished that when he saw Carmen in one of her moods, saw how she treated their mother, he wished he could find a way to make her see how ugly she was. Something to turn her back to the sweet girl she used to be. Diego loved his sister. He could admit that. But—qué coraje!—she sure could be la cabrona.

"D!"

Diego scanned the plaza in front of the school to see who called his name. He spotted Carmen seated on a stone bench under the oak tree with her group of friends. As he walked over, all their eyes fluttered over him like butterflies. They all thought Diego was tan chulo.

"I need some lunch money," Carmen said.

"So?"

"So, I need a couple bucks."

"Y qué?"

"Diego!" Carmen said in that little-girl whine that used to work on her brother when she really was a little girl. But these days, ya, he was through with it."

"Why didn't you get money from 'Amá?"

"Because I didn't." And then, because her brother kept staring at her, "I forgot."

"You forgot?" Diego plucked a five from his pocket. Carmen reached for it and Diego raised it over his head. At least two heads shorter than her brother, la chaparra reached for the bill but could never hope to snatch it.

"That should be my tip for not telling on you," Carmen said. Diego paused, wondering if his sister really knew where he had gone earlier in the morning.

"How is Sonia? Did you carry her books to school?" Carmen asked, todo smirky. Her circle of friends eyed each other and began acting like they weren't interested—which, of course, was a lie. They wanted to know all about Diego's business. One began flipping through her math book, the other stared into her cell phone, and the third—oh, she didn't even bother to pretend. She was staring right at Carmen and Diego like a little kid ready for what was next.

"None of your business, Carmensa," Diego said. The girls exhaled an "ah," which started at zero, zoomed up like a bottle rocket, and circled back, landing among them with a silent bang. In the short silence that followed, they looked at each other wide-mouthed, then burst out laughing.

"Mira, Dieguito is turning red," one of the girls said. Patti, Mari, Alicia? Diego didn't know which. They were all the same to him—annoying.

"Carmen, ven acá," Diego said, using his older-brother voice.

"What for?"

"Just come 'ere." When Carmen didn't move, he added, "You want your lunch money, don't you?" Carmen slowly stood up and walked away from the shade of the tree and from her friends to the center of the plaza with her brother. Students passed them like water around two stones, rushing from the parking lot to class, or stopping to meet friends on the steps in front of the school.

"Qué tienes?" Carmen asked.

"You need to quit."

"Quit what?"

"You know."

Carmen clucked her tongue and rolled her eyes.

"Everyone knows you like her, D. Get over yourself." Diego didn't know that everyone knew he liked Sonia. That made him nervous, but he pushed back to what he really wanted to talk about. "I'm not talking about her, I'm talking about 'Amá. You need to treat her better."

"Says who?"

"Carmen! Things are messed up enough as it is. Why are you acting up?"

An old school bus lurched into the drive in front of the school, and Carmen watched the tired students drop from the bus one by one, trudging toward the school like zombies. "I don't like how things are," she finally said.

"Me neither, but you don't see me acting all chiflada. You're giving her an ulcer. Why don't you chill?"

"Can I have some lunch money, or not?"

"Carmen! You don't even know what's going on."

"Do you?"

Diego stared down at his little sister. He knew as much as his sister did about what had happened between their parents, which was nothing.

"She ruined everything!" Carmen finally blurted. "That's what everyone says!"

"Everyone who? Who says that?"

"Tío Marcos, y las tías. All of them."

"When?"

"Whenever!"

"You don't know!"

"I know!" Carmen said as if that was all that needed to be said.

Diego knew that of all of them their tío Marcos was the worst. He was Ana's older brother and always had something to say about everything. Diego also knew that his tío had—how they say?—good intentions. He had Ana's best interests in his heart, even if what he said came out lopsided and served with a jab. He told Ana she was lucky to have a husband like Esteban—a good man, a good provider. Marcos made sure of it. He kept Esteban working steadily in his construction business, even in slow times. Esteban was a good worker, had good skills, and was a good man "in the old ways," Marcos said. Diego believed all those things about his father, but he also knew his mother was good. She worked hard, too. She was the first girl in the family to go to college. It took her longer than most, because she was working and taking care of her babies—first Diego and then Carmen, two years later. At first, there was talk that Ana had no business going to school with two babies at home. But with Beatriz helping out and all her professors encouraging her, and Ana making herself ignore the heavy sighs when she asked a tía or a cousin to please, please, *please* watch her kids while she studied or went to class, Ana got through it. And wouldn't you know—when Ana walked across that stage to get her diploma, all those clucking tías and cousins watched con todo cariño, tears in their eyes, saying, "Mira, la Ana. She really made something of herself." A good husband, a good job at the university, her nice house, good kids—all those things spelled success to the family. Ana had it all. They had helped her get that life. Why would she want to give it up now?

What they—including Carmen y Diego—didn't know is that it wasn't exactly the life Ana wanted. She had wanted to study art. She wanted to travel and see all the world's great museums. She wanted to run a gallery, or an art school, and learn how to paint. *Maybe that would come after*, Ana thought. After marriage, raising children, and taking care of all the other responsibilities the oldest daughter, a good wife, a good mother, and now a—cómo se dice?—a career woman . . . maybe that's when all those other things would come. Ana carried those dreams burning like a vela. They brought her comfort. But as time ticks forward, dreams have a way of turning into regret, trampled under the routine of daily life, verdad? Ana would be the first one to say she had a good life. Pero it just wasn't the one she was waiting for.

"Come on, D! The bell's going to ring pretty soon," Carmen whined.

Diego shoved the bill deep into his pocket as his cell phone rang.

"Tell Sonia I said hi!" Bianca said, as she walked up behind him. Diego ignored her and walked off to take his call. Bianca and Carmen walked back to the girls sitting under the tree.

"Tell her she can teach you how to dance at Carmen's quince!" Bianca called over her shoulder to Diego.

"You're having a quinceañera?" a girl in Carmen's clica asked. The girls all looked at one another, each wondering if she were the only one out of the know.

"No!" Carmen said. "Shut up, Bianca."

"Oh, please, please, please have a quinceañera," one of the girls pleaded. "I'll do it."

"She'll have one," Bianca announced. "She has to!"

"No, I don't," Carmen said, plopping herself onto the bench where she sat before. "I don't want to."

"Why not?" another girl asked.

"What's wrong with you?"

"Yeah, qué tienes? Every girl wants to have a quinceañera."

"I don't."

One of the girls gasped.

"It's not that bad," Patti or Mari or Alicia said. "I had one. The best part is picking out the dress."

"That's the first thing to take care of," Bianca said. "And as you can see by my skills, I am the one to take care of designing the dress." Bianca waved toward Carmen's bag.

"You made that?" one of the girls asked. When Bianca nodded, the girls oohed and ahhed over it, while asking a thousand questions Carmen did not want to answer about the when and where of her quinceañera. Carmen glared at her cousin, but Bianca smiled like she didn't know why Carmen was throwing her the mal de ojo.

Diego had made his way to the far side of the plaza and was leaning against a bike rack as he spoke on his phone.

"Son, some of the men said you were looking for me."

"Yes, 'Apá," Diego said. "I thought I would catch you before you started work. But it was getting late and I had to leave for school."

"Why didn't you just call me?"

"Because," Diego stammered, "because you always say important business is best discussed face-to-face, como un hombre."

There was silence on the phone as Diego dug up the courage to ask his father what he wanted to know: Why did he leave, and when was he coming back home? But even with only his father's voice to confront, Diego suddenly felt the courage he'd built up on the long walk to his father's construction site sputter like a kid's balloon.

"Qué pasó, mi'jo? Did something happen?"

Diego always felt the pressure to please his father, something that seemed to come easy to his sister. Diego cleared his throat and swallowed his questions.

"Diego, qué pasó?"

His courage shriveled, Diego said the first thing that came into his mind.

"'Amá wants to have a quinceañera for Carmen."

"Okay."

"Well, Carmen is being, you know." If Diego thought he could get away with calling Esteban Ruiz's little girl the Queen of the Cabronas, he would have.

"She's disrespectful," he blurted. "I try and tell her to be, you know, because, you know. Things are kind of weird now." Pobrecito, his mouth went dry. "She won't listen to me and she doesn't listen to 'Amá." When he finished, Diego cringed.

"Oye, son. I appreciate the call. I know you're doing your best. I'll take care of it."

"But . . . okay."

"Is there something else, mi'jo? 'Cause I got to go."

"No. That's all."

"Bueno pues, bye."

Diego starred at his father's blinking number on his cell phone, another one of the daily reminders that his father was gone. He turned off the phone and slid it into his pocket.

"I would make better use of that phone," Carmen said. She had just walked up to Diego, anxious to break away from the pack of chattering girls getting themselves more and more worked up about her quinceañera, thanks to Bianca.

"Yeah, well, 'Apá gave it to me to take care of business. You know. Since I'm at the house."

"Yeah, yeah, yeah. I know. Because you're the man of the house," Carmen said, todo smarmy. Diego turned red. *Maybe Carmen should be the designated man of the house, the way she struts and swaggers,* he thought. *Maybe Coach should be recruiting her.*

"Okay, Mr. Man of the House, can I please have some lunch money?"

Diego pulled out his five and handed it to his sister. "This is all I got. Bring me the change so I can eat, too."

"Don't worry," Carmen said. Pero Diego already knew that Monday was Carmen's lab day, so he wouldn't cross her in the hall before his lunch period. He already knew he'd be hungry the rest of the afternoon, as he slunk off to class.

≫ FIVE ≪

Monday afternoon was as good a time as any to have a paleta break, Ana decided. At the end of the day, Cynthia did as Beatriz said and brought her boss a paleta with the colors of the Mexican flag: red, white, and green. She didn't have to explain. Ana recognized it as pura Beatriz.

The day had been filled with meetings and phone calls. The expected and unexpected things that happen early in the school year had kept the office busy, especially with a distinguished guest in the department. Mocte had returned to the office after leaving in the middle of the day for his classes, while Cynthia managed to hold her own. At four thirty, when Cynthia walked in with the paletas, Ana said, "Ya!" and everyone stopped what they were doing to discuss what was accomplished and what was left to be done as they happily sucked on their frozen treats. Ana was about to return to her office when something peeking out of Cynthia's bag caught her eye.

"What is that?" Ana asked. Cynthia turned to look.

"It's *Your Quince* magazine."

"Wow. Where did you get it? I want to plan a quinceañera for my daughter. This might come in handy."

"I borrowed it from one of my girls," Cynthia said, pulling it from her bag and handing it to Ana. "We're trying to do more of those events."

"More of what events?" Mocte asked from the corner of the room, where he was finishing off the last chunk of his mango y chili fruit cup.

"Quinceañeras," Cynthia said, careful to say each syllable, ironing the "nyeh" with her tongue. "I'm in a mariachi, Las Florecitas Fuertes."

"Really?" Ana asked. "'Strong flowers?'"

"Yes. We were going for the paradox. But we might change the name."

"No, I like it."

"You play mariachi?" Mocte asked, with a little tip of his chin. "You like it?"

"What's not to like?"

Mocte nodded with approval.

"How long have you been playing?" Ana asked.

"Just a couple of months, but we're getting pretty good and we're about to start advertising. We're going to play this week at Cascabel's for a birthday party. You should come hear us, see what you think. You know, the most important part of the quinceañera is the mariachi."

"N'ombre, it's the cake," Mocte said. The two women turned to look at him. "That's what my tía says. She's the Q-Cake Queen."

"Your aunt is the Q-Cake Queen?" Cynthia gasped. "Wow. I've seen her cakes! They're like dancing sculptures. Almost like they're on hydraulics or something."

Mocte was impressed that this white girl from Kansas knew what hydraulics were.

"And they taste good, too," he said. "The chocolate-raspberry *rawks*."

Cynthia and Mocte continued to talk—she saying a recommendation from the Q-Cake Queen herself would help Las Florecitas Fuertes get work, and he saying that his aunt's business was booming and that the rest of the family was joining in to build a cottage industry—dressmakers, limo drivers, hairstylists, caterers, designers, y más.

Ana got a little dizzy listening to them talk. The quinceañera she had in mind was small. She wanted it to be a time when she and Carmen could talk to each other all cozy like they did before the separation, when her daughter would speak to her without the fangs in her words.

"Buenas noches, miss," Mocte said, slinging his backpack over his shoulder. Cynthia was right behind him.

"If that's all, ma'am . . ." Cynthia asked.

Ana looked at the clock. It was already after five thirty. "Sure, I didn't mean to keep you," she said as she handed back the magazine.

"You can keep it," Cynthia said. "That's from last month. I have the newest one at home."

As Ana walked down the hall to her office, flipping through the pages of *Your Quince* magazine, something wilted inside her. The young girls in the magazine looked like women, not girls. Sí, her little girl was becoming a woman. She knew Carmen would grow up one day, but with all the drama and Carmen working to send her poor mother to an early grave, Ana still found herself thinking, *How did it happen so soon?*

Ana was pulled from her thoughts by a ringing phone.

"Oye, mujer! I heard Steve Jordan is playing an extra show at Saluté! Let's go!" It was Beatriz on the other end. "Come on. We work hard for the money, honey! And we can talk."

Ana liked the idea of relaxing, listening to Steve Jordan

draw fire from his accordion; always familiar, but always different, depending on his mood. It was, as Beatriz always liked to say, comfort music for the Tejano soul.

"I told you, I have a meeting with Esteban." Ana didn't like the silence she heard on the other end of the phone and changed the subject. "So, you're coming Sunday?" Before Beatriz could answer, the other line was ringing and Ana put her on hold.

"Ana Ruiz."

"Habla Esteban."

Ana felt that quiver. That piece of physical proof that she still loved him in spite of all that had happened.

"Oye, I'm on my way," she said.

"That's what I called about. I can't come."

"Why not?"

Esteban paused. "Este . . . you know."

Ana heard the beep of his truck as he put the keys in the ignition, followed by the music of Esteban's favorite Tejano radio station in the background. The quiver Ana first felt turned to an ember. Like always, she expected to fill in the blank as to why Esteban could not meet her, and because it was easier to do that than to keep trying to get a straight answer from him, she let it go.

"We've still got the house to discuss. The lawyer says—"

"The lawyer? Why do we need a lawyer?"

"Well, if you want to talk, let's talk," Ana said a little louder. "It's just mortgage stuff. Don't worry. I can handle it on my own. I do everything on my own," she said, her temper flaring like a match.

"Ana—"

"I've got to go."

Ana dropped the phone into its cradle and immediately switched into what Beatriz called heat-seeking mode, when she poured all her attention into one thing, blocking out the rest of the world. It had made Ana's past bosses call her a go-getter, but it was also how she dealt with pain, anger, and disappointment.

Ana straightened the top of her desk furiously. Drawers were opened and slammed closed, old notes thrown in the trash, important papers swept into folders. She re-sorted the long line of files that ran from one end of the credenza to the other, working faster and faster, the rustling of papers like leaves in the wind.

As she worked, she got angrier and angrier. She saw a form that needed her signature, and when she picked up a pen to sign it, it was bleeding. *It's just a stupid ballpoint pen. They're not supposed to bleed*, she thought, looking at the gooey mess on her hand.

She stormed out of her office with her hand held out in front of her, down the hall to the supply closet. The office was quiet now. Everyone was gone. She found a container of wipes and cleaned her hands. The ink came off, except for a dribble of it that had seeped under her thumbnail. And something about that ugly stain of blue ink was enough to bring up the tears she'd choked down all day. She was tired of holding them back, and she let them come. She covered her eyes with her wrists. Gulping and snorting; her eye makeup drooling—she didn't care anymore. After five or ten minutes of this, she took a deep, calming breath, ran her fingers under her eyes and through her hair, and pulled down the hem of her jacket. Her eyes were swollen, but she was at least presentable, she thought. And then, she felt—cómo se dice?—an eerie sensation. She could feel she was not alone.

"Disculpe."

It was Carlos Montalvo, standing in the doorway staring at her. "I . . . the door was unlocked and I heard a sound . . ."

Ana's heart began to jump.

"May I help you?" she asked as blandly as she could.

"This paper . . . the dean asked me to, but I . . ."

Montalvo fumbled through the folder he had in his hand, peeling through the papers, turning around as if what he were looking for was behind him. He turned back to Ana sheepishly. "Discúlpeme, por favor. I must have left it behind."

When Ana saw she was in the supply closet with Montalvo blocking the door, a shot of anxiety ran through her.

"Excuse me," she said, as she plowed by him back into the main office.

"I did not mean to intrude—"

Ana was not like the people Montalvo was used to. The bigger he got, the more they worked to cover their true thoughts. The more famous he got, the more their smiles hid their real emotions. But Ana's pain was what he would call delicate, plain, and raw; or, as her kids would say, for real. He thought about leaving Ana to her private tears, but it didn't seem right to ignore someone who was honestly wounded.

"Por favor, perhaps—maybe you will let me take you for coffee?" Montalvo stammered.

"Coffee?" Ana snapped. "I don't have time for coffee." Ana wasn't trying to be rude. But she distrusted Montalvo's invitation as an injured animal might mistake a helping hand for danger. And Montalvo was dangerous, as far as she was concerned. Amazingly handsome, alone in a new city; the university had met his every need—except for one. Ana had heard the chisme about women on campus, their hearts bloated with hope by a visiting dignitary, only to be dropped like a used rag, left behind without so much as a "it was nice while it lasted," once a visiting dignitary had finished his stay and moved on to the next campus, where he would be greeted with the same parties and aplausos, and then begin to prowl for his next companion. Ana wanted no part of it.

"I have two teenage children," Ana said, and just like that her cell phone rang.

"'Amá?"

Ana was relieved to hear her son's voice. Diego gave his mother the rundown of his and Carmen's after-school plans. Ana hoped he would keep talking long enough for Montalvo to get bored and go away.

"'Amá, are you okay?" Diego asked, when he heard his mother sniffling.

"I'm fine, mi'jo," Ana said. "It's just the allergies. I have some last-minute work to finish. I'll be home soon." When she hung up, Montalvo was still there.

"That was my son. I have a son and a daughter. I have a family. They are waiting for me at home. I come here to work. So, no, I don't have time for coffee now, or anytime, anywhere."

"I did not think . . . I think, I thought . . ." Montalvo sighed. "I did not see a ring. I should go."

"Yes," Ana said. "Do you mind?" She was now at the office door, pulling it open and standing there like she would not take no for an answer.

"Of course. Buenas noches." When he went through the door, Ana closed it, latched it, and pulled on it to make sure it was locked. She returned to her office for her things, and as she stuffed her briefcase, her anxiety began to grow. She didn't mean to be cold to Montalvo. She remembered what Beatriz said about her dean and the university president wanting to keep him on campus. Would he complain about her to the dean, or would he hold what just happened over her head, using it to get more than he needed or deserved? Her stomach began to churn, and she almost started crying again, but then she remembered she'd left Beatriz on hold. Of course, when she returned to the phone, Beatriz had hung up. Ana thought about calling her back but decided she didn't want her to know what happened. Ana went through her briefcase for the mortgage papers she and Esteban were supposed to have gone over, shoved them back into the case, and angrily zipped it closed. Then she grabbed her purse and headed for her car.

The campus was nearly empty now. The cart where Cynthia bought Ana's lunch was closed up for the night. The woman who ran the paleta stand across the street had pushed her cart to El Mercado, down the block, where she would sell her fruit cups, paletas, and neon-colored mounds of ice to tourists. Ana kept glancing over her shoulder, half-expecting to see the dean and Montalvo following her—Montalvo wagging his finger and the dean glaring at her. She tried to put what happened out of her mind and to look forward to a quiet night at home, but then she remembered that that was a pleasure of the past. Who knew what kind of mood Carmen would be in when she got home? And since Diego had band practice, the house would feel much more hollow than usual. Ana wished she could get on the highway and drive until she was in the country, far out of town, until she reached the Gulf of Mexico, and she would drive right in. Sitting in her car, Ana tried to calm down. *It wasn't as bad as I thought, was it?* she asked herself. She sat in her car a long time and began feeling silly, then finally started the car to go home, determined not to let what had happened make her crazy. But as she drove off she could not shake the idea that what had happened was going to come back to haunt her.

SIX

The kitchen was the alma of the Ruiz house. In fact, Ana and Esteban bought their house because of the kitchen, even though it was in worse than bad shape when they first saw it. Her brother Marcos (el mero mero consejero in these things) had said they were crazy for wanting to redo the kitchen themselves. Afterward, though, between Ana's very particular design and color choices (tropical green walls with a cocoa-brown trim), and Esteban's easy way of learning most anything he needed to know to do a repair, the kitchen became the most loved part of the house. And to think it started from a hole in the ground. (Really! They have pictures.) Well, even Marcos was impressed when they finished.

Since Esteban left, the Ruiz kitchen was where Ana and Carmen circled one another como growly cats and where Diego—trying to fill up the hole made by Esteban being gone—acted like a puppy, eager to bring alegría y cariño back into the room.

Because Diego and Carmen had grown up in the house, they had gotten used to it having a familiar feel to it. The Ruiz kitchen was where the day began and ended for them. But it was more than that. It was where birthday cakes were baked and tamales were made assembly-line style by the family at Christmas. At the kitchen table was where buttons were sewn on (the light was good at the east-facing windows), where bangs were trimmed, hair braided, bills paid, multiplication tables learned, boo-boos made better, and pictures colored and then displayed on the refrigerator. So it was not a good thing for Carmen that Esteban left them from the kitchen. Late one night, when both he and Ana thought their kids were asleep, Esteban took the duffel bag he'd packed and stored in the closet, threw it over his shoulder, and made his way through the dark house to the kitchen, the place where their nest opened to the outside world.

It was not just that her 'apá was leaving them that shocked her but how plainly it was happening, with no emotion (claro que, she didn't know the half of the story, but try telling that to a fourteen-year-old girl who thinks her world is coming to an end). What really made Carmen angry, though, was how she thought her mother was without feeling, while Esteban was silent and brave (she was, as they say, her daddy's girl). Pero, oh no! She didn't know the storm that was blowing inside Ana and Esteban; that storm that only two people who have loved each other can know without words or music, como in the movies, to tell you how they feel. Porque love that is losing its life, like flowers gone dry, is still beautiful, no? It still holds the memory of what once was, entiendes? Well, Carmen didn't either.

"Do what you have to do," Carmen had heard Ana say to Esteban. When he leaned in to kiss her (Carmen didn't notice he was aiming for her cheek, not her lips), Ana pulled back, something Carmen found so ugly and heartless, she wanted to scream. Pero, she would come to understand, years later, when she would be the cause of someone's broken heart.

Even with Bianca in the kitchen now—filling up the space with her excited talk about her bolsas, her ideas for Carmen's quinceañera, and whatever else came into her head—the kitchen felt as if it belonged to some other family. Ana and her children were bumping into things and each other, as if someone had rearranged the furniture. No one could explain this strangeness to them or tell them if it would pass. But to Carmen, any mal aire that filled the once-comforting Ruiz kitchen was all Ana's fault.

Diego was reading the instructions on a box of spaghetti and holding a can of black beans when Bianca noticed him.

"What are you going to do with that?"

"Nothing, Bianca."

"Don't you all have whole wheat pasta?"

"Don't you have your own house?"

"Ay, don't be mean. I'm here to start planning Carmen's quinceañera."

Carmen frowned. "I thought you were going to help me with my algebra."

"We'll get to it. Come on, Dieguito. Don't make whatever mess you're thinking of making. Let's order pizza!"

"That sounds good," Carmen chimed in.

"Oh, yeah? How about we pay for it with the change you were supposed to give me at lunch, eh, Carmen?"

"D'oh!" Carmen said. "I forgot I had bio lab today, so I didn't see you."

"Yeah, whatever." Diego was so hungry he would have eaten the beans straight from the can if he didn't think Bianca would have something annoying to say about it.

"C'mon—you guys make a salad and I'll get the pizza. I have my dad's credit card."

"No, I'll make dinner," Diego said. He felt it was his responsibility. If his father were home, he would have fired up the grill by now, grilled some sausages, diced some onion, heated up some tortillas, y ya! Not a green thing on the plate, but his kids would be fed. But Esteban hadn't gotten around to showing his son the way around a grill. Diego looked out the window and saw it lurking in the far corner of the backyard. He wanted to go fire it up, but the thought of doing it without his father made his stomach grind harder and tighter. He saw a bag of corn chips on the counter and began to wolf them down.

"I'm serious, B. I need help with this stuff," Carmen said, pushing her math book across the table toward her cousin.

"Don't worry. Once you get it, you got it. Let me show you something." Bianca pulled out a sketchbook of drawings she had done for Carmen's quinceañera dress. "I did more, but these are the ones I like the best," she said, nervously looking at Carmen to see what she thought.

"These are nice," Carmen said. "But they're kind of low cut. My chichis would fall out of that one."

"It's a good thing you don't have any, then," Diego said.

"Shut up!" Bianca snapped. "You don't like these? We have time. I was just drawing what came to me. I have lots more ideas."

Diego was relieved when Ana came home with take-out food from the grocery store deli. He and Bianca helped Ana empty the bags. Carmen moved away from them and sat in the bay window looking out to the backyard, studying the sketches. It was her favorite spot in the kitchen because it overlooked the pond her father had built on her sixth birthday, filling it with glittery goldfish to mark the occasion.

"C'mon, Carmen!" Diego ordered his sister. Carmen closed the sketchbook and laid it on the wide windowsill. She pulled her knees up to her chest and watched the fish swirl in the pond beneath her.

"B, can you help me with my algebra or not?"

"Can't we eat first? I'm starving!"

Bianca was family and of course was always welcome, but Ana couldn't help but notice that this was the third time Bianca had eaten dinner with them in a week.

"Bianca, does your dad know you're here?"

"He's at work."

"But does he know you're here?"

Bianca shrugged. Ana's patience was going thin.

"Bianca, call your dad. Carmen, clear the table. Diego, get the silverware and napkins."

When Carmen didn't move, Diego shot her an angry look. Carmen ignored him and stayed where she was, watching the fish. Diego slammed the forks on the table and moved toward his sister. Ana put her hand out to stop him.

"'Amá!" he said under his breath.

"Don't start, mi'jo. I'll take care of this."

"But 'Amá—"

Bianca interrupted them.

"Tía, my dad wants to talk to you."

Ana gritted her teeth and picked up the phone Bianca held out to her.

"Bueno?"

"Ana! Cómo estás?"

"I'm fine," Ana said, wanting to make the call short. "You know, Bianca is welcome here anytime, but I wanted you to know she was here. I'll send her home right after we eat. Bueno pues . . ."

"Thank you, pero wait, wait, wait . . ." *Qué coraje*, Ana thought. She hated what would come next. "Tell me, how are things, 'manita?"

"I told you. Fine, Marcos. I have to go—our dinner is getting cold."

"Ay, you can nuke it," he said. "You know what I mean. When are you and Esteban, you know, going to patch things up?"

"I don't know, but thanks for asking," Ana said sweetly so the kids would not know she was having one of those talks with her brother.

"Your husband walks around the job site like he's got the weight of the world on his shoulders. He feels bad, Ana. Real bad."

"Is that so?" Ana was desperate to tell her brother that it was Esteban, not her, who cancelled their meeting earlier in the evening.

"You know, I hate seeing my men like that. When they've got home problems on their minds, that's when accidents happen." Híjole, Ana didn't know what was worse, hearing what her brother said to her or watching Diego shovel half the potato salad from the take-out box into his mouth.

"Marcos, I have hungry kids to feed. Can we talk later?" But Ana didn't really want to talk. She didn't want to listen to another lecture about marriage from her older brother. It's not like he was an expert. His first wife died early in their marriage, the second one left him because he was a workaholic, and the third—Bianca's mother, a woman much younger than Marcos—well, he still held out hope that she would return to her former self and they would go back to their life as it was. Everyone knew better, but in this Marcos was as starry-eyed as his daughter. That was the only reason

Ana could think that he pushed so hard for her and Esteban to get back together. Sometimes, it seemed, he wanted it more than anyone.

As soon as Ana got off the phone with Marcos, Diego announced it was time for his band practice. Ana groaned.

"Gimme the keys. I can drive myself," Diego said.

"I know you can drive yourself, but we haven't worked out the insurance yet. It's one of the things I need to talk to your father about," Ana said, as she put out the dinner rolls. "I'm sorry, mi'jo. I know you've been waiting a long time."

"I can take him," Bianca said. "It's just a mile or so, right? I'll take him then come back to help Carmen with her math."

Ana was thankful. It had been a long day, and the thing with Montalvo was still gnawing at her.

"Sure, go. Be careful. Call me and I'll pick you up later, okay, Diego?"

When the two of them left, Ana made a plate for her and for Carmen and set them on the table.

"Carmen, comamos!" she called. The girl was still sitting in the bay window and Ana could see that she didn't want to move. Trying to have a regular family dinner was one of the ways Ana thought she could keep some order in the house. But Ana could tell Carmen was going to fight her all the way. When Carmen finally rose from the window and went to the table, Ana was relieved until—would you believe it?—Carmen picked up her plate and turned to leave the room.

"What are you doing?"

"Going to my room."

"Siéntate, Carmen."

"I have homework."

"Sit down and eat your dinner."

Carmen set her plate noisily on the table and turned to leave the room again.

"Okay, then—I'm not hungry."

Ana knew she had to stand her ground.

"Carmen. Sit down. Now." Carmen slowly slid into a chair as far away from her mother as possible and crossed her arms. (Ay, muchacha!)

"Have you thought about what I asked you about this morning? The quinceañera fair on Sunday? Remember I showed you the ad?" Carmen shrugged. Ana took a deep breath. "It would mean a lot to me if we could go."

Carmen began pulling apart a dinner roll and spreading pats of butter onto the pieces, arranging them on the plate in front of her. Ana sat back in her chair.

"Is it really so terrible to sit here with me and have a meal like a regular family?"

"We're not a regular family anymore, and it's just you and me," Carmen said, todo sassy.

"Whoever comes to the table, that should be enough, whether it's two or twenty. Entiendes?"

"Something is killing my fish."

"What?"

"The fish. There used to be ten, now there's only four," Carmen said.

"Are you sure?" Ana crossed to the window to look out to the pond. "Oh, mi'ja!"

Ana still had a picture she carried in her wallet of Esteban and the children the day he put in the pond. Esteban was on his knees. Diego's knotty elbows and knees popped out from a pair of coveralls cut off at the knees. Diego was leaning into his father, proudly holding a spade and with one leg on top of a bucket while Carmen stood before them covered in dirt, the glow of her smile shining through the grime as she held up to the camera the first bag of goldfish to be put into the pond. It was a family project, but because it was Carmen's birthday, she had told everyone it was her pond. Ana knew that sitting next to the pond, either at the window or outside, was a favorite pastime Carmen shared with her father.

"I wonder what's happening to them?" Ana said. "It's probably just a passing thing." She crossed back to the table to comfort her daughter, but as she put her arm across her shoulders, Carmen shrugged her off.

"'Apá would know." Carmen rose from the table. "I'm not hungry. Can I please go to my room now?"

Too exhausted to argue with her, Ana let her go.

When Bianca returned, she was whistling along with the music she was listening to on her iPod. She sat down and started to spoon green bean salad onto an empty plate. Ana watched her silently, her elbow on the table, her chin cupped in her hand. Bianca took off her earplugs and laid them in her lap.

"Thanks for dinner, Tía."

"De nada, mi'ja," Ana said into her hand. "Carmen's in her room. You can take that with you, if you want."

Bianca's heart sank, seeing her aunt wilted and alone the way she was.

"That's okay. I'll stay here with you," she said. Ana rose to make some tea.

"So, you're going to that quinceañera fair on Sunday?"

Ana didn't mean to ignore Bianca, but she was lost in the comfort of making her tea.

"Tía?"

"I'm sorry, mi'ja. What?"

"The quinceañera fair—are you going?"

"You know about that?"

"Carmen told me you want to go," Bianca said. "Can I come?"

"If Carmen won't go, there's no need for me to go," Ana said, stirring honey into her cup.

Bianca looked at the kidney beans Ana had picked out of her three-bean salad and pushed to the rim of her plate. Bianca knew exactly how they felt. Part of the salad, but always pushed off to the side.

"I'll go, and I'll make sure Carmen goes, too. How's that?"

"You think you can do that?"

"Sure," Bianca said, not knowing how she would keep her promise but knowing she would give it all her attention.

Ana drank her tea and Bianca ate slowly so her aunt would not be alone. Later, she found the apple pie that was left in the bag and cut slices for both of them. Ana picked at hers as Bianca sat across from her, chattering about whatever came into her head—all the time thinking of ways to convince her stubborn cousin to have the quinceañera she so wanted her to have.

SEVEN

By the time Carmen got to her room, her tears had dried into a stubborn knot. She slammed her door and stood looking around her room. Whose idea was it to paint it buttercup yellow, as her mother called it? Probably her mother's, Carmen thought, and the idea made her feel stuffed in someone else's skin. She saw herself in the big mirror that stood in the corner of her room and moved closer to look at her moon-shaped face. With her high, round cheeks and her bright, wide eyes, she was still on the niña side of being a woman. She wanted to look like someone who should be taken seriously!

That was why she demanded the new haircut. It meant more work than letting it grow schoolgirl style—long and straight, or pulled back into a neat chongo like her cousin Bianca. Pero Carmen wanted to—how do you say?—stand out, be bold, and not look like she was following her cousin in all her ways, which she did when they were little. She was the baby of the family, used to being oohed and ahed over. She liked it all right, but she wanted to be heard! The only way to do that was to have a tantrum, but even Carmen knew she was getting too old for that.

She just didn't know any other way. She shook her head and ran her fingers through her bob; parted it on one side, then the other, tucked her chin down to make the swing of her bangs jut forward, como un rock star, her eyes peeking from behind a wedge of hair. Then she pulled all her hair back, away from her face. *I look like a fat-face baby*, she thought and threw herself onto her bed.

Ay, por favor! Carmen wasn't fat. She was shaped like an American Latina, with a small waist, broad hips, wide shoulders, and just enough on top. Her skin was creamy and smooth. But of course, every small bump here, every tiny mole there looked like deformities to her—another reason she liked her new bob. She thought the way it swung forward covered all her flaws.

She cranked up the stereo on her nightstand, already loaded with a Gustavo Alberto CD set to play "Dónde Vas?" If Diego were home, he would be pounding on the wall between their two rooms, sorry for the day he introduced his sister to the Chilango rocker. He would ask her to listen to something else, anything else—even La Conquista (which he called the "bubblegum cumbia chicas"). It was just last year that Carmen played their music like crazy. This year, they fell to the bottom of her pile, replaced by the razor-edged Girl in a Coma, the Spanish rapper Mala Rodríguez, and la chica de Tijuana Ceci Bastida. But Gustavo, he was her boy. When she listened to him, she thought it was like being with someone who knew how it was for her.

How it was for Carmen was different from her brother. Why wasn't he angry? Their father was gone! Couldn't he feel how wrong that was? But that was where *she* was wrong. That Diego's pain cast a different shadow from hers didn't make sense to Carmen. It was her—how they say?— blind spot, made worse because the baby of the family is always used to their needs getting all the attention, ver-dad? It got worse when her father left and Carmen's ability to feel for others exploded into self-absorption. It would pass, but not soon enough for her brother and mother.

Carmen rolled onto her stomach and reached under her bed for the book of saints she kept there. She thumbed through the curled pages, flipping between the stories that appealed to her, landing on St. Joseph the Laborer. She read the description, decided this was the one, and picked up the phone.

"'Apá?"

"Mande."

"Listo?"

"Siempre, mi corazón."

Carmen carefully read the description of St. Joseph the Laborer to her father. This nightly reading was a ritual they had started when she was a little girl. It was some-thing Esteban had learned from his mother, who prayed to her favorite saint as she put Esteban—her youngest son—to bed. As a father, it was how Esteban helped his daugh-ter learn to read (improving his English, también) and was a way to get close to the daughter he would, for the rest of his life, find enchanting. Confusing, but enchanting. Never did Esteban Ruiz imagine he would become the father of the little dove they placed in his arms fourteen years ear-lier. Boys, yes—he was ready for sons. He had come from a family of ten boys and a long line of uncles who all worked with their hands and taught him and his broth-ers all the skills they could use to hold a job and support a family. But Carmen, a thing so precious he couldn't believe she came from him, held Esteban in—cómo se dice?—her thrall. She buffed all his flinty edges, softened all the cal-luses, made him happy to be alive after a grinding day of working in the sun, crawling through tight places, hanging upside down, or suffering whatever work had worn down his back and his spirit. When the only thing he wanted to do was get home, eat, and go to bed, it was the sight of his little girl tugging at his pant leg as he washed his face and hands that brought him back to life. To Carmen's delight, he would scoop her up with one arm and hold her close, inhaling the freshness of her life. She giggled, and Esteban Ruiz didn't feel like another hand, a pair of arms, a back, or a worker. Yes, that little girl made him feel like a king.

"Dime mi'ja, why did you choose that one?" Esteban asked, when Carmen finished reading the entry.

"Because he reminds me of you."

"Ay tú. I'm no saint, mi'ja."

"No, but you're an honest man like him. A worker. You work hard, and you help people . . ." Carmen could not finish her thought. "'Apá," she said after a moment. "The fish are dying."

"What do you mean?"

"I mean they're dying. Se fue! Just like that," she said.

"Oh. A bird probably ate something bad and flying by, you know, made a drop into the pond, and the fish ate it."

"Yech!"

"These things happen," Esteban said. "I'm sure it will pass."

"Yeah, okay." Carmen was quiet for a long time, wondering how she was going to say what she needed to say. "I think they miss you," she said.

"Quién?"

"The fish. They miss hearing you talk to them in the morning before you go to work."

Esteban chuckled. "You know about that, eh?"

"Yeah, 'Apá. So, I think you should come home before

all the fish die." Carmen said it with a wink in her voice, but Esteban knew it was no joke. A lump swelled in his throat.

"Ay, mi'jita . . ."

"Okay, 'Apá? Just come back."

"When you're grown up—"

"I'm almost grown up now!" she said a little too bold, but the only thing Esteban heard was his little girl trying to sound brave.

"Yes, you are almost grown. I heard there's talk of a quinceañera. I heard you didn't want to do it. Is that true?"

"Yes," Carmen stammered. "No. I don't know."

"Oye, I've never been to one, but you get to dress up pretty and have cake. There are other things that go along with it that you might like," Esteban said. "There is a lot of tradition there. This is the kind of thing a daughter should do with her mother, entiendes?"

Carmen didn't want to disappoint her father, but she didn't like the idea of doing something to make her mother happy, either.

"Well, I guess I could go to that fair she keeps telling me about."

"What could it hurt, mi'ja?"

"If I go to the quinceañera fair, that doesn't mean I'm going to do it, though."

"Ay, Carmen," Esteban said, before putting on his most serious, fatherly tone. "Don't treat your mother bad because you don't like the way things are with us," he said. "Show her some respect."

Carmen was quiet for a long time, and Esteban thought he'd lost her when she finally said in a voice the size of a teardrop, "Come home."

Híjole, her voice was that little key to unlock all those memories, all those fears, all that alegría that came with being the father of one little girl. It was the voice that reminded Esteban that Carmen would be his most precious angel forever.

"Mi'ja, no te preocupes. All you need to worry about is doing good in school and being a good daughter. You can do that, verdad?" Carmen wiped her eyes with the back of her hand just as Esteban was doing the same. "Por favor, mi corazón—for your old padrecito?"

"Okay," Carmen said.

"Bueno pues, buenas noches, corazón."

"'Apá! The quinceañera fair is Sunday. I'll go with you to Mass before, okay?"

Esteban wanted to say yes, but even his everyday life was filled with uncertainty. Still, he didn't want to disappoint his angelita. He wanted to put that off as long as possible.

"Okay, mi'ja. Hasta el domingo próximo."

"I'll see you before then, won't I?" Carmen asked in a twisted voice.

"Por supuesto, sí," Esteban said. "Por supuesto."

But the truth was, he didn't know.

When Ana pulled up in front of the Castañeda house, Rafa, his sister Sonia, Diego, Tomás, and a boy she didn't know were inside the open garage, packing up and drinking sodas. The boy who played the congas was passing in front of Ana's car when he saw her and, like a good boy, gave her a polite nod.

"Oye, Tomás," Ana called, as she stepped out of her car. "Who's that boy?"

"Oh, some gabacho," Tomás said. "I mean, he's the guy who called from the flier we put up, looking for a bass player." The boys had been trying to form a band for a while now, but they hadn't found the right mix of musicians yet. Ana leaned against her car.

"Is he any good?"

"Yeah, he's good," Tomás said sadly. Ana frowned.

"That's good, isn't it?"

"Yeah, except I think he's interested in other things."

Ana looked back to the garage and saw that the boy was leaning in a little too close to Sonia Castañeda, Rafa's sister. Ana suspected her Diego had a crush on Sonia. In fact, she knew it. It was splashed all over his face. Diego stood a few steps away from Sonia and the boy as he spoke with Rafa, but all his attention was on the new boy.

"Where is he from?" Ana asked.

"I think he said he moved here from Austin," Tomás said. "Bueno, señora, my ride is here."

Ana waved to the driver who came for Tomás as she walked up the drive to get a better look at the new boy. He was dressed todo in black except for his white belt y los wristbands con silver studs, and big disks filling up both his earlobes (él dice, plugs). He had a piercing on his lip (ay, ay, ay!) and another on his brow. Compared to the boys, his facial hair was thick—which wasn't saying much, with those two weedy sideburns. What surprised Ana was that he had tattoos covering one arm with work started on the other. He was either older than the boys or had found someone who did it outside the law.

The new boy was acting todo suave, hanging over Sonia like a spider, waiting for the perfect moment to drop. Sonia was sitting on a cooler, tuning a guitar resting on her knee. Ana could see she was more interested in what she was doing than the boy, but Diego wasn't as sure. He kept throwing looks over at the boy to make sure he was keeping his distance from Sonia, and he was relieved when Mr. Castañeda came into the garage. Then the boy turned his attention from Sonia and purposely went up to the man to shake his hand. Sonia took the opening to pack up the guitar and hand it over to Diego. Mr. Castañeda took the boy's hand, not even trying to pretend he wasn't looking the boy up and down. He spent so much time checking out the boy, he didn't know that Sonia was already inside the house when he told her to get inside. Diego was relieved.

Ay, mi'jo, Ana chuckled to herself. *You have nothing to worry about.*

Diego quickly gathered his things when he finally saw his mother standing in the drive.

"What's this?" Ana asked, as Diego put the two instruments—the guitar and his sax—in the backseat of their car.

"A guitar. Sonia is letting me borrow it. She got a new one."

"That was nice of her," Ana said. "You're going to teach yourself?"

"She's going to teach me," Diego said. "She's really good. You should hear her play, 'Amá. I've never seen fingers move like that. She's like la Gabriela, each finger like a match, striking a different fire." Diego's voice grew more and more excited as he spoke.

"Gabriela?" Ana asked.

"Yeah, from Rodrigo y Gabriela."

"Who?"

"Don't worry. You'd like them," Diego said. "I'll make you a tape." Ana could see Diego's smile, bright inside the dark car, and they drove for a moment in silence.

"How did that new guy work out?"

"He thinks he's all that because he's played in Austin and has done some studio work."

"Well, is he?"

Diego sighed.

"Yeah, he's pretty good. The best one we've seen so far. But we'll see."

Ana glanced at her boy, tall and lean, with black curls tumbling over his head. She thought Diego was all that, too.

"'Amá, how come girls like boys like him?"

"What do you mean?"

"You know, all 'bad boy.'"

"What girls do you mean?"

"Girls. They always like those dangerous types. He even said he started playing bass because of all the attention he gets. I think it's because of his tight pants, cutting his huevos in half."

"Diego!" Ana laughed. "Not all girls like those kind of boys. I bet Sonia likes nice boys like you." Diego sank into his seat, staring at the dashboard.

"Sonia? She's Rafa's sister," Diego said.

"So, she's a girl, isn't she?"

Diego shrugged and Ana knew she needed to speak carefully.

"If you ask me, I don't think she's that impressed with him. And I think I remember something about being a girl."

Diego needed to change the subject.

"Yeah. Speaking of girls, how's la cabrona?"

"Diego!" Ana was shocked at her son's language as well as the fact that she knew exactly who he meant. "Watch your language, son."

"Disculpe, 'Amá, pero . . . when's she going to stop being so . . ."

Ana sighed. "I don't know, Dieguito. She's angry."

"But she's so—" Diego said. "I don't like how she talks to you."

"Thank you, chulo. I appreciate it. Try not to let her get to you. Let me worry about her. You just worry about school and all your projects. So, is Sonia going to play in the band now, too?"

"No, she just came out to give me the guitar when El Rey decided to make his movida," Diego said.

"El Rey," Ana laughed. "You better be careful. You might forget and call him that to his face."

"That's what he *wants* us to call him. You know, like Elvis?" Diego did his best Elvis impersonation, which even Ana had to admit was—cómo se dice?—lame.

Ana began thinking as they drove through the park near their house.

"Mi'jo. You're doing okay, right?"

"Yeah."

"I mean, it must be strange with your dad gone. I would understand if you were angry, too."

"I'm not mad. I mean, I don't really know what's going on, so . . ."

Neither do I, Ana thought. "Well, when we get things figured out, you kids will be the first to know."

But even Ana didn't know if that was true. How long would Esteban keep avoiding her? How long should she wait? She was as in the dark as her children, the only difference being she was supposed to know what was going on. If the authority known as "They" knew how much she drove by the seat of her pants, she was convinced They would be horrified and swoop in and take her children. She could organize things and events. She had a talent for planning and putting things in order, making sense out of nothing. It was what made her good at her work. But this thing with Esteban, with its messiness, and his silence, and the confusion about their situation, left Ana helplessly poking through the remains of their marriage. The only thing that made sense to her were their children. For them, Ana knew she would do whatever she had to do to protect them from the heartache she knew they would feel if they really knew what was going on. And the best way to do that, she decided, was to keep them busy with their own lives.

"So, Diego, can you help me with something? Can you help get your sister to agree to having a quinceañera?"

"I guess. I don't know what to say to make her get excited about it, though. You know how she is. Even if her hair is on fire, she'll say she likes it that way."

"That's exactly what I mean. She'll only go along with it if she thinks it's her idea. Make it sound like it's the most rad thing you've ever heard of."

"'Rad'?"

"You know, fly. Dope?"

Diego smiled and shook his head. *Qué cute*, he thought.

"You know, Carmen's going to need a court. I'm sure we can arrange it for you and Sonia to be a pair."

"Huh?" Diego felt like someone pulled down his pants on the playground. "I thought this was *her* deal. What does this have to do with me?"

"You're her brother. You should be involved."

"Can't I take tickets or hand out balloons or something? Why do I have to be in it?"

"You don't. I just thought it might be nice—you and Sonia as a pair. Think about it."

Diego was blushing so hard he thought his ears would start leaking. Pero, he liked the idea. He liked the idea a lot.

"Just help me get her talking about it, okay?"

The outside light came on when Ana pulled into their driveway, and they saw Carmen standing in the back door all ready for bed, arms crossed tight against her chest.

"Now what?" Diego said.

"Quién sabe?" Ana said. She put the car into park and helped her son with his instruments.

"I'll go to the quinceañera fair on Sunday," Carmen announced, as Ana and Diego reached her. "I'm going to Mass with 'Apá first. So, I'll meet you there after." And with that, she turned and left Ana and Diego standing at the door, blinking at each other.

"You're welcome," Diego said to his mother as he walked into the house.

≫ EIGHT ≪

Ana Ruiz was not escared of much. Mice, those flying palmetto bugs that aim for your face, and getting stuck in the elevator were on the top of the list. But after walking into the Henry B. Gonzalez Convention Center on a postcard-perfect Sunday afternoon, there was a new thing to add to her list: the quinceañera fair. It wasn't that it wasn't what she expected. She got what she expected and more. Way too much more, like a pretty girl with too much lipstick. It wasn't because it was big (the convention center is huge, but the fair only filled one of the small halls). What Ana wasn't expecting was the rush of mothers, girls, and 'buelitas, the vendors who swooped over her, Carmen, and Bianca everywhere they turned, and the this-is-a-once-in-a-lifetime-event-so-you-better-do-it-right ambiente covered in sparkling sugar, big smiles, and a no-refund policy. Everything you could want for the quince—and chingos of cosas Ana had never thought of—were brought by jewelers, bakers, caterers, tuxedo shops, evening-gown boutiques, stylists, decorators, makeup artists, manicurists, florists, printers, DJs, limo services, hair-care wholesalers, dermatologists, cosmetic dentists, photographers, videographers—all there to cut a good deal if you made a down payment with them right then and there. And that was not even counting the more traditional things that Ana knew of: the quince pillow, the quince muñeca, and the tiara. Nowhere did Ana see anyone showing a quince Bible or rosary.

Mothers and their daughters roamed the hall scribbling notes on fliers, in small spiral pads, and, for one girl, on the palm of her hand. Ana had to admit it was a good idea when some of the girls pulled out cameras to snap pictures of things they liked: "I like these flowers, Mami!" *Click*. "Look at this cake!" *Click, click*. "This table is perfect! Go stand next to it." *Click, click, click*. Everyone was excited, laughing and talking loud, drunk on all the pink and pastel, the lace, and all the pretty cositas that caught your eye no matter where you looked. But just as one girl got sucked into the charanga, there would be someone's yawny-eyed tía, or the 'buelita you had to drag from her novelas, whispering complaints into her shoulder.

"They call that queso?" a 'buelita asked her daughter, a woman whose future quince was scooping the orange glop out of a small cup with a corn chip and licking her fingers. "I make better queso than that!"

"Sí! If you want to be making queso for five hundred, go ahead!"

The few fathers shadowing their babbling wives and daughters were shell-shocked, their hands shoved into their pockets (with their fingers vise-gripped around their checkbooks, you can bet). As the fair went on, their expressions got more and more dazed as the cost of each "necessity" was added to the final bill in their heads. Some of the men were vendors, including two hairstylist/party-planner cousins who had the most lavish display of them all: three booths wide, with lavender tulle looped from end to end with garlands of pink flowers, and spotlights that twirled and changed colors. The cousins were the most popular after the food vendors, because they were giving out silver plastic tiaras for free and five-minute updos for girls whose names were pulled from a basket. So between all the mothers, tías, cousins, and abuelitas, a baby-faced girl walked by with her new do sprayed and clinched with a fake crown, looking like Miss America arriba but dressed in jeans and chanclas abajo.

The cousins were todo serious, working fast, chomping on their gum, wagging their combs at any girl who thought she might have something to say. (Oh, no, you get what you pay for, esa.) The cousins took their time when they did the models' hair for the fashion show. That's where they really showed their stuff, working like crazy hormigas, but fast—comb, spray, pin, y ya! Instant princess!

Ana and the girls sat down just as the next fashion show started. You didn't need a watch to know it was going to begin. The music announcing it was pumped up so loud it made your teeth vibrate.

Pobre Ana had a headache. Not just because of the noise or because her attention was pulled from here to there like a pinball machine, but because Carmen was being more cabrona than usual, and Bianca—ay, Bianca! Ana thought that Bianca had a hand in getting Carmen to the fair. She knew it was right to include her, but to be real, she wished it could have just been the two of them, a mother-daughter thing, Ana and Carmen on their own. *But of course, Bianca should be here*, Ana thought. *If only she would stop talking!*

"Oye, look at that one," Bianca said, doodling in her esqueche pad, looking at a model making her way down the runway in a pink tube trimmed in chocolate brown.

"The fabric is crap, but the cut is nice. I can make it better. Híjole! Aren't those shoes ugly?"

"Bianca! That lady over there is looking at you," Carmen whispered into her hand.

"I can make you something so much better than this stuff!"

How Bianca was heard over the music and the noise was a mystery of nature, like those places where balls roll uphill. Ana smiled at the woman who'd been glaring at Bianca, but the woman shot mal de ojos back at her. Any other time, Ana would have ignored her, but la mujer was hard to miss. Those huge brisket arms of hers were crossed over her panza, which was draped in a purple housedress embroidered with bloodred flowers. Ana wasn't sure why the woman was looking at them so mean. Maybe she'd just put down a payment on that dress for her own daughter; or maybe she, like Ana, was tired of hearing everything Bianca had to say. When it came down to it, Ana would fight for the girl as if she gave birth to her herself, but híjole, Bianca didn't know when to shut up.

"Let's go," Ana said, when the fat woman would not stop shooting mal de ojos at them. Ana stood up and the girls followed, all of them cutting through the crowd, taking cake samples and brightly colored fliers, whether they wanted them or not. They finally found themselves in a less crowded part of the hall, where a lonely woman had a small booth piled with her own line of clutches, purses, and bags. With most everyone ignoring her (no quinceañera bolsas?), the woman was happy to have someone to talk to when Bianca stopped to look.

"So, what do you think?" Ana asked Carmen.

"It's loud," Carmen sighed.

"Yes, but your quinceañera doesn't have to be big and

loud. I was thinking of something smaller. It's not just about the cake and the dress and all the stuff. It's about recognizing that you are becoming an adult member of the family, ready to enter the world. It's an old tradition."

"Then why didn't you have one?" Carmen asked, todo snarky.

"We were poor," Ana said plainly. "I had a cake and I got some new earrings, but . . ." Ana's voice trailed as she noticed a vendor demonstrating a miniature Cinderella coach outlined in blinking lights that changed colors from bright white to brilliant blue, fast and slow, then off and on, all from the turn of a dial. A circle of girls with new updos was watching, clapping, and squealing, looking like happy ice-cream cones made of hair and Aqua Net.

" . . . it was nothing like this. I was reading about the history of the quinceañera online. Some say it has roots in Aztec ceremonial rites . . ." Ana stopped when she saw that Carmen wasn't listening. She knew it wasn't just the noise. Ana could feel the distance between them getting wider. It was becoming normal, as if it had never been warm con cariño, like when Carmen was a little girl and she gave her mother hugs just because she wanted to. And in that moment Ana felt that Carmen was sailing out of her reach. She panicked. She was losing her girl, so she grabbed for the only thing she could think of, which was to talk about something she knew Carmen would want to talk about.

"How is your dad?"

Well of course, this would be the day when that was the wrong question to ask. Carmen's temper flared like Ana had poked her finger at a bruise.

"He wasn't there," she said coldly. Ana could almost see the horns sprout on Carmen's head.

"What?"

"I said, he wasn't there," Carmen said. She was annoyed she had to repeat herself. Ana couldn't believe what she had heard.

"He wasn't there? What do you mean, 'he wasn't there'?"

"I mean, he wasn't there. He didn't show up."

Ana went from heartache to worry. "How did you get here?"

Carmen acted like she couldn't hear her mother.

"Carmen! How did you get here?"

Carmen nodded toward her cousin. And then, just to be dramatic, she said, "But it took me forever to get her on the phone. I almost had to walk."

"Where was she?"

"I don't know! I'm not in charge of her."

Ana gritted her teeth.

"Why didn't you call me?"

But of course, Ana was the last person Carmen would call. The idea worried Ana more than it hurt her feelings.

"You should have called me," Ana said. "I can't believe him!"

"It's no big deal," Carmen said. She was trying to put no te preocupes in her voice, but the truth was she was trying to fool herself more than her mother. "I probably misunderstood which Mass he wanted to go to. He probably went to the Spanish one, and I just assumed . . ."

"Did you call him?" Carmen clucked her tongue and rolled her eyes.

"What are you getting so worked up about?"

"Carmen, did you call him?"

When Carmen would not answer, Ana fumbled in her purse for her phone.

He might not want to deal with me or our marriage, but our kids? I'm not letting this go! Ana thought.

"Yes! Yes! I called him," Carmen finally spit.

"What did he say?"

"Nothing. His phone was off. You're making a big deal out of nothing!"

"You were stranded!"

"Only for an hour, and I was at church, not in a dark alley. Chill! I'm here, aren't I?"

Ana stopped digging in her purse and tried to calm herself. The two of them looked over at Bianca, asking the purse lady 1,001 questions, which the woman answered once she saw Bianca flash a platinum card. Ana wondered how her brother, Bianca's father, could be so easy with his daughter. Cars, credit cards, clothes—the girl wanted for nothing, and his rein on his daughter was loose.

"Besides, the Mass was good," Carmen said. "The father's homily was about family and honor and stuff. He talked about the sanctity of marriage and honoring marriage vows. You should have been there."

Ana could hardly believe it. Was this fourteen-year-old girl really trying to give her mother a lesson on marriage?

"He was saying how people take marriage for granted and that divorce isn't the answer, and that he was leading a marriage-renewal seminar next month for couples who need to be reminded of what their vows meant. I got you a flier."

(Ay, por favor!)

Ana looked at the bright blue flier Carmen pulled from her purse. *What does this girl know about marriage?* she thought.

It had been years since Ana had gone to Mass. It wasn't that she didn't believe, but she practiced her faith "a mi modo"—in her own way. Until the separation, Carmen had nothing to say about how her mother expressed her faith. Besides, Carmen loved going to church with her 'apá. It was another one of those times when she had him all to herself. Maybe because Ana had an altarcito set up in the house, no one asked her why she stopped going to Mass. Ana loved the ceremony and rituals, the candles and the incense, the calming image of La Virgen, the murmuring sound of prayers by the faithful. She even liked the bake sales. But after a time, she began to feel the weight of the church pressing down on her. Faith she would keep, but church? No, her home altar was where she, and thousands, maybe millions, of other faithful women like her, felt closest to God—in those quiet moments when it was just her, preparing a meal or drinking her tea in time with the creaks and sighs of her house and the silent flicker of a single vela. That was when God came to her.

After a while, it was ordinary for Esteban to go off to church with the kids, while Ana (and later Diego) stayed at home, expressing her thanks and petitions at her altarcito, then preparing a large breakfast they ate together when Carmen and Esteban returned.

Ana looked at the paper Carmen handed her again. Maybe if she'd gone to Mass, she and Esteban wouldn't be in this situation. She shoved the flier deep into her bolsa as she felt a throb sprouting deep in her head. She massaged her temple with the heel of her hand.

"I'm going to sit down," Ana said.

"Can I have some money for a soda?"

Why don't you ask your dad for the money? Ana thought. But she held her tongue and handed her daughter some bills.

"I'll be out there," Ana said, pointing to the outer hall where the noise was lower.

Ana found a large window looking into a courtyard and sat down, leaning against the broad sill.

"So, here you are!"

Ana gasped, as if the sky had opened and delivered an angel to her feet. "Mira!" She stood up and threw her arms around Beatriz.

"Mujer, I've been walking around this barn for a half hour. I called but you didn't answer!"

"You did? I didn't hear the phone! You hear how loud it is out here? It's louder in there! Siéntate conmigo. I can't go back in there." Beatriz sat with Ana, glad not to enter the noisy hall. "I didn't think you were coming," Ana said.

"I wasn't going to, but I couldn't leave you hanging. So, where is your little angel?"

"She's in there somewhere," Ana said. "Her cousin is in there, too. They'll watch out for each other, which is good, because she doesn't need me," Ana said stiffly. "You don't know how lucky you are to have boys. They're no trouble."

"Are you kidding? For all the broken bones and sprains and split lips and all the crazy cosas boys get into? They built a wing onto Santa Rosa Hospital thanks to my Carlos alone."

"Yeah, but I would take a broken arm right now over all this. A broken bone, you slap a cast on it, it heals, and you're done. With this . . ." Ana dropped her head. "She's driving me crazy."

"So, why don't you tell her?"

"Tell her what?"

"Tell her the truth."

"No—it's not—I can't do that."

"Don't tell her everything, but just enough to let her know it's not just about you."

Ana's heart fell.

"The sooner she learns her father is just human, the sooner she'll grow up a little."

"But I don't want her to—I mean, no, I can't do that to her."

Beatriz put her hand on Ana's shoulder warmly. "Mujer, why are you taking all the chingazos?"

"I'm not," Ana said, unconvincingly. "I'm not! It's complicated." She paused as Beatriz began digging in her huge bolsa for the aspirin she knew Ana needed. "Esteban is a good man. He is! Carmen adores him. I can't—I don't want to be the one . . ."

Ana was embarrassed to say it, but she was a little jealous of Esteban, of how he was the moon and the stars to their little girl, of how he would always be the one she loved most of all. But Ana also knew that if her daughter knew the truth about her father, it would break her heart. She wanted to protect her daughter—both of her children—from the truth as long as possible. She knew Carmen had to grow up someday, but did it have to happen with so much disappointment and heartache?

"Ay, mujer," Beatriz said. "So, how did your meeting with him go last week?"

Ana bit her lip and looked out the large window down toward the clusters of girls and their mothers leaving the quinceañera fair. They each had a white shopping bag, thanks to *Your Quince* magazine, filled with souvenirs, fliers, y otras cosas from the fair. A skinny girl had her spindly arms wrapped around her mother's thick shoulders—the woman in the purple housedress who had been giving them the mal de ojo earlier. The girl gave her mother un besito on the cheek, and the woman wrapped her flabby arm around her niñita, pulling her in close so her girl's face rested against hers, petting her daughter's other cheek with her fat palm. Even though the girl had to crumple down to receive her mother's affection, she walked with her, cheek to cheek, like she was supposed to be there, like she wanted to be there, like there was no better place for her to be. Ana felt that pang, as small and sharp as a paper cut on her heart, and looked away.

"We're going to try again this week," she said. "We still have a lot of financial business to sort out. He's just—and I've been so busy at work. You know. How do you and Larry do it? How have you lasted all these years?"

"Bourbon," Beatriz said.

The truth was Beatriz Sánchez and Larry Milligan were completamente loco about each other. They both thought finding each other was like winning the lottery. So not to invite bad luck, they told old ball-and-chain jokes about each another. But deep in the secret folds of their hearts, they still truly, deeply, madly loved each other after all these years.

"You guys don't even fight," Ana said.

"We fight," Beatriz said. "But never about the big things. Somehow, we always agree on the big things."

Beatriz wished she could tell Ana what the secret was, she wished she had a magic formula to offer, but it was simple. It was Beatriz + Larry 4-ever, just like it was when they first met at the University of Michigan.

"Ay, 'manita," Beatriz said, as Bianca and Carmen came toward them. Carmen had a large soda, and Bianca carried a fistful of fliers, her sketchbook, and one of the white *Your Quince* magazine shopping bags on her arm. Bianca was chattering as they walked up.

"What do you mean you're ready to leave? I'm not ready to leave. Are you ready to leave, Tía?" Bianca asked.

"Say hello to mi comadre," Ana said.

"Hola," the girls said in unison.

"There's still one more fashion show. Can't we stay for that?"

"Why? You don't like anything," Carmen said.

"I get ideas. I've gotten lots and lots of ideas, just from walking around and watching everything. Come on, there are still some good seats in the front."

"How lovely to see you!" Beatriz sang as she lifted the soda from Carmen's hand. "Thank you mi'jita." She handed the drink to Ana along with the aspirin, urging her to take it. Carmen stared at Bianca with her mouth open. Pero Bianca was no tonta. She knew when she was out of her league. She looked back at Carmen with an expression that said, *You're on your own, esa.*

"I would love to join you," Beatriz said, "but I have to run. See you later?"

Ana looked at Beatriz blankly.

"The barbecue at the president's house? For Montalvo?"

"I thought that was next weekend."

Ana was lying. She had no plans to go to the barbecue and had done everything she could to avoid Montalvo all week. Thankfully, his studio was in a warehouse across campus, not in her building, like most of the others. She was still embarrassed about how he found her that day in the office, how she pierced him with her sharp words, and how she choked with dread afterward. Ana was hoping that if enough time passed, he would forget about it and forget about her.

"You should come. Really, you should come," Beatriz said, looking at her watch. "Ya me voy. I'm late already."

Beatriz took the soda from Ana and gave it back to Carmen. Then she raised herself up to her full four feet, eleven and three-quarters inches, and leaned in close to

Carmen. She wanted to make sure that the girl caught her meaning.

"It's so sweet your mother brought you to this. I can't wait to see what you all pull together. I'm sure it will be wonderful." Beatriz smiled, and Carmen had no choice but to smile back. To tell you the truth, she liked Beatriz, but la mujer could make the hairs stand on her neck with a wink. Beatriz gave Ana un abrazo goodbye and did the same with the girls and was gone as quickly as she had appeared. That Beatriz. Just like Glenda, the Good Witch, except that she came and went like the Wicked Witch of the West: with a bang.

"There's still so much to see!" Bianca said.

"You know what? I have a headache," Ana said. "You two go ahead and I'll wait for you out here." Ana sat down again and Carmen plopped herself down, far enough away so that someone passing by would not think they knew each other. Having them seated in front of her inspired Bianca. She'd been cooking up her plan all week, and being at the fair made her more sure of herself.

"We don't have to go back in there. Oye, so first, we rent a nice place. And I'm thinking Carmen enters in a cloud of smoke under an arch made of white feathers, and then more feathers fall from the sky like little kisses . . ."

"Goose feathers?" Carmen asked.

"White feathers."

"I'm allergic."

"You're allergic to white?"

"No, to feathers, like the ones in 'Buelita's pillows."

"Okay, no feathers."

"But I like feathers. Maybe if the feathers are dyed green or blue, or glow in the dark! Can they dye them glow-in-the-dark like the rosaries we got at confirmation?" Carmen smirked.

"Okay! No feathers!" Bianca said, working hard not to let Carmen get on her nerves. "So, if no feathers, what?"

"Glitter?"

"No, you'll be washing it off for weeks, and if you inhale it, it's worse than the feathers."

"Then, how about Ping-Pong balls?"

"Shut up."

"They won't go up anyone's nose."

Bianca would not let her cousin win. She pushed on, describing a quinceañera that sounded like a cross between a Las Vegas floor show and Disney on Parade. Ana could feel the aspirin burning a hole in her stomach. She hadn't eaten, so taking the aspirin was a bad idea. When Bianca got to the part with live doves and white horses, Ana knew she had to speak.

"Bianca! Who do you think is going to pay for this big production you have in mind?"

"All of us," Bianca said. "It's supposed to be a family thing, right? My dad will help. Just tell him what you need, and you can have padrinos y madrinas para this and that, and I'll help organize the whole thing. That's the way it's supposed to be."

Coraje! Ana thought. It's not that she didn't want the family involved, but since everyone had something to say about the separation, she was not looking forward to making phone calls and hearing remarks on her life:

Pray to La Lupe every day, mujer . . .

I know a curandera who can work miracles . . .

Get a makeover, girl!

What did you do?

And then, from her brother Marcos:

Get over it!

"Ok, I'll make the phone calls," Bianca said, as if reading

Ana's mind. "I can do it! Really!" She looked at her cousin
to jump in, but Carmen was more interested in her soda,
mashing the ice at the bottom of the cup with the straw.
Bianca plopped herself between the two and became very
calm. Ana could hear the gears cranking in Bianca's head.
Finally, Bianca reached into her white shopping bag and
pulled out a copy of *Your Quince* magazine. She slowly
turned the pages until she found what she was looking for.

"Look what it says here," she said. "'You and Your
Father on Your Special Day.'" Carmen leaned in as Bianca
read from the two-page spread with a big photo of a
quince dancing with an older man in a tux.

"'Your father deserves some recognition, too. This is
best accomplished during the quinceañera waltz . . .'"

Ándale. Dale gas, girl, Ana thought.

By the way Carmen was listening, Ana could see that
Bianca had found the magic words. It made her heart
swell, but she was a little sad, too. She had wanted this to
be an event they planned, a way for them to grow close
again, not another way for Carmen to be Daddy's Girl.

Carmen kept her eyes on the magazine as Bianca read
some more. Ana could see Carmen had her own ideas
cranking, también. All she wanted was for her 'apá to
come back home. If it meant getting all made up and going
through a big party to do it, why not? She hadn't thought
about her parents as a couple, the way she thought of
movie stars or even kids in school, full of romance and
gooey stares. She'd never even seen them hold hands.
The only thing she knew was that her father being gone
felt like the sun had gone black and the moon had fallen
from the sky. It was just not the way the world should be.
Maybe the quinceañera dance would be where they came
to their senses, where they would forget whatever stupid

thing had split them apart and come back together again. Maybe there would be a second wedding! Now *that*, Carmen thought, she would like to be a part of. Maybe the quinceañera was a warmup to that. It was worth a shot. And besides, some of the dresses she saw were pretty, no matter what Bianca said.

Carmen snorted when Bianca got to the part where the father helps the quince change from her flats to a pair of high heels. "I'm not doing that! I'll wear flip-flops."

"Flip-flops!" Bianca shouted. "Be serious, Carmen."

"I am!"

Ana had had enough. She sat up and turned to Carmen.

"Look," she said, getting herself ready for a fight. "If you don't want to do this, we won't do this. There's no point in spending time and money on something you're not interested in. So just tell me now, do you want a quinceañera or not?"

Carmen didn't want to show it, but she was excited. She wondered if there were other ways to make her father's part in the quinceañera bigger.

"Okay," Carmen said meekly.

"Yes!" Bianca said, pumping her fist in the air and jumping to her feet to face Ana and Carmen. "So, it's settled. Carmen is having a quinceañera! And I am the official quinceañera planner pa' todo!" Ana glared at Bianca, and even Carmen shot her a mal de ojo.

"Okay! Okay! I'll be the assistant quinceañera planner, but I'm in charge of the damas and the dresses. And the chambelanes. And the tuxes. I can be in charge of the tuxes, can't I?"

Ana closed her eyes and leaned back against the sill again. The spot in her belly felt like it was glowing.

≥ NINE ≥

Ana's Monday was wall-to-wall meetings, each worse than the one before it. A hiring meeting, a tenure meeting, a budget meeting, a meeting to discuss space (always a touchy subject), and another meeting to discuss why there were so many meetings. By three o'clock, Ana was starving. As she walked back to her office, she decided to send Cynthia out for a snack so she could sit in her office with her calendar and calculator and go over the fliers and business cards she got at the quinceañera fair. She needed a plan. Bianca could call herself whatever she wanted, but Ana knew she was the one to make sure it came off without too much drama—or expense. But when Ana returned to her office, she found Cynthia waiting for her with her purse on her arm and her car keys in hand.

"Oh, thank goodness! Here." Cynthia handed Ana a thick folder and headed for the door. "My appointment is in twenty minutes."

"Oh! I'm so sorry!" Ana had forgotten that she'd told Cynthia she could leave early. "I should have told you to go ahead and leave even if I wasn't here. Go, go! But what's this?" Ana asked, looking at the folder.

"Some documents the president's office sent over. They need Montalvo's signature by five o'clock today. I would take them, but I really, *really* have to go."

"That's okay. Mocte can go—"

"He's not here today, ma'am. I was here by myself and I didn't think I should leave. I thought you would be back earlier . . ."

"Oh, no. Cynthia—could you please take care of this? I really, really can't—" Ana stopped talking when she saw Cynthia's confused look and took a U-turn. "No. You know what? You go ahead. It's okay."

"I'm sorry, ma'am. This seamstress is going to make our trajes for Las Florecitas Fuertes. We've been waiting for months to get on her schedule. I couldn't cancel."

"Don't worry," Ana said as her stomach twisted into a knot. "I'll take care of it."

Ana had to drive to the far end of campus to find Montalvo's studio. He was the only artist to have a building all to himself, a request she thought the dean would not give. Instead, he called in several favors and turned the campus upside down to find a space that met Montalvo's needs: a barn-sized A-frame building with exposed crossbeams. The building was scheduled for demolition but had kept mowers and other machines and was a meeting place for maintenance workers. Because of the visiting artist, the maintenance crew had been split up and moved to spots across campus, making Montalvo the talk of many coffee breaks.

When Ana stepped into the building, it took her eyes a while to adjust to the shadows of the warehouse. A small group of students stood at the far corner of the space, looking up into a dark corner of the ceiling. At first she thought they were staring out the large windows, which let the sunlight spill over them. But that wasn't it. What were they looking at? She couldn't see. As Ana got closer to the group, she noticed how quiet they were, and as she got even closer, she could hear her heels clicking on the cement, like she'd walked into a church during prayer. She began to walk on her tiptoes. Ana could hear Montalvo's voice, but she couldn't tell where it was coming from. She turned around, thinking he might be behind her. When she didn't see him, she turned back to the students, confused, before she heard a screech and rattle, and she finally saw what the students were captured by: Montalvo was hanging over them in a harness. As he lowered himself he came into the light, looking like a large spider slowly twisting in the air. Wide leather straps were cinched around his waist, thighs, and buttocks, and a large pulley hung just over his head, threaded with the thick rope he used to control the speed of his fall. He let the rope glide between his leather gloved hands, lowering himself quickly to the ground but landing with a light tap. The students reared back and aahed.

"It's very easy when you understand how it works," Montalvo said. "So, if you do not like heights and the feeling of freedom, you might not want to do this, but I think you are all adventurous, yes?" The young women in the group giggled. "Upper-body strength is helpful, but this is designed in such a way that you do not have to be, how do you say . . . ?" Montalvo took a weight lifter's pose, and several of the girls said together:

"Strong."

The one girl who said "sexy" made all heads turn toward her, and she sank into a puddle. The young men sized each other up like they were in gym class. Montalvo began to hoist himself up again, and Ana noticed the ripple in his fore-arms and the thicker muscles under his T-shirt. Sweat had made his T-shirt damp so the cotton clung to him, showing the outline of his chest and his hard, chocolate-brown nipples. (Ay, madre santa!) He stopped talking when Ana's cell phone chirped loudly. She didn't have to look at it to know it was Bianca. All eyes turned to look at her. She winced and held up the folder.

"I'm sorry, I didn't mean to interrupt. I have some paperwork for you."

"If you want to leave it over there, I will look at it when the class is finished," Montalvo said. Ana couldn't tell if there was coldness in his voice or if he was sharing information, nada más.

"Yes, but I have to get your signature before the end of the day. I'll wait over here." She moved away from the students to a small meeting area that had been set up near a drafting table. Her phone chirped again, and she turned it off as she walked away from the class. She stopped near the drafting table and, seeing the plans for Montalvo's next project, remembered why he needed the large space. He was a sculptor who made large-scale fiberglass pieces famous for their bright colors and—how they say—muscular, undulating curves. He favored images of men and animals, and one lavish piece featured two Ballet Folklorico dancers in mid-twirl, the woman's skirt billowing proudly and the powerful, trim body of the male dancer slightly arched over her, his hand lightly touching hers as he guided her turn. (Hermoso!) Ana forgot that this was one of Montalvo's works. She first saw it in a book and marveled at how she thought it captured power and grace. She would have been bien wowed if she'd seen the piece in person, it standing two stories tall. The piece had traveled all over the world, and Ana wondered what they thought of it in Prague, London, Berlin, and Rome, places she wanted to see someday.

A swell of laughter and applause let Ana know that the class was over. The students milled about, talking to each other. While Montalvo unhitched himself from the harness, Ana wondered if she should go over to him or keep waiting where she was. She pulled at the sleeves of her blouse, straightened her collar, ran her hands through her hair, and finally leaned against a table, trying to look aquí estoy y nada más. She suddenly felt goofy and stood up again. When she did, a splinter from the old table caught the back of her skirt. She felt a tug at her backside and then a small snap of thread.

Crap! she thought, looking at the small pucker on the back of her skirt. She was pulling at the fabric when she could feel that someone was standing near her. And when she turned around, there he was, toweling off his arms, sweat glistening on his face and neck.

"I'm sorry to keep you waiting."

"No te preocupes," Ana said. Her voice was down to business. But inside, the híjoles were jumping all over because even though he was todo sweaty, el hombre was still bien good-looking.

"I hope you did not ruin your skirt."

"No, no. It's just a pull," she said, nervously brushing her backside. "I brought some papers for you to sign. I need to get them back to the president's office before five."

"What are they?"

"There's an I-9, a health insurance form, a payroll form. Nothing unusual."

Montalvo sat down and looked at the papers. Ana kept standing, her hands clasped in front of her. Montalvo looked very different from the day she met him. His skin was still smooth and dark, but his hair was ruffled. His recent exertion made a hum around him, as if all his muscles, still hot from having worked so hard, were winding down like a huge machine shutting down for the night. Montalvo wiped his face and neck with the towel.

"All of these papers need my signature?"

"Yes," Ana said, assuming that was correct, and Montalvo flipped through the papers.

"I'm sorry. I do not see where." Ana moved to examine the folder and when she got closer, she smelled Montalvo's aroma, the smell of sweat before it sours and stains. There was nothing artificial in it, no perfume or cologne that she could name. It was simply him. If the flavor of his skin were identified by his scent, Ana would have to say it reminded her of something surprising and thrilling, like chocolate with chipotle or mango slices dipped in wet chili sauce, or, like she heard the woman at the fancy store say about a perfume she liked: it had notes of leather (ay, tú tú!). She cleared her throat and put her fingers to her mouth, a habit she had when trying to figure something out. Here she was, working hard not to let everything about Montalvo—his neck, those nipples, his brazos like thick branches—make her drunk. But Montalvo got the wrong idea.

"Discúlpe," he said after a moment. "I must smell like a horse."

"Oh no—not at all," Ana said, thinking that Montalvo must have taken her habit the wrong way. He got up and moved to the other side of the table.

"I'm sorry. In my kind of work, it is to be expected to get what they call 'ripe.'"

"Oh no. You're fine." Montalvo plucked at the neck of

his T-shirt to air himself. That only made his aroma stronger, and Ana felt light-headed. His scent dazzled her, made
her feel unlike herself y—cómo se dice?—feral.

"Would you like some water?" Montalvo asked. He
could see Ana was woozy. "I will bring you water." He
trotted over to a small refrigerator for a bottle of water.
As he twisted off the cap, Ana imagined Montalvo pour-
ing the water over his head, letting it glide over his face,
down his neck, over his chest, down his belly, and into the
sudden thatch of hair she imagined just below. (Híjole!)
The idea of this made Ana turn red, and, if she were to be
honest with herself, she would say she felt that tension,
deep between her legs. Part of her wanted to cry with joy.
It had been so long, she thought those sensations had left
her forever.

"Maybe you should sit down," he said, afraid that his
stink was suffocating the poor woman. "Please, just put
marks where I am to sign and push the file over to me."

Ana could not believe what was happening to her. She
gulped the water and began to look at the file. Her vision
was blurred and she began to feel faint. Before she knew
it, Montalvo was offering her a carton of orange juice.

"Drink this. I have some dried fruit, también."

Ana chewed on the raisins he offered her and began
to go back to herself. She drank the rest of the juice and
blinked her eyes.

"When was the last time you ate?" Montalvo asked.

Ándale! La mujer had only had a cafecito early in the
morning.

"I—I'm so sorry. I'm fine now. Let's get back to this."

"No," Montalvo said. "Those papers can wait. Would
you like me to take you—is there someone I may call for
you?"

"I'm fine, really. You're right. I haven't eaten today and I have been running around and it's hot in here, isn't it?"

Montalvo jogged to the far end of the warehouse to turn on a fan, which whined and coughed but finally cooled the air.

"Please, I would be happy to call someone for you. Perhaps Sra. Milligan, or your husband."

"No, no. That's not necessary." Ana was now all herself. The mention of her husband and Beatriz, and remembering that time was ticking and the papers were still not signed, made her sit up, push back her light-headedness, and get down to work. When she got a good look at the file, she saw that his signature was only needed on the last few papers.

When Montalvo finished, Ana picked up the folder and turned to leave. She was partway to the door before she realized she hadn't bothered to say goodbye.

Coraje! she thought, as she stopped and turned back to face Montalvo.

"I'm sorry," Ana said. "I'm so very sorry. I—you are very kind and I was very—the other day, I mean. You caught me at a bad time, and I'm afraid I made it worse. I have been under a lot of stress lately. It has nothing to do with you."

"I did not mean to intrude, but when I saw you, I recognized your pain. I . . ." Montalvo turned to roll up his plans, fumbling as he tried to slide them into a tube. He knocked over a barrel holding other tubes, making them all spill like fat straws across the floor. Ana went to help him, smiling a little at how this man, *qué elegante*, could be so clumsy. They picked up all the tubes and put them back as they were.

"I was not trying to be forward," he said. "I think with my English not being very good and coming to this unfamiliar place, and because I work alone, my manners are very poor."

"Oh, no," Ana said, feeling a drop of sweetness toward Montalvo. "Your English is really very good. And you were so good with the students earlier."

"That was part of the reason I took this job, to have more direct contact with people, with young people. And because Bowb was so persistent."

Ana had to think for a moment before she knew he was talking about her dean, Robert Priestly. She chuckled.

"Did I say his name wrong? Is it 'Boob'?"

"Oh, no, don't call him Boob!" Ana laughed. "But we say 'Bahb.'"

"Bowb."

"Bob."

"Bowb."

"*Bahb*."

"I'll call him Robert." The two of them laughed, the stiffness from before floating off into the shadows.

"I should go," Ana said, picking up the file. "They are expecting this before the end of the day."

Montalvo walked Ana to her car and opened the door for her. The color had returned to her cheeks, and she felt good to drive.

"It's not a good habit, not to eat."

"I know. It's just sometimes I get so busy I don't think about it."

"I do the same thing, but I eat small snacks throughout the day. I don't like to stop working when I'm in the air," he said. "Getting light-headed up there is not a good idea."

"No, I don't imagine it is."

"Perhaps you could tell me of some places near here to have a cafecito and one of these breakfast tacos people tell me about?"

"Yes, I can do that," Ana said. She stared at her lap, then back up at Montalvo. "I'll ask my husband. He works all over town and knows the best places to go."

"Bueno." Montalvo looked off toward his studio. "Would your husband mind if we had coffee one afternoon? I have many questions about this campus and this city and the students. Sra. Milligan is very encouraging, but I need more thoughts. If it is not too much trouble."

"Of course," Ana said. She wanted to help. She had to help, pero she started to wonder: was she making the first prick into the cloth to embroider something big and complicated? Así no! Ana was not going to be like those other women. "I think that would be fine."

As Ana drove off she looked in her rearview mirror. Montalvo was still standing where she left him. And then, ay mujer! You'll never guess what he did. He took off his T-shirt and tossed it over his shoulder as he turned to head back to his studio. Seeing his naked chest, Ana couldn't help herself. (What living woman could?) She felt—how would she say it?—euphoric. Pero, not for long, because then it came—the guilt, hard and heavy, like a fist.

≫ TEN ≪

A y, ay, ay! Bianca was on what they call a roll. Her cell phone así, her esqueche pad acá, and Carmen's clica all around, waiting for what was next. Y Carmen? She was taking her math test. You would think it was Bianca planning her own quinceañera. That's exactly what Diego thought when he ran into her in the school plaza during a study break. He would have rather not got wrapped up in her tornado, but after he saw what she was up to, he was glad he did.

"Sí, sí. No. Sí. A deposit? How much? But you're going to be here already you said. Okay. I'll call you back." Bianca slapped her phone shut and crossed "DJ Juana" off her list. Las chicas groaned.

"So, she's not coming?" Mari or Alicia or Patti asked.

"Probably not. I don't know. I'll ask my dad," Bianca said, writing a note on her pad.

"Who's not coming?" Diego asked.

"DJ Juana," one of the chicas said.

"DJ Juana? From New York?" Diego asked.

"Who else?" Bianca said.

"Yeah, right!" Then Diego remembered he was talking to his cousin Bianca. "Bianca! You can't do that!"

"Why not?"

"A DJ from New York? Who's going to pay for her to come all the way here?"

"My dad," Bianca said, like it was nothing, which it wasn't, pos . . .

"This isn't *your* quince," he blurted. The girls threw each other slanty looks.

"I know!"

"Does my mom know you're calling New York? 'Stás loca?"

"I'm not crazy," Bianca snapped. The girls sat up, waiting to hear what Bianca would say next. "I just want my cuz to have a nice party. What's wrong with that?"

And then one of the girls—la Alicia or la Mari, one of them—asked, "So how *is* your mother?"

All heads turned to look at the bigmouthed girl. Los mal de ojos were flying so fast, you could feel the whoosh. The other girls clucked their tongues and pulled away from the hocicona, but the truth was, all of them wanted to know the chisme about Bianca's 'amá. Las chismosas!

Knowing what she had done, the girl pulled her books together and stood up.

"I got to go to class," she mumbled.

"Yeah, go to class and learn something, mensa," one of the other girls said. The chicas sat there, todo uncomfortable, till one by one they each came up with a reason to go do whatever it was they should have been doing already.

"I left messages for your mom, but some of this stuff can't wait," Bianca said to Diego.

"Carmen's birthday isn't for a while. What's the hurry?"

Bianca clicked her tongue and whipped her ponytail from over her shoulder to her back.

"You should be thanking me!" she said. "I talked to your novia last night and she said she would be a dama. But I had to say you would be on the court or else she would have said no."

"Bianca!"

"What?!"

"Things aren't so good right now. It's all messed up, and you being all crazy doesn't help. We're not like you."

"Like what?" Bianca asked, jutting out her chin. "Like what?"

"You know!"

"No, I don't. Like what?"

"My mom is worried about money, and don't go telling your dad I said that, either."

"Why not? He's her brother. He likes helping out."

Diego hung his head. He didn't really know what was on his mother's mind, but he saw the fat folder she always carried around with the bills and other papers. He knew that it had been a while since she told him he could drive the car once they got the insurance worked out. But with things the way they were, he didn't think it was right to bother her about it. It wasn't so bad, he told himself. He could get around; he had friends. He tried to not let it bother him . . . but it was bothering him, being seventeen years old and having his mother drive him around all the time, or getting rides from his cousin.

"I just want to help," Bianca said, bien sweet.

Diego knew that was the truth.

"I'm just excited because, you know . . ." Bianca began picking at the corner of her sketchbook. Diego hoped he would not be sorry for what he asked next.

"So, really—how is your mother?" Pero Bianca didn't

start spitting chingazos at him, or crying, or calling him names, but went through her sketchbook to the last page.

"That's how she is," Bianca said. A pencil drawing of her mother looked out from the page at him, and Diego almost didn't want to look at it. The woman's face was bien pretty but fierce también. Bianca put a lot of time on the eyes and the pencil marks creased the paper like scars.

"Is she better?"

Bianca shrugged.

"Is she worse?"

"It depends."

"When was the last time you saw her?"

Bianca closed her book and put it into the bag she had made from sky-blue suede. "She doesn't miss me. She doesn't care if I come or not."

Diego was thinking of his own ache from not having his 'apá around. He wasn't like Carmen. He carried his sorrow softly, hoping no one would notice the crook it put in his smile or the wobble in his throat.

"Come on. Don't be like that. She misses you," Diego said, trying to sound todo wise. He had not seen his tía, Bianca's mother, since—quién sabe?—not since she ruined Bianca's quinceañera before it even began. He tried to remember the last time he saw his 'apá in person. When he counted three weeks, it felt like a stone fell onto his chest.

"I have one more class. If you wait, I'll give you and Carmen a ride home," Bianca said, as she stood up to go.

"I got somewhere else to be," Diego said.

This would have been when Bianca would usually tease Diego about trying to go see Sonia, but no. Because she had her own stone to carry, she could feel the weight of her primo's también.

"Okay. Thanks for asking, D."

. . .

Beatriz was facing the window when Ana entered her office and dropped the Montalvo folder on her desk with a loud *thwack*. Beatriz twirled to see Ana staring at her with her fists on her hips.

"Qué pasó?"

"Here's your important file that you had to have by five o'clock." Beatriz was confused. She looked at the folder, then back at Ana.

"I sent this over, but I didn't say we needed it by five."

"That's what Cynthia told me."

Beatriz called for her assistant, Raquel.

"She's gone," Ana said.

"I told her to send the file over, but I didn't say it was a rush. One of them must have misunderstood. Híjole! Sit down, you look like hell." Beatriz's office was todo fancy, in colors from the earth and bright colors jumping from the paintings on her walls. Patssi Valdez was her favorite artista. Her cozy settings in electric colors was pura Beatriz, Ana liked to say.

"I'm fine," Ana said, falling into the tan leather couch near her. "I just came from seeing Montalvo, and it was hot in that place where he's set up, and I got faint."

"You fainted?"

"I felt faint. And Montalvo—"

"Caught you? Gave you mouth-to-mouth? Ay, mi dios!"

"No! He gave me some juice. I was so embarrassed." Ana thought about telling Beatriz about the time before with Montalvo in the workroom, when she lost her temper, but that embarrassed her even more. When her cell phone chirped, she wanted to throw it against the wall.

"Ayyyyyy, déjame!"

"Qué, qué, qué!?"

"It's Bianca. You know she's left me ten text messages today about the quinceañera? I should have never included her. I should have asked for her help later. But now she's planning a big pageant!"

"What do you mean she's planning a pageant? I thought this was yours and Carmen's thing."

"It's supposed to be, but I let Bianca help because, you know, what happened to her quinceañera."

Beatriz frowned before she remembered. "Oh! She was the one?"

"Yeah, she's the one."

"Pobrecita . . ."

"Well, pobrecita or not, I need her to calm down. She's a good girl, but when she sets her mind on something she doesn't let go."

Beatriz got up to make some tea.

"And that girl loves to spend money."

Beatriz passed Ana a gold box with dark chocolates sprinkled with tiny bits of dried cherries.

"Please, help me eat them before I eat them all."

"Where did you get them?"

"Montalvo gave it to me."

Ana surprised herself. *Why did Beatriz get a gift from Montalvo?* she wondered. Maybe he had a gift for her, too. Maybe that's what he came to bring her that day when he caught her in the workroom. Maybe he was unsure after what she had said. *Why do I care?*

"He gave them out at the barbecue. You should have come. Mocte was there."

"He was?"

"Montalvo invited him. He really likes that kid. He told me he wants him to be his graduate assistant."

"Oh! That would really mean a lot to him."

"Well, yeah, except he's still an undergraduate."

Ana lay back to rest her neck on the arm of the couch.

"Don't worry. I'm working on it," Beatriz said. "Come on, take one before I eat them all."

Ana picked one of the squares and put it on her tongue. Beatriz dropped onto the other end of the couch, the rich chocolate melting in their mouths.

"Oh, my God," Ana said.

"I told you!"

Ana began to remember Montalvo's brown nipples through his T-shirt and wondered if they tasted the same. (Ay, mujer sin vergüenza—y qué?)

"You know he's not married."

"Well, I am," Ana said, still looking at the ceiling. "We're separated, not divorced. The subject hasn't come up."

Beatriz swallowed the last of her chocolate and sat up, bracing herself in the corner of the couch.

"Things have been bad for a long time," Beatriz said. Ana kept staring at the ceiling. "Two, three years now?"

"Why do you keep trying to bury my marriage like it never happened?" Ana snapped.

The hot pot Beatriz had plugged in began to grumble. Ana sighed. She did not want to argue with her friend; she just wanted to make her understand. "You don't just throw away twenty years. And I think he still loves me," she said.

"You *think*?"

Ana bit her lip to keep it still.

Beatriz spoke gently: "You're the mother of his children. You will always be connected to him, but maybe it's time to get on with your life."

"My life is with him."

"Really? Do you really believe that?"

The hot pot was now screaming, but Ana kept her eyes on the ceiling. It had been a long day. Her emotions swerving back and forth made her tired. On the outside, she stayed calm, but inside, a storm blew through her. She sat up and took another piece of chocolate.

"I want to. I want to believe that."

"Why?"

"What do you mean, 'why'?"

"I mean *why*?"

Ana didn't know what to say.

Beatriz got up, shut off the hot pot, and poured the hot water over hibiscus tea she had spooned into a squat green teapot. Ana had given it to Beatriz for her sixteenth birthday. It was the first thing Ana bought with her own money, the year they each got their first summer jobs— Ana working at a dry cleaner, Beatriz waiting tables at the Blanco Street Café. The teapot was nothing fancy. The lid was cracked and the inside was stained, but it was one of Beatriz's most precious things. She used it every day but knew it had to be handled with care.

"I got married in the church, and I still believe in my vows," Ana said. Even without looking at her, Ana could hear what Beatriz was thinking. "Yes, I know, I know! I don't go to Mass, I'm a bad Catholic! I'm a bad woman! I'm a bad—"

"Stop it! That's not true. You're not bad, but this doesn't make any sense. You're so good at moving past the things that hold you back. I've seen you do it a thousand different times. Oye, I'm the first one to say that no one knows what goes on in a marriage but the two people in it, but—"

"Esteban is not holding me back. He's just not interested in what I do."

"And that's the kind of marriage you want to have, where you are two ships that happen to be in the same port? Anchored by what? Your kids?"

"If we split up, they won't want to be with me. They'll want to be with him."

"Oh, that's not true!"

"It *is* true! Look at how Carmen is with me now! And Diego, he's growing up and he'll be going to college, and . . ."

Even Ana could hear how todo lopsided she sounded.

"Ana . . ."

Ay, ay, ay! Ana knew that when Beatriz said her name, what came next was going to be la palabra, la verdad, the truth, sin feathers to make it tickle or cushions to soften the edges.

"I know he respects you, and I think he cares about you, and I think he wants to do the right thing, but you need to face the truth. He wants out. He is out. I think if you think about it—really, really think about it—you want out, too."

"No, I . . ." But Ana couldn't finish. She felt the tears coming, and she pulled a tissue from a nearby box and held it with her fingertips in the corners of her eyes.

"Ya mujer. Déjame, por fa'."

"Okay, okay. I'm sorry. Here," Beatriz said, handing Ana her cup of tea. "You don't have to decide today, and you don't have to explain anything to me, but please—don't spend too much longer being unhappy, okay?"

Ana took the cup of tea from Beatriz and inhaled the fruity steam. She tried to take a sip, but it was too hot. And besides, she wanted to keep the taste of chocolate in her mouth as long as she could.

"I'm sorry if I tease you too much about Montalvo," Beatriz said. "But damn, he's a good-looking man. I can't believe you didn't notice."

"Maybe *you* should go out with him," Ana said.

"Well, that's not going to happen, but don't think I haven't thought about it."

Ana dropped her chin to her chest.

"Hey, I'm with Larry to have and to hold and all that, but that Montalvo—he can make you think all kinds of . . . thoughts," Beatriz said.

Ana blew on her tea and kept her own thoughts about Montalvo to herself. Beatriz went back to the couch, sitting slowly so not to spill her tea.

"Oye, you think Cynthia can help Raquel arrange the Montalvo reception?"

"Another reception? What was at the president's house?"

"That was his private campus thing. I'm talking about the public artist-in-residence reception. Remember?"

"Oh," Ana said. She thought contact with Montalvo was finished. "Well, she's good, but she's new. I don't want to overwhelm her. Can't Raquel do it?"

"She's going on maternity leave the week after, but I think she's going to drop that kid sooner. I don't want her to be the point person. You want another chocolate?"

Ana looked at the shiny box, the last two pieces next to each another bien cozy. *What could it hurt?* she thought. Pero no. Ana knew what she had to do.

"No, I better not," she said. She took a sip of her tea, washing away the last taste of chocolate in her mouth.

The two friends sat, the way old friends can, without words, familiar and contentas. They drank their tea, chatted about small things, and watched the shadows of the late afternoon make shapes on the walls. Something about the change of light made the piles on Beatriz's desk look como un landfill.

"Ay! I have so much work to do!" Beatriz whined.

"I know the feeling," Ana said.

"Do you think Sister What's-Her-Name would believe this? Remember how we used to complain about homework? And look at all this!" Beatriz said, nodding toward her desk. "Sister is probably laughing at me from the other side as we speak. I bet she never imagined I would have this kind of job."

"You? What about me?"

"Oh, everyone always expected good things from you. But I always thought you were going to travel the world and take many lovers," Beatriz teased.

"N'ombre! I always thought that would be you!" Ana said. "I never thought you would get married, let alone be a mother. Remember how everyone used to cruise down Military and turn around at the river? No one crossed that river. You were the only one who crossed and came back with a nice Highland boy."

"Yeah, by way of the University of Michigan," Beatriz laughed. "I would have never met Larry had I not gone to grad school."

"And I would have never gone to college if you hadn't gone first."

"And I would never have gone to college if you hadn't helped me with that bio class I nearly failed."

"And I would have never taken my first art class if you wouldn't have driven me that one summer . . ."

"Oh yeah . . . every Thursday and Friday, three to six o'clock."

"I was so scared. And you never missed a day. You weren't even late."

"Yeah. Your teacher sure was cute!"

"What? All this time I thought you were doing it because you wanted to support me!"

"I did want to support you," Beatriz said. "But that teacher was yummy. What was his name?"

"I don't remember."

"Me neither."

Ana and Beatriz finished their tea, silently going through the long list of scenes they saw with each other—los novios, lost loves, false friends, their weddings, the births of their children, the deaths of Ana's parents at too young an age, Beatriz's miscarriage, new jobs, promotions, money problems, sick children, the once-in-a-while arguments, and the return to the fold of their friendship, where it was safe and familiar, como familia—the family you choose, the ones who can leave but don't.

"Wow. We've been friends for a long time, eh?" Beatriz said.

"Uh-huh."

"You know I love you, and I love Esteban, but it's your back that I always got."

"And I've got yours."

"Don't forget that."

"How could I?"

When Beatriz stood to take their empty cups, she searched Ana's face.

"Better?"

"Yeah, I'm good." Ana stretched her arms, feeling todo relaxed until she looked at her watch.

"Damn! I've got to go."

"Where are you off to?"

Ana sighed. "To meet Esteban. It's got to be done. There's too much stuff to take care of."

"Well, I hope things turn out the way you want," Beatriz said. And it was true. She wanted her friend to have a good life, to be as content as a cup of tea. Ana left, her heart warm and her mind clear from her time with Beatriz. And now, she was determined that her meeting with Esteban would not end in uncertainty.

ELEVEN

Ana got to the taquería on time, but Esteban was late. The place was only half full, and Ana stuck out because she was the only one dressed for office work. A couple and their young family sat in the middle of the room waiting for their meal. Their four small children had been told how to behave in public. Their faces and hands scrubbed clean, their feet dangling over their vinyl-covered chairs, their big eyes took in every corner of the restaurant. The woman's smallest child nestled in her lap, while her man, who looked like he'd worked in the sun every single day of his life, slowly sipped a beer.

A group of young men, not much older than Diego, sat in a nearby booth, all dressed in the same T-shirts and white painter's pants splattered with green spots. The one covered with the most paint was chosen to buy the first round with a slap on his back and a playful shove. The other customers were middle-aged couples, now so used to each other they didn't bother trying to impress any-more. Some of them came in with in-laws: older, creakier versions of themselves. Ana was always touched by the old ones, noticing how few words were said between them. Had they run out of things to say, or had they moved past language? These were the couples that would die within a few months of each other, Ana thought. The one left behind, surprised at how deeply rooted his or her love was for the departed and thrust into loneliness, would will him- or herself to join the passed beloved en el más allá. When she was young, Ana thought, *Well, you just start over.* She had read stories of eighty-year-olds swimming the English Channel or ninety-year-olds learning how to fly when they found themselves alone once again. But since her separation from Esteban, she wondered if those people were the exception to the rule.

Maybe something in the old ones' silence would tell her something about love. Crinkled, stooped, half-blind, or nearly deaf, leaning into walkers or balancing with canes, the old ones clung to each other through who knew what. The ones that held hands like teenagers used to make her sigh, but lately she'd been thinking, *Were they staying together out of love or because they knew no other way?*

And then there was the time Ana saw a viejito give his wife's sagging behind the squeeze (todo sneaky).

"Qué chiflado!" the woman had hissed. She swatted at her viejo's hand, but she liked it. He knew she liked it. And because she knew that he knew, she began to giggle como un schoolgirl. Ana smiled. *Is this what "to have and to hold till death do us part" is supposed to look like?* Ay, mujer. She could barely remember the last time Esteban touched her.

Ana looked around the restaurant remembering why Esteban liked it there. It was clean, friendly, y puro rascuache. Neon-lit beer signs hung on the mango-colored walls. A cooler near the kitchen was filled with Mexican sodas and milk jugs refilled with homemade aguas frescas and a plastic bowl with pico de gallo. A list of specials was written on bright pink poster board and taped above the register, and near that hung a line of signed photos from Tejano musicians. The owner's wife was an Emilio Navaira fan and near the door was a small shrine to the singer, who nearly lost his life in a bus crash driving back from a Houston concert. The food was comforting, and the main language was Spanish. The owner saw Ana when she entered and, as she seated herself in the corner, he insisted she have an horchata made fresh that morning. That was really Esteban's favorite drink, but she accepted it, thanked him, and took a few sips of the milky drink to be polite.

The painter chosen to buy the first round was told to pick a Navaira song on the jukebox. The boys at the table called out song titles, but the boy at the jukebox got confused. It wasn't a Navaira song that played but Lydia Mendoza, singing one of her sad, fist-beating-her-chest love songs, "Besando La Cruz." And, right on the mark, that was when Esteban walked in.

Ana could tell he was freshly showered, his jet-black hair still damp and shiny. She knew the Western-cut shirt he wore. It was her Christmas gift to him last year. The shirt was black con red piping, and she knew he would like it because, as he exclaimed when he pulled it from the box, "Mira! Now I can be como Rick Treviño!" (He was his favorite Tejano singer.) She liked it because she knew it would show off his broad shoulders and narrow waist.

And ay, how Esteban could fill out a pair of jeans! Worn, but still dark blue, they hugged his hips and his powerful thighs. He carried a stiff cowboy hat, his fingers dark and rough against the smooth, vanilla-white brim. Except for a few lines around his eyes, he didn't look that different from when they first met. She was working in the office at Marcos's first construction site, and he had just joined the crew after working on an oil rig in Alaska, landscaping in Michigan, working the rail yards in Omaha, and, finally, making his way back to Texas—where, he said, it felt like home. The other men on the site saw how he looked at el jefe's sister when she handed out the paychecks and teased him without mercy.

"Ask her out, hombre! You know you want to!"

Ana noticed him, too. His gentle eyes, his skin deep brown from working in the sun, his worn hands that he made a point to make extra clean on payday, digging the dirt from under his nails with a penknife. He did not want to extend a dirty hand to Ana when he took his paycheck. The men on the worksite teased him about that, too.

"Oye, Esteban—do you want someone to paint your nails, ése?"

Esteban ignored them. The day he finally got the nerve to ask Marcos if he could ask Ana out, Marcos told him he could do what he wanted, but Ana could decide for herself. So when Ana said yes, Esteban was floating como un hot-air balloon. He worked hard, pero Ana could see he was—how she said—arrestingly gentle. After a time, when it was clear they were crazy for each other, Esteban told her that he was not always going to be working construction.

"Why not?" she had asked. Her father had started the construction business Marcos would later take over and turn into a big business. "It's honest work," she told him. Ana had just finished at the community college and was taking her first class at the university. He told her he wanted to take the firefighter's exam so he could work for the city, put in his years, and retire. Maybe buy a boat. With Ana's "buena suerte," he took the test, ready to make this first step toward their life together. But when the letter came telling him he did not pass—ay, Esteban!—he felt like he had fallen into a hole he could not climb out from.

"You're not the only one, mi amor," Ana had told him. "I hear it's tough."

He told her it was the physical part that kept him back, but really it was the paper test that kept shooting him back to the end of the line. Ana could have helped him, but he just could not make himself ask her. He just couldn't. Maybe that was the first drop in the pool that would, over time, turn into the wave that would rock their marriage, quién sabe?

The city had stopped the call for firefighters one year, and then the next. By the time the city put out another call, Esteban had already settled into steady work with Marcos, and Ana got her first part-time job as an administrative assistant at the university, and went to classes at night. That was the year they decided to buy a house and start a family. When Ana found out she was pregnant with Diego, they both believed life could not get better.

Esteban looked around the dining room, saw Ana in the corner, and walked over to her just as Lydia sang:

"You are the only one for me / There was never anyone else . . ."

Esteban leaned down and kissed Ana on the cheek and then sat down. Ana would have liked to believe he was dressed up for her, but she knew he always dressed like this whenever he went out—to church, to the grocery store, out to eat. It was his way.

"Cómo estás?" he asked.

"Bien. Y tú?"

"Bien, bien. Did you order?"

"No, but you go ahead," Ana said.

Esteban ordered his usual: tres tacos de lengua, arroz, jalapeños, and the pickled cabbage salsa that the owner's Salvadoran wife made for the few patrons who liked it. He ate quietly, nodding as Ana went through her file. She asked him how he wanted to handle the household finances now that they were living apart. He had few suggestions. She was the one with the solutions; he had no worries about how she wanted to handle things.

"So that's it?" Ana asked, when they got to the bottom of the papers.

"You know what you're doing," he said, shoveling some lengua y arroz into his mouth. "You don't need me."

Ana sat back in her chair.

"Well then, maybe you can help with the kids."

Esteban reached into his shirt and pulled out a rumpled envelope with several $100 bills inside and slid it toward Ana.

"It's a little less than last time, but I can get you the rest later."

"No, I mean, thanks. I mean, your kids miss you," Ana said. And then she decided, what the hell. She dove headfirst into the deep end of the pool.

"I miss you."

Esteban didn't know what to do with these words. They were small words, simple words that he knew Ana said honestly, but they made him go dumb. He knew that was not what she meant to do, but he did not know any other way to hear her. This wasn't always the way it was. He didn't know when it changed, and that made him feel worse. If Esteban had taken the time to really think about what Ana was saying, he would have come up with his own simple words: he missed their life; he missed the way things used to be. He missed that his kids weren't small and full of questions he could answer. He missed the Ana he met when they were young, the woman who needed him, who found strength in him, who needed to know what he thought, the woman who didn't need anything else in her life but an honest man, good kids, and a nice house to come home to.

Esteban wiped his mouth with his napkin. Even though he was clean-shaven, his whiskers rasped the thin paper napkin. Ana remembered how his cheek would do the same to her face when he kissed her full with desire, when they were young, before children, work, buying a house, and all the other things that brought them to this sad place in their lives. Esteban wadded the used napkin into a ball and dropped it onto his empty plate. Ana began to squirm, left hanging in the air as she waited for Esteban to answer her.

"Did you hear me?" she pressed. Esteban could feel the shame and sorrow thundering under the surface and did what he could to ignore it.

"Are they still doing good in school?" he asked.

Ana felt like she had belly-flopped into the water and was being held under. She struggled, but she could hold her breath as long as he could, she decided.

"So far."

"Have they asked any questions?"

"Not yet. Diego worries too much, and Carmen . . . What happened to you on Sunday?"

Esteban leaned forward and rested his elbows on the table, rubbing his eyes with the heels of his hands. "Perdóneme. Tell her I'm sorry, por fa'—"

"*You* tell her you're sorry! You talk to her more than I do. The way she talks to me, you'd think I was the cause of everything wrong in the world."

"What does she say?"

"It's not what she says; it's her attitude."

Esteban looked at her blankly.

"Her tone, her mood. You know . . ." Ana struggled for the words in Spanish so Esteban would fully understand. Not finding them, she resorted to her old standby:

"The flavor of her words to me son muy picosos. Entiendes?"

"She disrespects you?"

"She's angry and confused," Ana said. "And yes, I would call her disrespectful."

"I can talk to her."

"Gracias, pero—what about, you know, what we talked about before?" Ay, no! Esteban was praying that Ana had forgotten. He leaned back in his chair like he was trying to get away from her question.

"The marriage counselor is waiting for an answer," Ana said. "He speaks English y Español, y él respeta confidentiality."

Esteban looked over his shoulder and then leaned forward and took Ana's hand. Her heart leapt. The way he could show tenderness from his worn hands always surprised her. Maybe her patience was paying off. Maybe Beatriz was wrong when she said Esteban had already left their marriage. Maybe he did miss her. Maybe . . .

"I know this is what you want, but I . . . I wish I had done things different, but I am trying to make things good. So, por fa'—"

"Be patient?" Ana snapped, before Esteban could finish. She took back her hand.

"Forgive me."

"I already have," Ana said. "What else do you want from me?"

Esteban didn't know how to answer this question without getting to the truth that would only hurt Ana more. And that was why Ana fell in love with Esteban Ruiz. He was kind. Underneath that thick male skin, he was tender. And maybe that was the part of him that got bruised when he saw that Ana didn't need him for the things he thought a man should be needed for: to support his family, make things better, and to keep the order. He didn't like hearing that Carmen was not acting right, but he liked that he could bring her back to her old self. She was his angel, after all.

"I thought I could make things better by getting Carmen interested in having a quinceañera," Ana said. "But you have to be involved, okay?"

"Sí. When is it?"

"March, or early April. It depends on when Easter, la Pascua, falls."

Esteban stared into the air, calculating in his head.

"Qué pasó?" Ana asked.

"That's a bad time of the year for me."

"What do you mean, 'bad time'? Since when?"

Esteban rolled through the new information he had in his head. He wanted to tell Ana the truth, but he couldn't do it. Someone on the outside would have said he was a coward, a mal hombre, but the truth was he didn't want to hurt her any more than he already had. He needed to be sure he was straight in his heart and in his head before he made any more choices that would affect her and the lives of his children.

"I can't change when our daughter was born," Ana said, todo sarcastic. Her words cut deeper than she knew, and Esteban, again, sat dumbly. The two of them sat with their arms knotted across their chests, watching the water on the glass of horchata bleed into a puddle onto the table.

It wasn't an easy silence like Ana saw with the old ones. Their silence was bloated with sadness, a candle at the end of its life, its flame burning up the last drop of wax. Esteban belched a small, sad chuckle.

"What?" Ana asked.

"I was thinking how when Carmen was born, there was more hair than baby in the blanket. And now she's almost a woman." He pushed his empty plate to the end of the table.

Ana was running out of air. She pulled herself from the deep end she had dived into and began the long, hard swim back to the surface where it was safe.

"And Diego, también, but with curls," she said. Esteban heard the sadness in her voice, but told himself Ana was just being a sentimental mother.

Ana wanted to scream.

"And how did he get to be so tall?" he went on. "No one in my family is that tall. Who in your family is that tall?"

Ana shrugged.

"We're blessed to have two good kids, healthy, and smart," Esteban said. "You did good with them."

This made Ana angry. "*We* did good with them," she said. She was not going to let Esteban off like that, let him believe that he was always on the outside. And she didn't like feeling that all this talk of their past was a long—cómo se dice?—bittersweet eulogy for their life, their marriage. Things were bad, but she wasn't ready to let go yet.

"It was you," Esteban pushed. "You were the one who took them to those classes and put them in that school they go to now. Took them to the library y todo. I never thought about those things."

"You're an important part of their lives."

"Gracias, pero . . . okay." Esteban stood up and dug in his pocket for his wallet to pay the bill. "I'll help with the quinceañera; just let me know what you need. I'm going to pick up some overtime once this other job is over."

Ana knew that when Esteban worked overtime it was his way to not face whatever waited for him at home. Pero that was only part of the truth.

He was the kind of person who worked out all of his problems as he hammered, sawed, hauled, and built things. Depending on the problem, he could work through and let go of his worries like a snake sheds its old skin. Esteban needed more time to clear his head, find the answers, and make some decisions. He didn't need no marriage counselor to hear his problems, he thought. He would work it out, como un hombre.

Esteban walked Ana to her car and noticed how rundown it was.

"Híjole, I can't believe La 'Onda is still runnin'!" he said, remembering that they bought it right after Carmen was born. "Take it to Estrada's, over there on Zarzamora. I'll tell my compadre to give it a look. Pero, it might be time to start looking for a new car."

"I don't want a new car!" she said. The tears were swelling in her eyes. "This one is good enough for me." Ana didn't tell Esteban that the "check engine" light had been glowing since he left. "Maybe a paint job."

"N'ombre! It might look better, but if it's going to go out, you don't want it to happen on the highway." Ana's tears made him uneasy. Was she sad about the car or something else? He knew the difference. He knew what the truth was. He couldn't let himself recognize her pain. Not now. There was only so much he could handle. He told himself Ana's tears were because of allergies, nada más.

"Well, as long as it's not giving you trouble. They don't make them like this anymore."

"No, they don't," Ana said, looking at her husband with a crooked smile. Esteban couldn't stand the way she was looking at him: a sadness, thick with want. Knowing he was the cause of this misery filled him with shame.

"Can I have a supper with the kids this week?"

"You can have breakfast, lunch, and dinner with them anytime you want. But this week, yes. They're expecting it. So, don't forget, okay?"

"No, I won't, and I will talk to Carmen," he said, feeling pride in the one thing, the last thing, he knew he could manage.

Ana got into her car and buckled herself in. She expected to see Esteban waiting to lean in and kiss her good-bye through the window, but he had walked off and climbed into his truck, his mind already on what was next. Loneliness came over Ana as she watched him start his truck and drive away. She was soggy with grief.

When she started her car and put her hands on the steering wheel, she noticed her naked ring finger. When Esteban took her hand, he didn't even notice her wedding ring was gone, and if he did notice, he didn't bother to ask what had happened to it. Or maybe he was glad to see it gone. Or maybe—and this was what Ana feared the most—he felt nothing. Ana leaned back in her seat as La 'Onda chugged roughly. Now, she understood why the old ones willed themselves to die after their beloveds passed. It was the only reasonable thing left to do.

TWELVE

If there was one thing Ana knew, it was that she had to keep Bianca from going toda loca. She called the girls together to talk about the quinceañera the following Saturday morning, and to make it feel like old times she decided to make buñuelos, just like she did when Carmen and Bianca were little girls. Carmen walked into the kitchen barely awake, her lavender robe thrown over the T-shirt and flannel shorts she liked to sleep in. Diego was right behind her, dressed for the day in his nicest pair of jeans and an Arhoolie Records T-shirt. When Carmen saw what Ana was up to, she said she was saving her calories for dinner that night with her 'apá.

"I want some!" Diego said. He was in a happy, happy mood, muy feliz. Ana smiled as her son gave her a big hug and kissed her on the cheek. "Calories? I don't care about no stinkin' calories!" Ana continued to roll out the dough and mix the cinnamon-sugar. Diego crossed to the refrigerator, where his sister was searching for some juice.

"She's just trying to be nice, Carmensa!" he whispered.

"Whatever."

Diego rolled his eyes. Ana was laying the first thin disk into the fryer when Bianca came in, hauling a white board and three presentation boards—one for dresses, one for the seating arrangements and table decorations, and the other for . . . quién sabe? They were on sale, and you never know.

"Dang, B. You couldn't get everything you needed on your PowerPoint presentation?" Diego asked. Bianca ignored him and set up her display as Ana continued cooking. Her plain three-ring notebook was puny compared to her sobrina's todo showy display, but that did not stop her from taking charge.

"Okay. Music," Ana began. "There are mariachi songs specifically for the quinceañera Mass, so I was thinking—"

"I don't like mariachi," Carmen yawned.

"How can you not like mariachi?" Diego asked. Ana and the girls looked at him. "It's mariachi! What kind of Mexican are you?"

"When it's bad, it's like a squealing cat, and in church it sounds like a giant squealing cat," Carmen said.

"I was talking to a DJ—" Bianca said.

"We can't have a DJ at the Mass," Ana said.

"What about at the reception?" Bianca asked.

"Why do we need a DJ?" Ana asked. "Diego, you can do that, can't you?"

"I guess," he said between gulps of milk. "Yeah, okay."

"Does that sound good to you, Carmen?" Ana asked. Carmen shrugged.

"But a DJ is better," Bianca said. "Besides, if Diego is in the court, when is he going to have time to DJ?"

"Wait, wait, wait—why do I need to be in the court? I can be the DJ. That's good enough for me," Diego said.

"But I asked Sonia to be a dama. So who's she going to be paired with?" Bianca asked todo obvious.

"Oh . . . you should be on the court, mi'jo," Ana said.

"'Amá!"

"Come on, son. You should be on the court. Carmen, who else do you want?"

Carmen shrugged. La muchacha was starting to get on Ana's nerves.

This is how it went for an hour—the food, the cake, the invitations. Carmen had no interest in anything until it came time to talk about the dress. Bianca pulled out her esqueche pad, using a chair como un easel to show her drawings. The girl had talent, but to put it nicely, each dress was showing more chichi than the one before it!

"Dang, Bianca! It's going to look like a puta parade!" Diego said, as he crossed to the small sunroom next to the kitchen, where he went to watch TV.

"Diego!" Ana scolded, but she could see what he saw. She turned back to the girls. "These are pretty," she said, todo diplomat, "but they're a little too showy for church, don't you think?"

"More like 'showgirl,'" Diego scoffed from the other room.

"And what do you know about showgirls?" Ana asked. Diego sunk into the couch and turned up the TV.

"This isn't for the Mass," Bianca said. "These are for the party afterwards. She can wear some frilly Easter dress for the Mass if she wants. I want to make the dresses for the party."

"No," Ana insisted. "We're talking about the dresses for the Mass and the reception."

"I'm not wearing an Easter dress," Carmen said. "I thought I got to wear something special."

"Well, what are *your* ideas, then?" Ana asked. "Did you look at any of these magazines I brought?"

Carmen shook her head no. Ana was going to dress her girl in a garbage bag and tights if she kept acting like this.

As Bianca and Ana wrestled over dress styles, Carmen licked her finger and picked the buñuelo crumbs from the bottom of the serving platter and ate them. Ana was not sure that Bianca could finish all the dresses on time, but Bianca begged her tía to believe her. When pushed, Bianca finally said that she might have to hire a dressmaker.

"*You* will hire a dressmaker?" Ana said.

"My dad will. He'll be the padrino de vestidos."

"Bianca, this is a lot of work. I think we should order the dresses from someplace. Did you look at some of these? They're cute!"

Ay, back and forth, back and forth, como Ping-Pong balls Ana and Bianca went. Carmen let them go like this, kind of listening but mostly not, until she found a pad Bianca hadn't opened. She flipped it open and took it to her mother and prima.

"I like this one."

Bianca and Ana turned to look at her. The picture Carmen found was a simple—how they say?—cocktail-length dress with an empire waistline. Not too low cut, not too tight. The one thing about it was it was colored in wild tiger stripes.

"That's not for you," Bianca said.

"But I like it," Carmen said. "It's got a simple cut, and I like the pattern."

Finally! Ana thought. She was happy Carmen had an opinion, and she didn't want to let the moment slip away.

"Okay, so what if we put the girls in something similar but only you wore this dress, the *cut* of this dress? Bianca, you can make *this* dress, but the dresses for the damas will be ordered." She wanted to talk her out of the animal stripe but decided to hold that for another time.

"I can make all the dresses, Tía! Tell her, Carmen."

"Yeah, she's crazy. She'll do it," Carmen said. "And I like her stuff. It doesn't look homemade. She can do it. I know she can," Carmen said.

"Why, thank you, cuz."

But Ana was not sure.

"Well, the girls have to be willing to wear the dresses. And they have to fit," Ana said. "Everyone has to feel good about what they're wearing. So, listen to me. We're going to create a budget and we're going to stick to it. No last-minute changes." Bianca could hardly stand still.

"Are you *sure* you can do this, Bianca?" Ana asked.

"I'm sure! I'm totally sure!"

"Okay . . ."

Bianca squealed before Ana could finish, jumping up and down around the room.

"Dang, Bianca," Diego said from the sunroom.

"Oye! Escúchame!" Ana said, peeling herself away from Bianca, who had tightly wrapped her arms around her. "Listen to me! We're going to pick a date sometime before the quinceañera. If the dresses aren't coming together by that time, or it's too hard for you to do this *and* keep up with school, then we're doing it my way. Got it?"

"Got it! Don't worry, Tía! You won't be sorry!"

"Now, let's talk about food," Ana said.

This was about as much girly excitement as Diego could take. That, and he was hopped up on all the sugar and honey he'd poured on his buñuelos. He was restless and needed to move.

"Hey, 'Amá, I'm going to walk to Rafa's house, okay? We're having band practice."

"You're going to walk over there carrying all your stuff?"

"I'm good." Diego would arrive at the Castañeda house

all sweaty and with a crick in his neck, but he didn't care. He needed to get away from the pink tornado. And he was anxious to see Sonia.

"Okay, but remember you're having dinner with your dad at five," Ana said. Diego kissed his mother on the cheek and shot his sister a look, as Bianca gave her ideas for centerpieces.

"What?" Carmen said to her brother.

"Be good."

Carmen rolled her eyes. Bianca had ideas about party favors and invitations. She spilled fabric swatches and piles of shiny magazine pages with her notitas before them. She began thinking out loud about the one thing that bothered her: cupcakes or a cake? Which was best? And the flavors! So many choices! Diego barely shut the door behind him when, like a werewolf, Carmen turned into her cabrona-self.

"Why can't we eat here?" she said, interrupting her cousin.

"You mean have the reception here?" Bianca asked.

"That would be nice," Ana said. "But I don't think the yard is big enough. If it's small . . ." Ana lost her thought when she looked out the bay window into the pond and saw a goldfish floating in the water.

"No, I mean why can't we eat dinner here tonight?" Carmen said.

"We haven't even talked about a theme!" Bianca said, trying to steer the talk back to the quinceañera. "If we talk about a theme first, that will help with everything else!"

"This is his house as much as it is ours," Carmen said.

"Eating out was your dad's idea, not mine," Ana said.

"So, we can eat here?"

"Why don't you ask him?" Ana said. She thought about what Beatriz said about telling Carmen the truth. She bit her tongue and closed her notebook.

"So, what do you think you'd like to make?" Ana asked. Carmen looked at Ana calmly. She had it all figured out.

"We could grill. He likes to grill. Or we could order pizza. It's not that big a deal. Bianca, you wanna stay and eat with us?"

But Bianca noticed the time and began picking up her things.

"I have something else to do."

"Where are you going? I thought you wanted to talk about a theme."

"I do, but you want to talk about dinner, and I have other things to do."

"But I want you to talk to my dad about the quinceañera. You can explain to him what he's supposed to do. Tell him how handsome he's going to look in a tuxedo, you know. Get him excited."

Carmen was annoyed. Annoyed with her brother, annoyed with her mother, annoyed with the world, but most of all she was annoyed with Bianca. How could she have something else to do?

"You know what? Most of the people I want on the court are at Rafa and Sonia's. You want to go over there now?"

"I guess," Bianca said, looking at her watch. "But you're not even dressed!"

"It won't take me that long." Carmen ran to her room to change. Bianca stayed in the kitchen with her aunt.

"Is that okay with you, Tía?"

"Sure, Bianca. It's okay. But if you have somewhere to be, I can take her."

"No, I'll do it. I'm just going home. I said I wanted to help, so let me help. You probably want a break from her, don't you?"

"You can tell?"

"*I* want a break from her!" Bianca blurted. "I'll take her. It's on the way."

When Bianca went to see what was taking Carmen so long, Ana rushed out to scoop the dead fish from the pond. *Would it be easier*—Ana thought, as she pulled the goldfish toward her with a rake—*would it be easier to tell Carmen, to tell both of the children, the truth about their father?* After the dinner she and Esteban had earlier in the week, she was beginning to wonder. But Ana knew her daughter. Carmen could talk tough, she could be mean and nasty, but when it came down to it, Ana knew Carmen would shrivel up if she knew the truth. Ana wrapped the dead fish in a piece of newspaper and walked it to the trash can near the garage. She buried it deep in the can so there would be no chance of Carmen finding it. The fish left some slime on Ana's hand. The smell made her gag. She quickly went back inside to wash her hands when Carmen came back into the kitchen.

"I'm going to ask him," she said to Ana's back.

"Ask who what?"

"'Apá. I'm going to ask him to have dinner here with us tonight."

Ana could still smell the stink on her hands and scrubbed her hands with the rough side of the sponge.

"Just so you know," Carmen added.

"Okay."

"I mean it!"

"I heard you, Carmen! You're going to ask your dad to eat dinner here. I didn't say you couldn't."

"Well, it wouldn't matter if you did," Carmen spat. "This is his house, too." La muchacha turned on her heel, very satisfied with herself. She was leaving the kitchen as Bianca came in from the other direction.

"C'mon, Carmen! I don't have all day!"

Through the living room window, Ana watched the girls drive off. The house was silent, and she sighed, a heavy sigh that should have blown out the windows. She knew Carmen wasn't a little girl anymore, but like a bird protecting its nest, Ana was going to protect her precious chick as long as she could—no matter how hard she was poking Ana with that sharp little beak of hers.

Diego was not happy when he walked up to the Castañeda garage and saw El Rey unpacking his gear with the rest of the boys. He was dressed all in black, like last time, but this time his sandy-brown hair was spiked and dyed black on the left side, bleached white on the other. Diego couldn't decide if the look was by accident or on purpose.

"Hey, man," El Rey said to Diego with an upturn of his chin.

"Hey," Diego said back. Rafa came out with some chairs and Diego pulled him aside.

"What the hell, man?"

"Qué tienes?" Rafa said, before he understood what Diego was talking about. "We voted, and you were outnumbered, man."

"Yeah, but . . ."

Sonia poked her head out the door and called to Diego: "Oye, Diego, did you practice what I showed you?"

Before he could answer, El Rey was already slithering over to Sonia, who pulled the screen door closed between her and the boy.

"Dude, I thought we went with that other guy," Diego hissed.

"Naw, man. He was the backup, remember? We didn't think this vato was going to say yes, but he did, so there you go."

Sonia laughed at something El Rey said. Anyone else would have known right away that Sonia was not even a little bit interested in El Rey, but pobre Diego, he watched the boy helplessly.

"Dude, you should make your move already," Rafa said under his breath.

"What?"

"Don't play like that. I know you like my sister."

Diego scoffed and Rafa looked at him like he was pitiful.

"Yeah, she's okay," Diego said.

"Oye, I don't think she likes him, and even if she did, my dad would make her change her mind real fast. And to be honest, I would rather have her hook up with a home-boy than with some tie-dyed Austin boy, 'tiendes?"

"I'm not livestock," Sonia said flatly. She had managed to get past El Rey and was behind her brother and Diego. Diego wished he could evaporate.

"We weren't talking about you, loca!" Rafa lied. He pushed past his sister and turned to look at Diego with a strong look. Diego began to fumble with the guitar Sonia had loaned him.

"Thanks for letting me use this."

"De nada. So, show me how you did."

"What?" Diego said stupidly.

"You practiced, didn't you? I know I didn't send you home with that for nothing," Sonia said.

Ah, even scolding him, she had the sweetest voice, Diego thought. "I practiced, but not that much."

"Why not?"

"Oh, you know. Stuff." *I sound so stupid!* Diego thought.

"Yeah, I heard about your mom and dad," she said in a low voice. "It's harsh, huh?"

Diego was surprised but relieved that Sonia knew about what was happening at home. "Yeah." He sat in a chair as he tuned the guitar, and when he looked up at Sonia's heart-shaped face smiling at him, things didn't seem so bad after all.

"So, show me."

Diego handed Sonia the guitar.

"No," she laughed. "Show me what I taught you last time."

Diego really didn't practice much, but he didn't do half bad.

"That's pretty good, but you need to practice some more." She took the guitar from him. "See, you're going to add that to this, and then to this, until you get this." By themselves, each chord she played was ordinary, but together, it was like the guitar was enchanted.

"Damn, that's hot!" El Rey said from across the garage.

"Yeah, she's pretty good," Rafa said.

"I'm damn good," Sonia said. Pos, it was the truth. She'd been playing since she was a little girl and knew plenty about playing the instrument that she would devote her life to.

"I can't play like that. I don't think I'll ever play like that," Diego said, marveling at Sonia's skill.

"Hey, I'd like a lesson. Are you giving lessons?" El Rey said. The vato made even plain questions sound todo smarmy.

"Oye, Rey, show me how this thing works." Rafa was asking about un wah-wah pedal Rey brought. Rey turned to Rafa, and Diego had Sonia to himself again.

"So, your cousin asked me to be a dama at your sister's quinceañera," Sonia said.

"Yeah." Diego didn't know what else to say. El Rey began to play wild and fast. Sonia turned to look at him.

"I thought you didn't know how to play," she said. El Rey didn't hear the "y qué" in her voice.

"Oh, I can play," he said, making a whiney wah-wah on his guitar using the pedal Rafa had asked about earlier.

"That's cool," Rafa said. "Show me how you work it." Rafa was working hard to keep Rey busy, but his efforts had the opposite effect. El Rey took it as a chance to show off and play even wilder. Sonia wasn't impressed, though. She decided she'd had enough.

"Okay, you guys have fun," she said, as she crossed back to the house.

"Ah, come on! Stay and watch. I do better with an audience," El Rey said como un flirt. Diego would have popped the baboso in the mouth, if he were that kind of boy.

"They can be your audience," Sonia said, waving out to the end of the driveway, where Carmen and Bianca were marching up toward them.

"Damn, there are some good-looking chicas in this town," El Rey said, as Sonia crossed down to greet the girls.

"Hey, man, be cool," Rafa said. Sonia greeted the girls and stood behind them as they all walked into the garage.

"What are you all doing here?" Diego asked.

"Dropping off your sister," Bianca said. "Your dad's picking you up here later. But I have to talk to you all about Carmen's quince, and I don't have a lot of time."

"Hi," El Rey said.

Bianca gave him the once over. "Quién es ese?" she asked no one in particular.

"That's Rey," Rafa said, greeting Bianca and Carmen. Tomás nodded from the corner where he was trapped behind the drums, and Rudy did the same behind his keyboard.

"Okay, so look, I'm glad you're taking a break, because I need you to listen up. We don't have the court all set up, but so far, we want Rafa and Patti, Tomás and Mari, Rudy and Alicia, and Sonia will be with Diego. Any questions?"

The boys were like deer in the spotlight.

"Are you asking or telling?" Rafa asked.

"What do you think?" Bianca said. "Don't worry. My dad is paying for the tuxedos, because of what happened last time." The boys were confused.

"At *my* quince," Bianca added. The boys nodded uneasily and instantly got busy with their instruments.

"So, like, is someone getting married?" El Rey asked.

"No, man," Rafa said.

"And what about you? Who are you getting paired up with?" El Rey asked Carmen. As soon as he asked, Diego looked over at his sister and noticed she had her full attention on the slick rocker. She was smiling so sweetly he half-expected to see a crown of birds flying around her.

"I don't know. Maybe *you* should be with me."

Diego was happy El Rey had his attention off Sonia, but when he saw he had moved on to his baby sister, he had an estroc.

"No!" Diego said. "I mean, Carmen, come 'ere." He pulled his sister outside the garage as Bianca continued talking to the boys. He didn't like it when he saw El Rey paying close attention.

"What do you think you're doing? That guy is way too old for you!" Diego scolded.

"I can ask him to be my escort if I want to!"

"Yeah, well, 'Amá's not going to like it."

"It's not her quince! Besides, all he has to do is escort me. We're not getting married and having babies! And I'm not even sure I want him. Chill out!"

But that was a lie. Carmen wanted him. She really, really wanted him. How she would work it—that was what she had to figure out.

"So, tell me more about this *keensinara*," El Rey called from across the garage to Carmen. "What do I have to do?"

"Hey, man, she can tell you about it later. We still got to practice," Rafa said.

"Don't worry. I'm not going anywhere," Carmen said. Diego shot his sister the biggest, meanest mal de ojo he could make.

"Qué tienes?" Carmen asked her brother, as she sat, bien cozy, on a stool close to Rey. Diego slunk to the opposite side of the garage, keeping a close eye on the two of them. Ay, qué no, he didn't like this. He didn't like this at all.

"Okay, ya me voy!" Bianca announced. "I got all your numbers, so I'll call you with more news later."

"You want my number?" El Rey asked in his slinky way.

"Yeah, dude, I got your number," Bianca said without looking at El Rey. In spite of themselves, the boys scoffed, one of them uttering a "Damn!" under his breath. But El Rey didn't notice. He was too busy checking out Carmen, and she was smiling her most appealing smile—thinking of the reaction her mother would have when she announced she wanted to have this strange and dangerous boy be her escort at the quinceañera. He was even a little cute, she thought. Oh yes, El Rey was the perfect escort for her— the perfect boy to drive her mother crazy.

THIRTEEN

Carmen was eating the last of her potato salad as she spoke excitedly about her quinceañera to her 'apá. Esteban listened con cariño as la chica went on and on, describing one thing after another. He could not get excited about dresses and hairstyles and all the things she was talking about, but he loved her. If she was happy, he was happy. Diego sat next to their 'apá, staring at his sister like she had horns on her head.

Carmen's plan to get Esteban back home for dinner had been forgotten, deflated by Esteban himself. Oh, sure, Carmen had asked her 'apá about eating at home, and he even went along, saying, "Why don't we get the food from the barbecue place and take it back?" But when they got to the restaurant, Esteban asked his daughter, "What do you think your mother would like?"

"My mother?"

"Well, she's going to be there, isn't she?"

Just as Diego was about to answer, Carmen pointed out that their favorite booth by the big fireplace was open, so why didn't they stay? Esteban agreed, and Diego went along. When the three of them sat down, Carmen was as happy as a little lamb.

. . .

"Mi'jo, are you sick?" Esteban asked his son, seeing that he had barely touched his #4 brisket plate.

"No, I'm not as hungry as I thought," Diego said. He looked at his sister as she dug into a peach cobbler smothered in vanilla ice cream the waitress had just brought to their table. Esteban was smiling and nodding, trying to keep up with his daughter, when she came to his place in the quinceañera.

"So, there's a dance after the Mass, and there's supposed to be a part when you dance with me and there's a shoe thing—but I don't want to do that. It's kind of weird. And there's a doll thing, but I don't know about that, either. I have to find out about it. But you're going to be there, right, 'Apá? You have to wear a tux, but when you're done with your part, you can change."

"I have to dance?"

"Sí, un—cómo se dice?—a waltz," she said, looking to Diego for help. He ignored her, picking up one of his cold fries and eating it mindlessly.

"But before that, there's the part of the Mass when you walk in with me. Down the aisle."

"With 'Amá?" Diego asked.

"I don't think so," Carmen snapped.

"Shouldn't she be there, too?" Esteban asked.

"Yeah, well. We haven't figured that part out."

"I don't know a lot about these things," Esteban said. "But I think this is a time for us to give thanks to God for our child and for you to show the people that you are ready to be a young woman."

Carmen sat silently, poking the ice cream with her spoon.

"So, dime," Esteban began slowly. "How is it at home?"

"Fine," Carmen said.

Mentirosa! Diego thought. "It could be better," he said.

"Qué onda?" Esteban asked. Diego felt his mouth go dry, but then with a sudden charge of courage, he heard himself say:

"It would be better if Carmen would be nicer to her."

Carmen nearly dropped her spoon.

"To who? Your mother? Is that true?" Esteban asked. When she didn't answer, he knew what he had to do.

"Escúchame. This business between your mother and me—it's not your business. It has nothing to do with you. This is a nice thing your mother wants to do for you, this quinceañera."

"But I didn't even want to do it," Carmen blurted. "It was all her idea. I never even thought about it."

"Well, then—if you don't want to do it, don't do it. But if you are, do it with respeto y gracias. Entiendes?"

Esteban turned to his son.

"Y tú. I know you've been waiting to drive. Just give me some more time. I'm going to fix this, okay?"

"I don't need to drive," Diego said.

"Yes, you do," Esteban said. "It would help your mother. Then you can get a job and start saving for school. I'm going to help as much as I can, but things are not good right now."

The three of them sat silently, the clattering of plates and voices bouncing all around them.

"I need you to be patient," Esteban began again, with a second wind. "And I need you to help your mother as much as you can."

"Why don't you just come back?" Carmen asked.

"Ay, mi'ja," Esteban sighed.

"Just come back." Her voice was cracking. "Perdón."

Carmen slid out of the booth and rushed to the ladies' room. Esteban sat back next to his son, each of them looking in opposite directions, neither one talking. Finally, Esteban got up and moved to the other side of the booth to face his son.

"Oye, I know this is hard on your sister—"

"It's hard on everybody," Diego said.

"Yes, it's hard on everybody. But I need you to know I am trying to do the right thing. It's not easy."

Diego and Esteban began picking at Carmen's half-eaten cobbler, their spoons clinking the bowl, one and then the other.

Diego had so many questions for his 'apá. Pero Diego had the kind of respect for his father that was rooted in fear. Not that Esteban had anything to do with that. The truth was, Esteban worried that Diego was embarrassed to have a father like him, a workingman who barely finished high school. Así no! Diego adored his father just like his sister did; he just didn't show his affection as plain as her. And unlike his sister, Diego was afraid of disappointing his father, afraid he was not the son his father wanted or expected. Coming from a long line of men who worked with their hands and their backs, Diego wondered if he could measure up, if he could ever hope to please him. And sitting there, eating the melting cobbler while the world spun around them, made Diego more anxious about asking the questions he had for his father. When it came down to it, he wasn't sure what to ask, and he wasn't sure he was ready to hear the answer. He was going to. He was going to try. Just as soon as they finished the dessert. But as soon as they got to the bottom of the bowl, Esteban dropped his spoon in the dish and told his son to go check on his sister. Diego groaned inside but did what he was told.

Carmen was sitting outside the ladies' room on a bench. She wasn't crying anymore, but she sat with her arms and legs tightly crossed, watching a pair of twins in highchairs at a table across from the restrooms.

"'Apá wants to know what's taking so long."

Carmen blew her nose and Diego sat down next to her.

"How come you're so calm?" she asked. "Like him being gone is nothing."

"It's not nothing to me, Carmen."

"Well then how come you're not upset?"

"I'm not like you," Diego said. "I don't know what's going on with them, but he says he's trying to do the right thing. I think 'Amá is trying to do the right thing, too. I think that's the difference. You want someone to be right and someone to be wrong. Maybe it's not like that."

Diego had no idea what the right thing was, but he knew he wanted to believe their father, and unlike his sister, he still had faith in their mother.

"And you're a daddy's girl," he added.

"Shut up," Carmen said mildly, even though she knew it was the truth. "You didn't see what he looked like when he left in the middle of the night like some kind of . . ." Her voice trailed off.

"No, but I see how they are now." He leaned his head against the wall and watched one of the twins drop his bottle on the floor. His 'amá leaned over and picked it up, and when she didn't give it to the baby quick enough, he began to scream. "You know they were only a few years older than me when they got married?" Diego asked.

"I'm going to wait till I'm forty to get married," Carmen said.

"Yeah, right!"

"Okay. Fifty."

"Shut up."

"I mean it!"

"Well, that's good then, because if you get mixed up with that crazy vato from the band . . ."

"I'm not going to do anything with him!" That wasn't exactly the truth, but Carmen hadn't worked through her plan.

Happy to be in this "no drama" zone, they stayed watching the twins. One was slathered in potato salad, the other had barbecue sauce in his hair.

"Do you remember being that young?" Carmen asked.

"No."

"I do."

"For real?"

"Yeah, I remember one day. I was in that walker thing, remember?"

"The green one?"

"Yeah, you used it before me, right? Anyway, I remember 'Amá put me in it for the first time and I remember looking up at her, and 'Apá was there next to her, and they were holding hands, smiling at me."

"You made that up."

"No, I remember! I was happy. They were happy."

"And then what?"

"And then I thought: Whoever had this ride before me sure did slobber a lot."

Diego shoved his sister lightly. "Come on. I think he's ready to go."

Back at the house, Ana was busy. She washed all the morning dishes. Watered the plants, refilled the hummingbird feeder, pulled the dead vines clinging to the side of the garage, and was getting out the ladder so she could brush away the leaves from that part of the gutter where they always got trapped. It was mindless work, but she welcomed it. She placed the ladder against the house and was climbing up when she heard a loud roar behind her. A huge, white troca with "De La Torre Construction" stenciled in arched letters on the door pulled up below her. It was her brother Marcos.

"Buenas, 'manita," he said, climbing down from the high cab.

"Buenas yourself."

"Shouldn't Diego be doing that?"

"He's not here," Ana said.

"Well then, shouldn't Esteban be doing that?"

And here we go, Ana thought. She climbed down from the ladder and gave her brother an abrazo, which wasn't easy porque Marcos de la Torre was shaped like a barrel: a broad face, a broad chest, and manners to match. He was the oldest of the de la Torre children. Between him and Ana, he looked like the largest in a set of nested dolls, and Ana would be one of the smallest ones inside.

"I have some ice tea inside, ven," she said.

"Bianca's not here?" he asked.

"She was a couple of hours ago. She gave Carmen a ride, and then she went home." Ana noticed an escrecha on her brother's neck. "Qué pasó?"

"Nothing."

"It doesn't look like nothing. Did that happen at work?"

"No, a little while ago, I was, I . . ." Marcos was stammering. "I was with Teresa. She was having a bad day."

"Híjole, Marcos. Let me fix that."

As Ana got the cotton balls and peroxide, Marcos looked around the kitchen and dining room. It was quinceañera central, with Bianca's presentation boards propped up, magazines all over the table, and notepads and otras cosas all over. Marcos whistled through his teeth.

"You got a little production here, eh?"

"Yeah. Your daughter has some big ideas."

"Thanks for letting her help. She's real excited about it, because, well, you know."

Ana began to dab a moistened cotton ball on her brother's thick neck. Marcos winced.

"That's enough."

"Oh, come on, you big baby. Hijo! She really got you." Ana ran a washcloth under some cold water and handed it to him. "Put this on it."

"Yeah, that's good."

"So, what happened?"

"I don't know. We were sitting there talkin' and then all of a sudden, she got mad and started swinging. It took two orderlies to take her down. I don't think she meant to. She just got, you know."

Ana put her hand on her big brother's shoulder. *Ay, pobrecito*, she thought. He was bigger and older than her, but sitting there in her kitchen, he suddenly looked like a boy.

"She got upset because Bianca wasn't there. I told her she was going to come today, and when she didn't show up, Tere accused me of doing something to her."

"Ay, Marcos."

"Bianca was supposed to go with me, but she said she would meet me after she came here to drop off something you needed. But she didn't come. And she hasn't been answering her phone."

Ana poured her brother a glass of tea, adding extra lemon wedges, just the way he liked.

"I know it's not Tere. It's the illness talking," he said. "It's hard to get Bianca there to visit because, well, it's hard for her."

"Does Tere try and hit her, too?"

"No. She cries and cries and cries for her, but then when she shows up, she says things to her, mean things. You know, how she was before we put her in there? I tell Bianca it's just the illness, but it's just too much for her. I'm happy she gets to spend time with you and your kids. I think it makes her feel, I don't know, balanced."

Ana felt guilty. Her house felt anything but balanced with Esteban gone and Carmen being—how she said—acting out. She was thinking of telling Marcos that Bianca might be spending too much time at her house, and that she was worried Bianca was too wrapped up in Carmen's quinceañera, but seeing her brother as tender as he was, she decided to keep those thoughts to herself.

"Bianca says you are the padrino de vestidos. Is that true, or did she volunteer you?"

"Sure. Whatever."

"Don't you want to know how much it's going to cost?"

"Well sure. Give me the bill."

"No, no, no, Marcos—"

"Business has been good. Which is why I'm here. I have to go out of town and was wondering if you would look after Bianca. I would ask if she could stay here, but I think you're running out of room," Marcos said, looking around Ana's house. "Plus, she might be more comfortable in her own bed."

Ana didn't like to think of Bianca all alone in the big house she shared with her dad. Having Bianca in her house would be better.

"How long are you going to be gone?"

"Three weeks."

"Three weeks! Where are you going?"

"Austin, Houston, and Dallas and then down to the valley. I can drive back and forth from Austin, but when I go north and especially down south, you know—it's a long haul."

It's going to be a long haul having Bianca in the house, Ana thought.

"I can give you some money for your trouble. And I was serious about helping with the quince. When is it?"

"March or April. We haven't picked the date yet."

"Well, I'll be the padrino de whatever. I'll help with the barbecue."

"The barbecue?"

"Yeah, because you know the most important part of the quinceañera is the barbecue after. Brisket, chicken, sausage—something more than that prissy food you girls like. The men quieren comer!" he roared.

"We haven't gotten to that part yet," Ana said, patting her big brother's panza. "And I don't need money to take care of Bianca. She practically takes care of herself, and she hardly eats a thing. But . . ."

"But what?"

"You know she's always welcome here, but when was the last time you spent time with her?" Ana asked.

"What do you mean?"

"I mean—she's here a lot."

"Yeah, well, I've been working a lot," Marcos said defensively. "I got to keep it up to keep the business going as good as it has been, and it costs a lot to keep Tere in that place. Her family is helping out, but this is the longest she's been in there since, you know, the first time."

Ana remembered when Marcos and Teresa got married, how he beamed next to his little bride. They met the year he was el Rey Feo and she was the Charro Queen at the annual citywide festival known as Fiesta. After a day of making one of his many public appearances as el Rey Feo, Marcos decided to go to the Fiesta Charreada, where Miss Teresa Armendariz, recently crowned Charro Queen, was making her debut. They met among the smell of hay, horse sweat, and dung, but you would think they were above the clouds. When they met, it was one of those once-in-a-lifetime lightning strikes that stunned everyone else but made sense to them. They were like Frida and Diego, only he had eyes for her and her alone. Marcos de la Torre was surprised as anyone else that this little dove would want him, and he considered himself the luckiest man alive when she agreed to marry him. He had no inkling of what was to become of his wife.

"Well, I'm praying that she's better in time for Carmen's quinceañera," Ana said. Neither of them had to say it, but both of them were remembering the year Teresa's illness came like a hurricane during Bianca's quinceañera.

Ana never forgot the look on her poor sobrina's face when she went to the room where she was to get dressed and saw that Teresa had cut and torn Bianca's quince dress into shreds. Teresa had some idea of what she'd done and tried to correct the situation by taking off her own dress and offering it to Bianca, forcing her into the dress, as Bianca begged her to stop. Ana and then Marcos had to pull Teresa off her daughter. The nightmare went on with Marcos picking up his half-naked wife and stuffing her into the car as she screamed at the top of her lungs in the church parking lot. The next afternoon, Marcos had a small family birthday party for Bianca in the backyard. Pero, with Teresa gone and Bianca hiding in her room, it was not a very happy birthday.

"So, I need to ask you to do something else for Carmen's quinceañera," Ana said.

"Mande."

"I need you to be there in case Esteban doesn't show up."

"What do you mean if he doesn't show up? He's not going to miss his little girl's quinceañera. What makes you say that?" Marcos said, refolding the washcloth and putting it back on his neck.

"I don't know. He said it was happening at a bad time of year for him. Do you all have a big job coming up at that time?"

"No, and even if we did, I would let him off for the quince," Marcos said. "You must have misunderstood him."

"I understood him fine," Ana said. "He sat right across from me and said it was a bad time. I just need to know that if he doesn't show up, you will stand in for him, okay?"

"Well, that's not going to happen. Esteban is very dependable. He's one of the most dependable men I have. He's not going to let his little girl down."

Ana could feel her temper bubbling. "Well, he stood up his little girl at church last week."

"N'ombre!"

"Yes, güey!"

Qué, qué, qué? Ana *never* talked that way to her brother, and his head snapped so fast to look at her she thought he would get the whiplash. Pero, she finally got his attention, and he could see she was not going to back down. Marcos decided to let this pass.

"Well, she must have misunderstood which Mass to go to," Marcos said.

"Why do you do that?" Ana said between her teeth. "Why do you assume I don't know what I'm talking about?"

"I didn't say that."

"No, but you act like he's a saint!"

"He's no saint, Ana, but he's a good man. You could do worse—"

"Ay, por favor, Marcos! Do you all take an oath to defend each other no matter what?"

"N'ombre! He's a good man, is all I'm saying. He made a mistake and he's trying to make it right."

"Verdad? Well, I've asked him half a dozen times to go to therapy, and he won't do it."

"Therapy?" Marcos scoffed. "He's not going to go to therapy."

"And you think that's okay?"

"That kind of thing isn't for everyone," Marcos said. "Cálmate, 'manita. Just give it some time."

Ana had been told to "calm down" and "give it some time" all her life. She had had it. Before she knew it, the thought that had been boiling in the back of her mind came out.

"Well, I think he's seeing her again."

As soon as the words were out, she wished she could suck them back in.

"That's not true," Marcos said.

"How do you know?"

"I know."

"How can you know?"

"I know!" Marcos said. "You think I'm going to let him treat my own sister like that? Hell, no! Trust me. I got eyes everywhere. I know what he's doing when he leaves work. Between being an altar boy and going to work he doesn't have time to mess around."

"An altar boy?"

"Hell, yeah—he goes to Mass every other damn day! Believe me, he's sorry for what happened."

"So you're sure?" Ana asked, suddenly feeling the full power of being Marcos de la Torre's little sister.

"I'm sure, 'manita."

That only made Ana feel worse. If Esteban wasn't back with that woman, what was he waiting for? Ana took the washcloth from her brother. It was hot from his body heat, a trace of red glaring up at her. Ana wondered what it would be like to lose control, to let loose the full force of her anger and pain like Teresa. Ana rinsed the cloth and hung it over the edge of the sink.

"Esteban is very particular, and so are you. He got confused."

"Confused? About what?"

"I don't know. Like he didn't know where he belonged."

"What are you talking about?"

"Men like Esteban, they have to be needed. I think after you got successful over there at the university, maybe he thought you didn't need him anymore."

"So he messed around because I'm successful?" Ana asked.

"No, but—"

"No, but what?" Ana demanded. "I'm supposed to stop being myself, stop doing what I'm good at because he feels threatened?"

"Well, no, but yeah—I mean . . ." Marcos didn't know what he meant. "I mean that, well, you know. You're not the same as when you all got married."

"People change, Marcos! Everything changes! Life isn't static!"

"I know that better than anybody, don't you think?"

Ana could barely believe that she and Marcos grew up together. How could she and Marcos, and the rest of the family, from what she could see, be so different from each other? How come she was told to do well, succeed, and work hard, only to be told later that she'd done too much?

"Your kids are almost grown, and when they're gone, what good is he? The truth is, you don't need anyone," Marcos said. "You are a strong woman."

Ana had also been told this all her life, and she didn't know where it came from. The way she dressed? The way she talked? She couldn't be sure, but she did know that since Esteban left, she felt lost.

"And that's why he left me, because I'm strong?"

"He left because you already left him," Marcos said.

Ana couldn't take any more. "That's the biggest load of crap I've ever heard!" she screamed. "I didn't go anywhere! Look around, Marcos! Who's missing? I'm still here!"

"Okay, okay! I'm sorry I upset you! Cálmate! Shit." Like the bull in the china shop, Marcos could knock over everything with every turn. But he couldn't stand what came after—the tiptoeing around to get out of the place without getting cut. He dug in his pockets for his car keys and jangled them nervously.

"You're not going to cry, are you? Por fa', don't cry."

Ana was too shocked to cry.

"If Bianca comes back here, send her right home, okay?"

Ana walked her brother to his troca and watched him hoist himself in. As soon as he was gone, she went back into the house. She walked through every room, setting picture frames straight, putting cosas back in order, straightening, rearranging, throwing out newspapers y junk mail. She wiped down every surface of the kitchen, then did the same in the bathrooms. She went into her children's rooms and picked up dirty clothes and put them in the hamper and then hauled it to the garage, where she sorted the clothes and began a load of laundry. She returned to the house and went into the bedroom she'd shared with Esteban.

The room was clean and orderly, the bed neatly made with clean sheets she put on that morning, the extra pillows bien fluffy and inviting. Ana climbed into the bed, thinking she would take a nap. Instead, she was tearing at the covers, pulling at the sheets, ripping the cases off the pillows, and tossing everything into a huge, rumpled pile on the floor. When the bed was naked, she sat on the edge of the mattress for a long, long time. What would her children think if they saw her like this? She didn't want to, but she stood up and remade the bed, pushing and tucking and stuffing, till everything was neat and in order—the opposite of how she was inside.

FOURTEEN

Ana decided she would plan the Montalvo reception. Compared to Carmen's quinceañera, it was nothing. It didn't matter that she had to work with all the calendars of all the university VIPs who had to attend, the egos of the local artists who needed to be included, the politicos y otro big shots who must be invited, or the 1,001 details that would put anyone who could not stand the mix of egos, power, and money on edge. No, to Ana Ruiz, planning the reception was like a walk at the park. She could almost do it in her sleep, thanks to Cynthia and Mocte and with the help of Beatriz and her assistant (who had her baby a week before the event, just like Beatriz said).

Because of the size of the reception, and because of the need to give it what they called a public face, it was held at the Museo Alameda, which of course wanted to connect with Montalvo, and he with them. It was one of those ideas that started as—cómo se dice?—cocktail chisme but could end up turning into something big with lawyers and agents and papers signed on the dotted lines. No one could tell when or if it would go from talk to a deal, so los players (and those who wanted to be) planned to be at the Montalvo reception with their feelers out.

Ana got there to check the final details and make sure everything was going as planned. Beatriz was already there, joking with the bar staff, sampling jalapeño martinis made especially for la pachanga grande.

"What are you doing getting all borracha before it even begins?" Ana joked.

"Hey, my boss is paying for the booze. It's my job to make sure they're of the highest quality." Beatriz gulped down a second glass, and as she began to reach for the third she paused, closed her eyes, and savored the flavor of sweet vermouth and the slight snap of jalapeño.

"Eso! This is the one. Make them all like this one," she commanded. The head bartender nodded and gave instructions to the others as Beatriz took the last martini and gave it to Ana.

"Here, you deserve it," she said. "You look great."

"Really?"

"That dress is fantastic on you!"

"Clearance rack at Dress for Less."

"You're killing me," Beatriz said. "I never have luck at that place." In her last-minute run the night before, Ana found a simple, black cocktail dress with a neck that fell in soft arcs to the middle of her chest. For work, she wore a jacket to cover her bare arms. For the pachanga, she traded the jacket for a sheer wrap dotted with small crystals and changed her shoes from plain pumps to strappy heels (bien chula!). It was the middle of November, but it was a mild fall; the evenings were clear and cool, but not cold.

"Y yo?" Beatriz struck a pose to show off her flared black slacks, a glittery black jacket over a pearly cream shell, silver jewelry, and a wide belt with a sparkly buckle that matched her shoes.

"You're *chiney*," Ana said. "You look nice."

Beatriz got a portfolio she had stashed behind the bar. "Where will the big boys speak?"

"Upstairs," Ana said. "Come, and I'll show you."

The large exhibit space on the second level had been transformed into a shrine to Montalvo's work. Huge photographs of his sculptures in places around the world were hung with their plans displayed next to them. A wall in the center of the room had photographs of Montalvo at work, surrounding a larger one of him hanging in his harness. He was looking away from the camera, a sleeveless white undershirt showing his powerful arms and chest, his long legs dangling from the harness. Mocte was in front of the display, giving—how do they say?—un quickie plática to a group of wide-eyed admirers dressed in caterer's uniforms. Even in two dimensions, Montalvo had a way of pulling attention, but what made him more attractive to this group was the fact that a dark-skinned Mexicano like them was the reason for the evening. The catering staff silently went back to work when Mocte excused himself and walked over to Ana.

"Mocte! Qué suave, mi'jo!" Ana said playfully to the young man, dressed in a crisp white shirt and a black suit that fit him muy bien.

"Thank you, miss. Is everything okay?"

"It's great! You did a great job! Didn't he do a great job?" Ana asked Beatriz, who was gaping at the image of Montalvo in the harness.

"Uh-huh."

"That was a good idea you had, to get these photos blown up, since we don't have any of Montalvo's work to show. Right?"

"That was your idea?" Beatriz asked.

"Yes, miss."

Beatriz turned to Ana.

"And whose office paid for this?"

"Ours did."

"In that case, te aventaste! It's fantastic!"

"Thank you, miss. And thank you for helping me get to work with Señor Montalvo. It's an honor."

"You thanked me already, pero de nada," Beatriz said, smiling warmly at the young man. Then she looked over Mocte's and Ana's shoulders.

"What's going on over there?"

They turned and saw Cynthia dressed in a worn traje de charro outfit she bought at an estate sale, unloading a huge harp.

"She plays . . . mariachi?" Beatriz asked.

"I hope so," Ana said, taking a final gulp of her martini.

Beatriz's smile fell off of her face.

"She brought me a CD," Ana said. "They sound pretty good, and they're not playing until later."

"Oh, good. Everyone will have had a few drinks by then," Beatriz said. "But the harp?"

"That's what I'm not sure about," Ana said, watching Cynthia wrestle the large instrument onto the small riser.

"Some of the early mariachis had harps, and she plays," Mocte said with authority. He excused himself to help Cynthia, who almost knocked over the microphone he'd set up for later.

"Who knew?" Ana said. "She's playing solo the first hour and the mariachi later. Her price was right, and I want to check them out for Carmen's quinceañera."

"So now Carmen wants a mariachi?" Beatriz asked.

"We'll see. I asked the girls to drop by to check them

out, but I'm sure Carmen will come up with some excuse not to come."

The women walked through the rest of the building, making sure everything was in place, and ended up in the small kitchen where the caterers were busy loading their trays. Things were going as planned, so they each took a plato of bocadillos along with another jalapeño martini and made their way down to the patio on the main floor.

"So, how is the quinceañera going?" Beatriz asked.

"It's going," Ana said. "Carmen is more involved, but her heart isn't in it. I think if she could do it without me it would make her happy."

"You know, you still haven't told me how you want me to help. I can be the madrina of something," Beatriz said. "How about la madrina de los pies y las manos? I'll pay for the girls to have manicures the week of—how's that?"

"Yeah, they should like that," Ana said.

"But after this whole thing is over, I'm going to be la madrina de la mamá!" Beatriz said. "We're going to go stay at the Guenther Hotel and order room service and get massages y facials y todo! Or better yet, we'll go to Austin and stay at the San José and bum around like we've got nothing better to do with ourselves. Speaking of which . . ." Beatriz saw her husband, Larry, coming in, escorting a withered woman dressed in winter white and weighed down in pearls.

"Time to go to work," Beatriz said. She walked over to her husband and greeted the elderly woman. Larry Milligan had met her as she was climbing the steps to the Alameda and offered his assistance. Ana recognized the woman as Mrs. Gruber, who they called an obscenely wealthy patron of the arts and a major supporter of the university. Mrs. Gruber was ancient. Some joked that she was there when the Alamo was built, that she had had a relationship with Davy Crockett, or that she was first of the Daughters of the Republic of Texas, the official gate-keepers of the Alamo.

Mrs. Gruber's husband had died two decades before, and unlike the old ones Ana watched, la viejita refused to die. She was invited to every major ay tú tú party in the city, and no one knew which ones she would attend and which ones she would not. Mrs. Gruber was—cómo se dice?—on the A-list, pero todo grumpy. Once inside the Alameda, la señora got a glass of wine and asked for help finding a place to sit for the rest of the night. Larry waved at Ana as he crossed to the bar for la señora's wine and later helped Beatriz escort the rickety woman to the elevator and up to the Montalvo room, where the program would be.

Ana saw how easy it was with Larry and Beatriz. While they gave their full attention to Mrs. Gruber, they gave each other a quick beso without making the woman feel overlooked. It was a brief, tender kiss, a moment Ana tried to remember having with Esteban.

The pachanga grande started at six o'clock. By six thirty, the place was packed, the booze was flowing, and everyone was in what Beatriz called high schmooze. Cynthia's harp sweetened the air above the bubbling crowd. Everything was going well until Ana looked at her watch. She pushed through the crowd to find Mocte.

"Shouldn't you have picked up Montalvo by now?"

"He said they would get here on their own," Mocte said. "He's staying at the Guenther Hotel this week. It's not that far, miss."

They? Ana wondered.

"Do you want me to go over there anyway?"

"No, no. We'll give him ten minutes."

"Hey, dónde está el hombre de la hora?" Beatriz said into Ana's ear. "The prez has to be at something else later this evening."

"The dean isn't even here yet," Ana said. She was getting anxious.

"Don't worry. I'll feed him another martini. That should buy some time."

Ana didn't want to be, but she was curious: Who was Montalvo coming with? She and Beatriz were worming their way to the bar on the main floor when Beatriz motioned for Ana to look toward the entrance. There they saw the dean and his wife coming in with Montalvo, who was dressed muy elegante, in a white tuxedo jacket and black slacks. A photographer who had been waiting for him started taking photos before he even knew he was the guest of honor. Montalvo was gracious, smiling that handsome smile of his, then he reached behind him and pulled forward a young woman. Híjole! La mujer was la mamasota! Todo hot stuff, como un siren, wearing an emerald-green dress that followed every curve (and there were many). The dress plunged deep in the front and deeper down her back. Montalvo asked the photographer to take a photo of them together. The young woman smiled como un movie star, and the photographer was suddenly more interested in his work. The flash of his camera brought the attention of the other photographers, who began to snap their own photos.

"Oh, *please* tell me that's not a student," Beatriz whispered to Ana, as she handed her another martini. The thought came to Ana, too, but something about the young woman's way didn't seem to her like that of a student. For one thing, she didn't shrink into the background, and Montalvo made no effort to hide her. The young woman was todo stylish and confident, posing for the cameras like she was used to having all eyes on her.

"He should be ashamed of himself," Beatriz hissed. "I'll get the prez and meet you upstairs. You snag the cradle robber."

Montalvo's private life was none of her business, Ana told herself. She pushed through the crowd to greet the dean and his wife, and then Montalvo, who was just about to introduce la mamasota to her when she stopped him.

"Perdón, pero the president is anxious to get started. We must go upstairs now." The group followed Ana through the crowd to the Montalvo gallery and to the riser where Cynthia finished playing a Peruvian song con mucha alegría. Ana stepped up to the podium to announce that the formal presentation was about to begin when she saw she was still holding the martini Beatriz gave her earlier. She looked around for a place to set it.

"I'll take that," Montalvo's woman said in a thick accent Ana didn't know.

"Are you old enough to drink?" Ana asked.

"I'm old enough for a lot of things," the young woman said. She lifted the drink from Ana's hand and peered over the rim of the glass at Montalvo as she sipped from it. He smiled back at her.

"Oh Ana! Always minding every detail!" the dean joked. The dean's wife looked at Ana with an arched eyebrow and turned away.

The presentation went as planned. The dean spoke, toasting Montalvo and saying how fortunate the university and the city were to have him. The president spoke, thanking all the supporters who made the event possible. Dignitaries spoke. It was, as Ana says, the typical litany of thank-yous and praise punctuated with light applause aquí y allá. The campaign to get Montalvo to stay in San Anto had started. But if someone could have read the minds of everyone in the audience, they would have discovered that most everyone had two burning questions on their minds: Who was that hot babe on Montalvo's arm, and where have I seen her before?

Finally, it was Montalvo's turn to speak. He stepped up to the mic, and the light hit him perfectly. The crowd was hushed. Even the catering staff stopped to hear what he had to say.

"Gracias todos for this lovely evening. I am so pleased to be in this great city. I have been treated with much care and respect at your fine university. I have found much talent among the students."

"We see that," Beatriz whispered into Ana's ear. They were standing near the edge of the riser, behind the speakers and out of the light but in a perfect position to watch the crowd.

"I am honored by this wonderful display of my work, thanks to my able assistant Moctezuma Valdez, but I am afraid one of my proudest creations is missing."

Mocte almost had an estroc, until Montalvo reached back for la mamasota's hand and pulled her forward. "I would like to introduce to you my daughter, Liliana Montalvo."

After a silent gasp, the audience put away any ideas they had had about what was going on between Montalvo and the young woman (cochinos!), and the crowd broke into applause that was part delight, part relief.

"She comes here from Italy to surprise me this very afternoon! So, the evening is more beautiful than I thought possible. But please, enough talk. I invite you to enjoy the lovely event that has been planned. Muchísimas gracias."

That is when Ana saw that the woman looked familiar because she looked like her father. The chisme running through the crowd was that Liliana's mother was an Italian movie star and that she was following in her mother's footsteps. Some said they recognized Liliana Montalvo from a small independent film made by an Austin filmmaker, while others swore they saw her on their favorite novela.

"Well, thank God," Beatriz said to Ana. "Let's have a toast!"

Ana and Beatriz stepped off the riser and over to the bar set up in the far corner of the Montalvo room. "Everybody who needs to be here showed up, and those that didn't will be sorry." They clinked their glasses, and Beatriz raised hers to salute her friend. "Congratulations, mujer. Te aventaste! You really threw yourself!"

A crowd instantly formed around Montalvo and his daughter. Those who weren't trying to meet him or get a close-up look at his daughter were listening to Mocte's plática. Whatever schmoozing or deal making to be done was out of Ana's hands. She decided to take a break from the clamor while Las Florecitas Fuertes set up and walked into another gallery where there were fewer people.

She was surprised to see a small balcony off to the side of the gallery. A couple had just finished their cigarettes and were returning to the reception through a glass door. Ana traded places with them and was relieved when the door closed, blocking the commotion from the gallery and allowing her to enjoy the gentle sounds coming from the street below.

A cool breeze fluttered her hair. She leaned on the wrought-iron railing and gazed at whatever caught her eye: couples strolling nowhere in particular; an accordionist playing in the distance; a pack of giggly girls eating raspas from paper cups; a pair of squat men, their bellies flowing over snakeskin belts that matched their boots, leaning against a brick wall and sometimes removing their cream colored cowboy hats to comb back their hair with their fingers. The tourists were obvious, Ana thought. They were the ones who didn't know what to look at first—the dazzle of colored lights crisscrossed above the Mercado, the mounds of souvenirs that tumbled from small storefronts, the freestanding carts where the aroma of grilled meat danced with the sweet smell of fried churros, or the whiz of flies around the chunks of Mexican candies made of pumpkin, mango, coconut, y nopal. The people below were more tranquil than the crowd was behind her in the Museo. Ana enjoyed watching them from above, but just as she thought she should return to the reception, the door opened. When she turned, she thought she would see another pair of smokers. Instead, it was Montalvo, looking bien handsome in the moonlight.

"Perdón, señora. Please forgive me! I neglected to thank you when I spoke earlier. I wanted to say how much I appreciate all the work you did to make this event," he said.

"De nada, señor."

"My daughter would like to thank you as well, pero I have asked Mocte to take her back to the hotel."

"Oh, is she all right?" Ana asked.

"The jet lag. I told her she should go back and rest." Montalvo turned to leave but paused. "Everyone is very kind, but I am not used to being around so many people," he said. "May I join you?"

"Sure." Ana watched Montalvo take in the street scene below. It calmed him as much as it did her.

"Your daughter is stunning."

"Thank you. She takes after her mother," Montalvo said.

"I can see where she takes after you, too."

Montalvo laughed.

"Really, the resemblance is strong," Ana said.

"Yes, yes. Everyone says that. I was thinking if you said that five years ago, she would tear your tongue out! It is only now that we get along," Montalvo said. "Her teenage years were"—he paused, searching for the best word—"unpleasant."

"Ah, yes, I understand!" Ana said, thinking of her Carmen. "But it looks like you survived. You said she came here to surprise you?"

"Yes. For Thanksgiving next week, we will fly to California. She lives in Italy but wants to move to the U.S. to be in the cinema, like her mother."

"Oh, yes, the actress," Ana said, suddenly feeling very plain in her clearance-rack dress. "Well, that explains it. Your daughter was a natural in front of the cameras, but after her entrance, I think the rest of us must look like frumpy old ladies."

Montalvo scoffed. "Youth has its appeal, but the most beautiful women I've met have lived life. They have the caress of worn leather, the elegance of antique furniture."

(Ay, tú tú!)

"With all the nicks and stains to match," Ana joked.

"The things women see as their blemishes, I see as embellishments."

The sound of Montalvo's voice in the moonlight was making Ana's skin prickle. She had to change the subject.

"Do you think your wife will like it here?"

"No," he said in a stony tone. Coraje! Ana wondered if she was being too personal, if this would be another thing between them that she would have to repair.

"I'm sorry," Ana said. "I wasn't trying to be too—"

"No, no," Montalvo said in a softer tone. "She has decided she would rather be a great actress than to be with me. She stays in Italy. There is no need to be sorry. Once you've seen your private life splattered in gossip magazines, the rest is nothing."

A sad veil fell over him. Ana saw him mindlessly massage the finger where he once wore a wedding band. After a moment, he caught himself, looked at his hand, and shoved it in his pocket. Ana was touched. She could plainly see that this part of his life was bruised and still healing. She was suddenly aware of the nakedness of her own ring finger and made a note to call the jeweler about her ring. It had been several weeks. What was taking so long?

"It was for the best," Montalvo said. "But Lili did not agree. Her mother's career started to take off when Lili turned fourteen. I kept her while her mother was making her films. But Lili wanted to be an actress, just like her mother. And she missed her terribly. I told her she needed to finish school, but I didn't want her to be tutored on the set. I wanted her to have as conventional a life as possible. But teenagers can be very . . ."

"Challenging," they said in unison. Montalvo laughed.

"So, you know about this?"

"Oh, yes," Ana said. "So, you raised your daughter through her teenage years alone?"

"Yes. Most of the time. She saw her mother when possible, between her films."

"That must have been difficult."

"Only because Lili was angry. Her mother left, but I was the one she decided to be angry at."

"Because you were the bad cop."

Montalvo was puzzled.

"The 'bad cop'—the parent who has to make sure they go to school, they do their homework, clean their room," Ana explained.

"Yes, I was this bad cop. With that and seeing your private life talked about in those shameless magazines, ay! But really, I don't blame her mother. She worked hard and got what she wanted. I understand the drive. It's the thing that brought us together and the thing that pushed us apart. I think it must always be the way: the parent who is not there is the one longed for the most," he said. "In the end, it was all worth it. She gave me one of my beautiful daughters."

"You have more?"

"Oh, yes! I have five!" Montalvo said proudly.

"Five!"

"Lili is the youngest with her mother."

Ana wondered if four other daughters meant four other women. "Five! I'm having trouble managing one! Well, two, if you count my niece. No sons?"

"No sons."

"Five!" Ana marveled again. "I should get tips on raising teenage girls from you sometime."

"Your daughter, what is she like?"

"She's a teenager." Ana said it like being a teenager was the most sinister thing in the world. The two of them laughed out loud.

"And her name?"

"Carmen, after my mother."

"Ay, qué linda! I love that name, like the character in the opera. The woman with the fiery temper who makes the men crazy!"

"You got the fiery temper right!" Ana laughed, "But she seems to spend most of her time driving *me* crazy."

"She's headstrong?"

"Headstrong, mouthy, stubborn, mean . . ." Pero Ana found herself getting sentimental. "But she's my girl. I had no idea it would be like this when she was a baby. Childbirth? That was hard. Taking care of a baby and a toddler, that was hard. Teething was hard, colic and diaper rash, measles and chicken pox—hard. I would take all of that, all at once, if I could trade it for what it's like now. So, tell me—how long do I have?"

"Quién sabe? Lili hated me for ten years. Thank God her half sisters were my angels."

"Oh! So you're the papacito of some daddy's girls."

"That is not good?"

"Oh, it's good if you're the girl or if you're the daddy. Not so much if you're the mommy."

"Really? So, your Carmen, she is the 'daddy's girl,' as you say?"

"Oh, yes. And I am that annoying woman who hangs around just to make her life miserable," Ana said. "I think if I fell off the face of the earth, she wouldn't notice."

"She would notice," Montalvo said. He was looking into the moon, the light bathing his chiseled face, and in that brief moment, Ana let herself enjoy looking at him.

"I'm sure she would notice," he said, turning to look at her. Ana realized she was leaning in close to Montalvo, and he was leaning in toward her. She stood up and moved away.

"Are you cold?" he asked.

"Oh, no," she stammered. "But I better get back inside." She turned back to him at the door. "It was nice talking to you."

"Yes, I would like it if we could do it again," Montalvo said. "Really."

Ana was about to leave when she thought of something: Montalvo was stranded. "Is . . . is Mocte coming back for you?"

"I sent him home for the evening."

"Do you need a ride?"

"Oh, I didn't think . . . I'm sure the dean and his wife will take me back."

"All right, then," Ana said.

Maybe because she learned that they shared something in common, or because she'd had too many martinis, or because the moonlight on Montalvo's face made him look—how you say?—dreamy, Ana allowed herself a small indulgence.

"Or, um, I could take you."

"Oh, no. I would not like to impose," Montalvo said, raising himself to his full height.

"It's no problem, but I have to take care of some final details, if you don't mind waiting. Or, I could take you now and come back. Either way is fine."

"Gracias," Montalvo said. "It would be an opportunity to meet your husband."

"Oh, no," Ana said, the dreamy cloud suddenly evaporating into the night. She looked inside the building to gain her bearings. A tipsy woman with maraschino red hair was waving an unlit cigarette as she spoke dramatically to an amused circle of effeminate men, dressed in, how Beatriz would say, their "cultivated edgy-artist best." A museum guard in a uniform one size too large watched la redhead.

The woman would not light the cigarette. She enjoyed keeping the guard on edge. La redhead was trouble, but Ana was glad to have something to pull her back into the world.

"He doesn't like to come to these things," she said. "He's more of a beer-and-tacos kind of guy." What Ana didn't say was that Esteban had only come to a handful of these kind of things, and when he did come he stood in the corner, staring at the walls or into his drink, until he finally disappeared to wait for Ana in the car.

"Oh! Did you ask him about the taquerías?" Montalvo suddenly remembered. "I am starving!"

"You didn't eat?"

"I have discovered, as the guest of honor you do not eat! I would like it if we could find a taquería on the way. If it's not too much trouble."

Ana smiled. "I think we can make that happen."

When Ana reentered the museo she immediately approached the redheaded woman and waved her and her friends to the balcony. The woman, who seemed always ready for a fight, decided to go without an argument when she saw Montalvo also come from the balcony. She looked Ana up and down, giving her that "quién es esa?" look, before she turned to Montalvo and ate him up with her eyes. He nodded politely and quickly left the gallery. As soon as he was gone, the woman's men cackled wildly and followed her out.

The crowd had thinned and the pachanga was coming to its natural end. As Ana walked into the Montalvo gallery, Las Florecitas Fuertes were just finishing a song to wild gritos y aplausos.

"Hey, they're pretty good," Beatriz said, walking up to Ana. "I think Carmen likes them, too."

"Carmen is here?"

Beatriz pointed to where Carmen was standing against the wall, casually dressed in jeans and a light sweater. Ana walked over to her daughter and discovered quickly that Carmen was furious.

"Where were you?" Carmen began. "I was looking all over for you."

"I'm working. And I didn't think you were coming."

"You said to come, didn't you? So here I am."

When was the last time you did anything I asked? Ana thought.

"They practically frisked me at the door," Carmen said from behind her curtain of hair.

"I told you it was a dressy event. I thought you might at least throw on a skirt. Where's Bianca?"

"She couldn't stay." Mentirosa! Carmen was lying. *Bianca better back me up if she asks,* Carmen thought. She didn't ask questions when Bianca suddenly had something else to do. And where was she that Sunday of the quinceañera fair? *Probably with some stupid boy, ignoring her cell phone,* Carmen thought. *She'll tell me when she's ready to dump him or wants to start bringing him around.*

"When can we go?" she asked.

"In a while. So, did you like the mariachi?"

"They were okay."

"Just okay?"

"Whatever. They were fine. Don't they have any food at this thing?"

"Carmen, you can see it's almost over. There was plenty of food earlier. If you would have come then, you could have eaten."

"When can we go?"

"When I'm done working!"

"Watching a bunch of snobs get drunk isn't work."
(Ay! Cabroncita!)

Ana shot la muchacha an impatient look.

"I'm going to the bathroom."

"That's a good idea," Ana said. She took a deep breath
to calm herself as the dean and his wife came up.

"Ana, we're leaving now," he said. "Montalvo tells me
he's getting a ride with you?"

"Yes," Ana said, watching her daughter, who had
stopped to look at the Montalvo photos. Ana was having second thoughts. Carmen was in one of her moods,
and she didn't know what to expect from her. Would she
be mute and sullen, or would she do or say something to
embarrass her? Ana wished there was a way to take back
her offer to Montalvo.

"Ana has offered to take me to the best taquería in
town!" Montalvo announced as he approached the group.

"Don't be silly!" a pinched voice said below them. It
was Mrs. Gruber. "I have a driver. You will come with
me," la viejita ordered.

"I'm sorry," Montalvo said. "I don't believe we have
met. I am—"

"I know who the hell you are," she barked. "You're all
I've heard about all night from the university people, the
museum people, the arts people—everyone has been telling me why it's necessary to keep you here. I should like to
find out for myself."

Everyone was todo edgy, including Beatriz and her husband, who had just joined the circle.

"Mrs. Gruber, is there something I can do for you?"
Beatriz asked, searching the faces for the reason why la
viejita had left her perch.

"No, I merely offered this young man a ride home. If he

were truly as gracious as everyone tells me he is, he would have accepted by now and we'd be on our way."

Even Beatriz had no words. The dean leaned down to Mrs. Gruber and explained that Carlos Montalvo was very tired and needed to rejoin his daughter, who was waiting for him at his hotel. Ana's stomach lurched. Mrs. Gruber didn't like hearing no for an answer; she hadn't been introduced to Montalvo the way she liked, and now she was—how they say?—irked. But what really set her off was Liliana Montalvo. No one remembered Mrs. Gruber when she was a young beauty, when her smile or the curve of her backside was as valuable as any endowment she funded. She couldn't say how she felt. Instead, the force of her frustration was being worked into a wad of chingazos she was getting ready to spit at the dean. But before she could make that first hack, Montalvo put out his hand to the brittle woman.

"You are very kind, señora. I *am* quite tired. If you are leaving now, I would be most honored to accept your invitation." Mrs. Gruber looked at Montalvo's hand, deeply contrasted against his snow-white jacket, and took his arm como la coqueta. Then, in her most educated, Castilian Spanish, she spoke directly to Montalvo and no one else.

"Come along then. I'm tired of these ridiculous people. I would like to hear why I should donate thousands of dollars to keep you in this town," she said boldly. "I've seen your work abroad. Tell me, why in God's name would you want to live here? Do you really think there are any students here worthy of your talent?"

Montalvo looked at everyone and with a nod of his head told them that he would be fine. Their leaving would have been faster if he had swooped her up and carried her under his arm (which she would have loved), but Montalvo adjusted his robust bearing to match her mincing steps, listening to her closely and responding to her in his own well-pressed Castilian Spanish, complete with a lisp.

"I am at your service. Ask me what you wish."

The two of them ambled off, and just as the elevator door closed Montalvo caught Ana's eye and winked at her.

"I don't know if that was such a good idea," the dean sighed.

"And you talking to her like she is an idiot was?" his wife snapped.

"I am so sorry," Beatriz said. "I should have introduced Montalvo to her sooner. But I couldn't wring him away from his adoring fans, and then he disappeared."

"I'm beat. Let's just all go home. We'll check in with him tomorrow," the dean said, looking at Ana. "Make sure the old crow didn't make a nest out of him."

Before she left for the evening, Ana made a point to thank the catering staff, the bartenders, and especially the museum guard tormented by the redheaded woman and her bunch.

"Them? I see them all the time. They're all show," the guard said with a wave of his hand. "They act like they're going to be bad, and I act like I'm worried about them. I wouldn't have anything to do if they didn't show up to these things!"

Ana was relieved the night was over. Her feet were killing her, and she couldn't stop yawning. When she and

Carmen walked to their car, she wondered how Montalvo was doing with Mrs. Gruber. But to tell the truth, she was glad to have an excuse to call him the next day.

"I'm hungry. Can we stop somewhere?" Carmen asked.

"We've got tons of food at home. I'll make you something when we get there," Ana said.

"So you'll take your boyfriend out for tacos but not me?"

Ana almost swallowed her tongue. "My what?"

"Your boyfriend. I guess everyone knows but us, huh?"

"What are you talking about?"

"That man with his pictures on the wall, looking all . . . sweaty."

"If you're talking about Señor Montalvo, he's the visiting artist that my department brought in for the year. Just like we've brought in other visiting artists in previous years."

"And were they your boyfriends, too?"

Ana didn't like the ugly tone in her daughter's voice. "Carmen, what do you think you're talking about?"

"I saw you! I saw you with him on that balcony!" Carmen said. "I was looking for you all over the place, and you weren't working. You were out there with him the whole time!"

"Carmen, we were just talking."

"I know what I saw!" Carmen cried. "Now I know why you kicked 'Apá out of the house!"

"I did not kick your father out. It was his decision to leave! And he didn't leave *you*, he left *me*!"

"Why would he do that?" Carmen yelled. "What did you do?"

Híjole! Ana couldn't stand it. She knew that telling Carmen the truth would hurt her much more than it would relieve her misery, but she was the parent and Carmen was the child. She would protect her no matter what.

"Carmen, I am married to you father. I want him to come back as much as you do."

"Really?" Carmen said, todo snarky.

"Yes, really."

"Then why doesn't he come back?"

"Listen to me. I'm sorry that what is happening between your father and me hurts you. I know you want to find someone to blame, but it's not me!" Ana would have done anything to steal back her words, but there they were, out in the open like a new cut.

"He's the one who's out there on his own, while you go out to all these fancy parties!"

"What are you talking about? You act like I'm running all over town every night! How many of these events have I gone to lately? When was the last time I went out, period?"

Carmen didn't know what to say, and it annoyed her. But she was annoyed before she even stepped into the museo. This new aggravation—fueled by her old anger and mixed with her crazy suspicions, all held together with the spit of her stubbornness—was all Carmen needed to dump a new wave of bitterness on Ana.

"If you went to that thing I told you about, maybe you could work it out already."

"What thing?"

"That flier I gave you when you dragged me to the quinceañera fair? The flier I brought from church about the marriage seminar?"

Ana dropped her head against the headrest. She would have laughed if she thought it would lighten the situation. But Ana could see that that was not the thing to do, even if she could laugh.

"You shoved it in your purse without even looking at it!" Carmen said.

"I know you think you're trying to help, but really, this is none of your business. This is between your father and me, and no one else!"

"You're not even trying!" Carmen yelled.

"Carmen, I just told you: this is none of your business."

"At least 'Apá is trying."

Qué coraje! Ana felt her head explode.

"He is? You think he is? Well, let me tell you something"—Ana had to stop, she wanted to stop, but she couldn't—"I don't know what you think your precious father has been doing, but I can tell you it doesn't include me."

"What are you talking about?"

"Damn it, Carmen! I don't have to talk to you about my business! Stop being such a self-righteous little bitch!"

Carmen tried her best but couldn't stop the explosion of tears. Ana leaned over to comfort her, but Carmen pulled away. Ana reached into the backseat for a box of tissues and tried to give it to Carmen, but she refused it. Ana had had enough. She wanted to take her girl by the shoulders and shake her. Instead, she dropped the tissue box on the floor in front of Carmen and got out of the car. She slammed the door and walked around the car, back and forth, back and forth, finally stopping at the rear of the car where she leaned against the trunk with her hands on her knees.

Please make her stop! Ana screamed inside her head. She wished she had a magic wand to make it all better. She wished she could crawl inside her daughter's head and help her understand that the world was not painted in crayons. Ana didn't want to kill Carmen's image of her father, but this was too much. If her daughter was this upset now, what would knowing the truth do to her? Ana knew the truth about Esteban would come out in time, but now, with it being kept quiet so long, Ana was beginning to worry she was doing more harm than good keeping Carmen and her brother in the dark.

A gust of wind blew her sheer wrap up and around her head. She fought it, like she was tearing through a cobweb. She could hear the rips in the tender cloth, but she didn't care. When she finally got control of the wrap, she balled it up and crushed it in her fist.

Ana felt as if something inside had cracked. Maybe Marcos was right. Maybe she had already left Esteban before he left her—not physically, not with another man, but by being a different person than she was when they first got married. Was it possible to be the person you were at eighteen, as you were at twenty-eight, as Ana was now, at thirty-eight? The idea bubbled up into her head like muddy water from an old faucet.

If Mrs. Gruber had been aware of Ana's situation, she would have advised her to find a man who could be trained with the right kind of encouragement, which in her mind was money. "You can buy all sorts of happiness with the right amount of money," she would say. Mrs. Gruber liked to create a stir among those who wanted her favor. But it was an old game that bought her less and less satisfaction now that she had outlived them all: her husband, her parents, her friends, and, perhaps cruelest of all, her children. There was no one left who wanted her the way a human wants to be wanted: for the simple pleasure of her company. She could buy respect, but affection? Only the fantasma of affection was real. In time the truth would reveal itself.

Ana began to feel cold and damp. When she looked up at the street lamp, she could see a fine mist passing through the light. She began to shiver and decided it was time to face her daughter. When she got in the car, Carmen had stopped crying, except for hiccups, which helped to make a foggy glaze inside the window next to her. She dabbed at her nose with a wadded tissue and avoided looking at her mother. Ana used the wrap to wipe the moisture off her arms and threw it in the backseat where it landed with a splat. She finger-combed her hair and wiped her hands on her lap, and waited for what was next.

"I want to go home," Carmen said bluntly.

Ana started the car. She was ready to pull out but something changed her mind. She turned off the car and sat back to find the words that were making their way out into the open.

"I hate this," Ana said quietly. "I really, *really* hate this, Carmen. How long is it going to be like this with us?"

"What are you talking about?"

"Oh, please!" Ana said.

Carmen could see her mother was talking to her in a new way. She wasn't letting her have her little tantrum without a comment, and Carmen wasn't sure how to act.

"I'm sorry I called you a bitch."

"You called me a *self-righteous* bitch," Carmen snapped.

"You *are* self-righteous!"

Carmen's mouth fell open.

"You are!" Ana insisted. "Ever since your father and I—you act like you're the only one with God on your side."

"Why are you talking to me like that?"

"Oye, chica, if you're going to throw chingazos, you better learn to take some punches."

"You're not supposed to talk to me that way," Carmen whined.

"And I'm not your personal punching bag!"

Carmen pulled another tissue from the box and wiped her eyes.

This whole freaking night has been one big mess, Carmen thought. When she opened her eyes again, she saw that Cynthia was crossing in front of their car, pushing a huge case that held her harp. The case was teetering on two puny casters that seemed too small for the job. Cynthia didn't see Ana and Carmen in their car. All her attention was on keeping the harp upright and a bag she'd flung over her back up and out of the way. Carmen flinched when she saw the pink hem of Cynthia's long skirt graze a thin pool of water she had stepped in without knowing.

"The mariachi was okay," Carmen said plainly. She wasn't trying to fight with her mother, but she wasn't trying to make up with her, either. She just wanted things to be normal. Pero, she wasn't sure what normal meant anymore. She didn't want to be treated like a little girl, but she had no idea, no real idea, what it meant to be treated like an adult. If hearing the truth about yourself was part of it, she didn't know if she liked it.

"You heard them play more than one song?" Ana asked, watching Cynthia load her harp in her car and close the door.

"Yeah," Carmen sighed. "It would be better if they had matching outfits."

"I know they're getting new outfits made," Ana said. "They should be ready in time for your quinceañera."

"Are they going to be like that harp girl's?"

"I don't know. I have no control over that." Ana wondered if Carmen would blame her for that, too.

Carmen slunk down in her seat, like a small animal licking its wounds.

"You know, this quinceañera is not just an excuse to get dressed up and have a party; it's supposed to *mean* something," Ana said.

"Yeah, I know. I'm supposed to be a woman and all that. Whatever."

"Not 'whatever'; it's a big deal," Ana said.

"It just seems that I get older and things get harder. I thought they were supposed to get easier."

Ana was heartened by this sudden glimmer of light, this little crack where she might be able to crawl in and reach her daughter without getting cut with barbed words.

"Not everything is harder," Ana said. "This is just bad timing. It's not always going to be like this. Bad things happen, but good things happen, too." Ana was afraid she sounded like something from a self-help book, todo corny, and she was relieved when Carmen spoke up.

"I'm tired. Can we go home?"

Ana started the car just as Mrs. Gruber's long, black sedan passed them. Ana couldn't see, but inside Mrs. Gruber was seated in the backseat with Montalvo, her veiny hand resting near his on the leather upholstery, still talking in that Castilian Spanish. La vieja would have been offended to know that Montalvo felt sorry for her. Somewhere inside, she did know, but she chose to believe he found her the most fascinating woman de la noche.

"Why didn't Bianca stay?" Ana asked, as she pulled into traffic.

"She had too much homework or something."

Mentirosa! Carmen was still lying.

She let her mother think that Bianca had dropped her off. But the truth was, she got a ride from El Rey, the boy she met in Rafa and Sonia's garage. It was a quick trip, no nonsense, straight from her house to the museo.

And wouldn't you know it, Rey was todo un gentleman. But when Carmen asked him to join her inside, he said no, leaving her on the corner of Santa Rosa y Commerce como un bus driver.

That was not what Carmen had in mind. She had wanted to make an entrance with the tattooed boy to upset her mother. She had it all planned out. So when Rey didn't play along, she—how they say?—was stumped. And then, seeing Ana with that man, and then having her own mother put Carmen in her place (órale!), all of it made Carmen wonder just what she would have to do to get her way—to *really* get her way. But compared to Mrs. Gruber, Carmen was un lightweight.

FIFTEEN

So, the reason Carmen could sneak out of the house with that rockero was because Bianca was off tending to her secret, as was her brother, Diego—whose secret wasn't really a secret, but try telling him that. Ana had told the kids to hold down the house while she was working. But they decided—as kids will do when given more rope than they maybe deserved—that what she *really* meant was for them to make sure she couldn't tell that things didn't go the way she thought they went when she was gone: Carmen sulking in her room, Diego doing his homework or strumming his guitar, and Bianca busy with whatever Bianca business she had flying.

The evening started innocent. Diego asked Bianca for a ride to band practice, and she jumped on it—but only because that made it easy for her to go take care of *her* business, without too much attention. Diego thought that Bianca was heading back to the house. She *did* go back to the house—just not right away. If Bianca would have been home earlier, she would have stopped Carmen from her crazy idea. She would have told her to forget the "Mexicon"—the name Bianca called boys who liked to be with Mexican girls because they were bien "spicy." She knew when she was eyed like the prize in the bottom of the cereal box. She would have set Carmen straight on all of that.

But there was something else on Bianca's mind that night. Something that had been with her for a while. She had been dreaming about her mother. Not nightmares, not even bad dreams. In them, her mother was her old self, the way she was before the year she lost it, doing ordinary things. In one, she was peeling potatoes. In another, she was threading a needle and sewing on a button. In another, she was matching and folding socks. Bianca didn't have any especial memories of her mother doing these things, but they were so calm and deliberate, the dreams began to nibble at her.

But those were dreams. In real life, Bianca knew it was wrong, but she didn't want to see her mother. She always found an excuse not to go with her father when he went to visit her in that place. Her father was patient with her. Everyone was. No one told Bianca she had to deal with her mother. Pero, something inside told her that she needed to. She didn't know how, but she knew she had to figure it out.

So, that's what Bianca was up to when Carmen was being la cabroncita, flexing her muscle without knowing what she was getting into. She'll learn the hard way, that one. But don't worry too much about her. The good thing about being bull-headed is that she might fall hard, but she won't break. And in this, she took after her mother, strong as a reed in a hurricane. But if you told her that, she would throw you a mal de ojo. Ay, Carmen!

When Bianca and Diego drove up to the Castañeda house, Bianca didn't notice the garage was dark. The girl barely slowed down for Diego to get out of the car.

"Laters," she said roaring off into the dark. Diego wondered what was her hurry as he walked into the house.

"Hey, man," Diego said, when Rafa answered the door. "Where is everybody?"

"N'ombre! Remember? Not tonight, man," Rafa said. "My dad wants to watch the Spurs game, and he says he can't when we're practicing. You want to watch with us?"

"Quién es, mi'jo?" Rafa opened the door a little wider so his father could see Diego, and Diego could see Mr. Castañeda and a compadre of his setting up their snacks for the game.

"Buenas noches, señor," Diego said.

"Buenas! Pásale, pásale!" Mr. Castañeda said. "Come in! The game is about to start. You want a soda?"

"Gracias, pero no, sir. I came for band practice."

"Hi, Diego," Sonia said, as she brought in a plate of nachos she had just nuked.

"Hey, man, I'm sorry but, you know," Rafa said, motioning over his shoulder to his father decked out in his Spurs jersey, hat, and workout pants.

Sonia was standing next to Mr. Castañeda, watching Diego. "'Apá, I've been teaching him. Is it okay if Diego shows me what he's learned? We'll be quiet," she said.

Mr. Castañeda gave Diego the once-over and then looked up at his daughter, who was trying not to look too excited.

"Go in the garage, but keep the door to the kitchen open. Rafa, go out there with them."

"Why?"

"Because I said so."

"Man, you all *so* owe me," Rafa said under his breath. The three of them passed from the living room into a hallway. Sonia broke off to get her guitar from her room, while Rafa and Diego kept going through the narrow kitchen and out into the garage. Rafa pulled a stool to the door so he could keep a lookout into the garage and still see the TV set in the living room through the kitchen. Diego unpacked his guitar as Sonia returned with hers, and the two of them pulled two old kitchen chairs under the light.

"Okay. So, show me what you got," Sonia said. Diego slowly played the chords Sonia had taught him.

"That's good, only try your fingers this way," she instructed. "Loosen your wrist; use this pick." Rafa was already caught up in the Spurs game, only partly watching his sister y Diego.

"That's good," Sonia said. She was a good teacher. "But now, add this." She added extra beats with her fingers, making it sound like she was three guitaristas, instead of one.

"Whoa! No way! How do you do that?" Diego asked. Her speed made his head spin—or was it her freshly washed hair? He couldn't decide.

"Okay, okay. I'll make it easier. You play these chords, and I'll do the rest." Diego struggled at first, but after the third try he surprised himself. Sonia added the extra notes along with the percusión.

"There, there, eso!" she said. "Now, faster." The Spurs had just—how they say?—rebounded the ball. Rafa was not paying any attention to them, cheering the Spurs silently as his father and his friend roared in the living room. Sonia and Diego were playing faster and faster, but when Diego felt how well he was doing, he got nervous and stumbled just as the Spurs player missed a layup.

"Mi'jo, bring me a beer," Mr. Castañeda called to his son, giving Rafa an excuse to leave his guard.

"That was good!" Sonia said.

"*You* were good; I'm trying not to embarrass myself."

"You don't need to be embarrassed." Sonia stopped to

adjust a string. "I'm glad we're going to be in the quincea-ñera together."

"Yeah," Diego said dumbly. He didn't know what else to say.

"Your sister doesn't seem that into it, though."

"Oh, she's being a pain in the ass since, um, stuff."

"Still the same?" Sonia asked bien gentle.

"Yeah. It's just weird, you know, because—everything was normal and now . . . it's all messed up."

"Yeah, I know," Sonia said, strumming lightly. "When my mom passed, it was hard for a long time. It's still hard." Sonia and Rafa's mother had died two years earlier. Diego remembered how windblown she and her brother had looked at the funeral, clinging to their father, who was a heaping mass of stunned pain. Diego heard Mr. Casta-ñeda bellow some coarse remarks to the referee for miss-ing a foul, echoing the same thoughts fans were yelling in living rooms and sports bars all over town.

"I'm sorry," Diego said.

"For what?"

"I don't know." He watched her fingers as she moved them along the frets and picked at the strings. What he wanted to say was that he was sorry he didn't know how to talk to her. He was sorry she made him feel todo goofy inside. He was sorry he couldn't come up with something he'd written in the journals he had hidden under his bed, something that would tell her how she made him feel. He was sorry he didn't know what kind of shampoo she used, because if he did, híjole, he would run out and buy enough to take a bath in.

"Hey, tell me what you think of this." She plugged her guitar into the amplifier and began to play a bluesy num-ber that Diego had never heard from her. The music yawned with ache and hit notes he could feel; emotions tender to the touch but plain enough to be the honest-to-God truth. She was just starting to get into it when Rafa came to the door, pulling it behind him to block the music.

"Hey, Dad says to stop."

"Okay," she said.

Rafa closed the door and went back to the game.

"That was badass!" Diego said. "I didn't know you could play like that."

"Not all the time. I'm not really a blues player, but this one came to me after my mom died. I played it a lot, and I don't know—it made me feel better. My dad hates it."

"But it's so—it really hits you, you know?"

"Yeah, that's what he says." Sonia turned off the amplifier and tried to play it again, but it wasn't the same. It was music that had to be played loud, like a howl. "I was thinking it needed lyrics," she said. "But I'm not very good at that."

Diego found that hard to believe. "I might have some that would work."

"Really?"

"I don't know. Maybe."

"Okay. I'd like to see what you got."

The two of them smiled at each other, the fireworks exploding in their eyes.

When Carmen and Ana were having their own explosion after the Montalvo pachanga, Bianca was in her car. She had a bag of fresh clothes, had walked through the big, empty house she shared with her father, sorted through the mail, checked the answering machine, and even called her father, who was now in Dallas, to let him know she was fine, todo está bien. But when he asked her where she was, she lied. She said she was at her tía's house studying. Where she really was, was outside the place where her mother was living, sitting in her car, chewing on a rope of cherry-flavored licorice (so she wouldn't bite her nails). Her Bug was hard to miss, and the hospital staff could see it from the window.

"Do you think she's coming in today?" an orderly asked another one, as they straightened chairs in a common room.

"I don't know. She better come on if she's going to. Visiting hours are over soon."

"She's not coming in," a third one said. "She just sits out there, waiting for who knows what."

"She's waiting to be ready," the first one said. "You got to remember these are just crazy people to us, but they belong to someone. It's not easy for some. At least she's trying."

"She's not trying!" the third orderly huffed. "She's just sitting in her car, listening to music, running down the clock."

"You don't know what's going on in her head, no more than you know what's going on inside some of these sad folks' heads," the first orderly said.

"Whatever."

"Well, there she goes," the second orderly said, watching the lights on Bianca's Bug blink on as she started her car and drove around and down the long drive to the main entrance.

"And just in time," the third orderly said. "Visiting hours are over right . . . now!" She turned to the others with her hand out. "Pay up." The two other orderlies pulled out their bills and slapped them into the winner's hand. This month alone, he was up twenty-five dollars.

≈ SIXTEEN ≈

M ontalvo's eight o'clock class was just ending when Ana drove up to his studio with breakfast tacos. As she entered with her bags of food, Montalvo looked up from the notes he was reading.

"Buenos días," Ana said timidly. "I hope you're hungry."

"Buenas, Ana! What is all this?"

"I didn't know what you liked, so I brought you a little of everything—tacos de lengua, tacos de huevo y papa, huevo y chorizo, tocino, gorditas, pan dulce . . ."

"You brought enough for the whole class!" Montalvo exclaimed. "Please sit. Was this Robert's idea?"

"Well, no. I mean yes. He wanted me to check on you after Mrs. Gruber kidnapped you last night, and since you didn't get your tacos, I thought I would make a special delivery."

"You did not have to, but how nice that you did. And Leonora was a gracious captor." It took a moment for Ana to figure out he was talking about Mrs. Gruber.

"Really? She can be very, um . . . trying."

"She is a character, but she was not so bad when it was the two of us," Montalvo said, poking through the bags Ana set on the table. "Please, I hope you will join me. I cannot eat all of this myself, and cold tacos are almost not worth eating." Before she could answer, he got paper plates and napkins and began to set a table for the two of them. She uncovered the to-go containers, and the aroma of coffee, warm tortillas, and fresh pico de gallo sprung up to tease them. They danced around the table setting things up, and when it was all ready, he invited her to sit.

"So, really," Ana began as she unwrapped a bundle of warm gorditas, "she was nice to you?"

"Yes! She can be very charming when she wants to be. She's not as awful as people say she is. Pobrecita, she is lonely. But you cannot guess so many words could come out of one little woman. She could not stop talking! I was exhausted when she finally took me back to my hotel."

"She didn't take you right away?"

"No, she made her driver take us around the city on the—what did she call it?—the Loop, and she told me the story of her family and her life."

"I thought she wanted to interrogate you."

"She did," Montalvo laughed. "But she saved that for last."

"You must have been dying by that time," Ana said, remembering that Montalvo had said he was starving.

"I was. She heard my stomach growl and made her driver take us to this place she called the Sonic? Is that right? She bought me a hamburger and papas fritas."

Montalvo found a container of lime wedges and squirted the juice onto his lengua taco, sprinkled it with bits of white onion and cilantro, refolded it, and took a healthy bite.

"Ah! But it was nothing like this. This is from heaven! Muchísimas gracias, Ana!"

The two of them continued to eat, talking about the

evening—he asking her about all the people he met, and she asking about his daughter, who was still sleeping at the hotel.

"She will be fine," Montalvo said, unwrapping another taco. "And you? How was the rest of your evening?" A small cloud came over Ana as she remembered her fight with Carmen in the car. She thought about telling Montalvo about it. Maybe he would have some good advice. But the whole thing made her sad, and she was having a nice morning with Montalvo. She didn't want to ruin it. And besides, she didn't want to get into what her daughter said about him, thinking he was Ana's novio. Qué loca!

"It was fine," she said, watching Montalvo enjoy his meal. "Let me ask you something. You said you have five daughters. Did you have quinceañeras for all them?"

"Oh, no," Montalvo said. "My girls weren't interested. I thought Lili would be, but even she said no to it. There was a party, but not the whole ceremony at the church y todo," Montalvo said. "Why?"

"Oh, just comparing notes. I've been trying to plan a quinceañera with Carmen, and it's been nothing but difficult. Very difficult. She's very . . ." Ana exhaled a frustrated growl.

"But I imagine she is lovely, like her mother."

Ana wasn't sure if Montalvo meant what he said or if he was trying to be as gracious with her as he was with Mrs. Gruber. She ignored the spark his words made in her belly.

"So, she is fourteen. And your son?"

"Diego is almost seventeen."

"And why are you doing it? Is this something you did when you were a girl?

"No," Ana said, picking through the pan dulce for the

smallest piece. "I was hoping it would be a nice way for us to try and get along," she said. "We—I . . ." Ana's voice broke off, and Montalvo searched her face for an explanation.

"I'm sorry. It's been a difficult time. My husband and I are—he is not living with us now. It's very hard on my children. Especially Carmen."

Montalvo could see it was hard on Ana también. He put his taco down and leaned forward to give Ana all his attention.

"These things happen," he said.

"I didn't think it would happen to me."

"Did you marry young?"

"Right out of high school."

"Ah," he said. "People change, hopefully to become the best person they can become. If that happens at the same time with another person, it is a miracle. But do not ask me. I am the last person to give advice on this."

Finally, Ana thought. Someone who was not going to tell her how to act, what to think, or how to feel about her situation.

"But don't worry, Ana, you are a beautiful woman. You will not be alone for long." It had been so long since Ana was told she was beautiful, she thought he was joking. She smirked until she caught Montalvo looking at her todo wistful.

"You do not know how beautiful you are, do you?"

Híjole! Ana began to nervously clean up the remains of their meal.

"Let me help you," Montalvo said. When he stood up, Ana got flustered and knocked over a half-full cup of pico de gallo, and it made a puddle in a pile of napkins.

"Ay, discúlpeme! I was trying to help," Montalvo said, even though Ana knew it was she who was the clumsy one. As he went to find some paper towels, Ana wondered if

Montalvo was one of those men who couldn't help but flirt with women no matter who they were or what they looked like, or if he was really trying to win her over. Ana could see how informal she had become with Montalvo and decided to direct their talk to less dangerous things.

"You said you and your daughter were going to California for Thanksgiving?"

"Yes. One of her sisters is there, and she will stay to meet with some producers."

"In Hollywood? Wow. I wouldn't be surprised if she were a famous movie star one day."

"Maybe. I would rather she were a successful actress instead of a starlet. But we will see."

Ana searched for a trash can. She found one near the table where Montalvo had his plans all laid out.

"Is this the piece you're working on?"

"Yes! Un momento." He ran to the far side of the warehouse and flipped a switch, fully lighting the cavernous space to expose a large skeleton of wood, wire, and rebar.

"Oh, my goodness! I didn't even notice that was there! You've done a lot of work since I was last here!" she said. "But what is it?"

"This is only the form," he said, running back to her. "It is almost finished, and then we will start applying the shell when it is ready."

"And the students are helping with this?"

"Some of the students. I have the rest of them doing smaller work over there." He pointed to a wall of shelves on the other side of the warehouse, where the student works were stored. "Mocte and another student are helping me with this."

"I bet Mocte is thrilled," Ana said, feeling very proud of him.

"I am thrilled. He has many good ideas and is very talented."

"But I don't understand how this works. You fly up there and they hand you material, or what?"

"Something like that. Come, I'll show you. But you will need to change."

"Change? No, that's okay. I'll just come back and watch you work with the students sometime."

"Oh, please, Ana Ruiz. Come play with me!" Montalvo puffed out his lower lip como un chico (qué chulo!). Ana laughed. "Please, Ana. I need your help."

"Well . . . what do I have to do?"

"There is a coverall behind that panel. Go put it on and I will show you."

Ana was unsure of what she was getting into.

"This is good. I have only thought of this new way of working, but I have not tried it out and should like to do so before I bring it to the students. In my own studio, this would be nothing, but I am still getting familiar with this space. Really, this is a huge favor for me."

Ana was worried but went behind the panel as he said and found the coveralls. As she changed, she could hear the squeal and jerk of the ropes and pulleys as Montalvo pulled them into place. She put on the large coverall quickly, but paused when she realized it carried his scent. Not a sour, used-up smell, but faint, like a caress. Ana tried to come up with a good reason to stop, but it was too late. Montalvo's scent filled her like a strong whiskey. Pero, la mujer pulled herself together and came out from behind the panel. Montalvo smiled and gave her his hand.

"I shouldn't be doing this," Ana said.

"It's all right," Montalvo said (bien dreamy). "I'll help

you. Now, put your legs through this." He was holding down the harness for her.

Ana choked.

"Oh please, please! It would help me very much. You don't want me to kill a student, do you?"

"I don't want you to kill me, either!"

"I assure you, you are in good hands. Please, let me help you." Montalvo helped pull the harness up to Ana's waist and attached a safety lead to another strap he had her place around her chest. Montalvo was all business, pulling and cinching and deciding the best way to secure her. The flurry of his hands over her body—madre santa— even with the coverall between her skin and his hands, made her heart gallop. She bit her tongue.

"'Stá bien?" he asked. "Are you ready?"

"Do I have any choice?" she asked, not sure what was going to happen next.

"All right then—ándale!" He pulled on a rope, and before she knew it, Ana was in the air, floating like a piñata over Montalvo's head. She thought she might fly into the structure, but just as she grazed it, Montalvo pulled her away by the other rope attached to her chest.

"'Stá bien?" he called to her from below.

Ana couldn't answer; she was breathless with excitement. As she swung the other way, toward the wall, she screamed, and then laughed, in spite of herself—a full laugh drenched with delight.

Below, Montalvo was worried. This was not working the way he had planned. He was making adjustments in his head.

"The idea is to have two students, one in the air, one on the ground, helping to navigate and apply the fiberglass pieces, which I will mold onto the frame with the heat," he said.

But Ana did not hear him. Flying up there made her feel as if every worry she had in the world had exploded and fallen away like confetti. She was breathing deeply out of excitement instead of fear, a thrill blowing through her body and bursting from her in streamers.

"Now, I will figure out how to bring you down," Montalvo said.

"What do you mean, 'figure out'?" Ana asked. Now she was escared. He made it look like nothing the day she first saw him in the harness, but that was when he was handling himself. Now he was working out how to instruct his students to work the harness-and-pulley system from a different angle.

"Ándale!" he said. Híjole! Ana was falling! Her stomach lurched, and the food she ate bounced to the top of her stomach. But just as quickly as she fell, she suddenly stopped—a foot above the ground. Because Montalvo was working as a counterweight to her, his feet were off the ground también. They circled each other in the air, both of them breathing deeply. He took hold of Ana's waist and pulled her toward him while taking the rope over his head. She could see the strain of him holding both of them in his biceps, in the flush of his skin, the gleam of sweat on his neck. And when his body working hard bloomed that scent of his (qué hombrazo!), Ana gasped.

"I have you," he said. He was afraid he might be hurting her, and the adrenaline rush made him work fast. He let loose a length of rope wrapped around his arm, finally bringing them both to the ground. He was still holding her, and he carefully let her body slide down his to the floor. Ana's heart was pounding in her ears, and Montalvo was breathing heavily.

"That wasn't the way it was supposed to work," he admitted. "But I think now I have a better idea of how to explain it. Gracias! Are you all right?" He looked at her dazed expression, worrying that he had handled her too roughly. "Are you all right?" he asked again.

Ana was more than all right. Pero, pobre mujer! She desperately wanted to be kissed.

Ana didn't see Montalvo again until Thanksgiving week, when she offered to drive him and his daughter to the airport. The trip was short and fast, y nada más. But over the break, oh, how Ana suffered! She was tortured with daydreams of him—his scent, the feel of his arm around her, the shape of his hands, the warmth of his skin, the caress of her breast against his chest as she slid down his body. Híjole! She was filled with desire and sick with guilt. She was married. She was married to Esteban, the father of her children, the man she had vowed to spend the rest of her life with. Didn't that mean something, anything, anymore? She loved Esteban, but being with a man who had lost his passion for her was worse than wounding; it had made her numb. Being close to Montalvo awakened a part of her that she thought was asleep forever. She thought her passion was like a small room in the attic: closed up, dark, and coated with dust. Now, that space was burst open, filled with light, the windows blown out, and every corner soft and round, humming with sensation. She felt alive, but this was worse than being closed up and forgotten. She had nowhere to unleash that blissful desire. So she stamped it down and tried to ignore it. The holiday came just in time.

Thanksgiving for the Ruiz family was not the same as always. Because of the split with Esteban, it was decided that the big meal would be held at Marcos's house instead of Ana's. Marcos manned the outdoor grill to make the brisket and ribs, while Ana made the turkey and a few side dishes inside. Ana didn't like cooking in a strange kitchen, but trying to make her way around the unfamiliar room was a useful distraction from her daydreams about Montalvo—and especially from the flock of tías, primos, y hermanas who came in from the Valley, Corpus, and Laredo with their covered dishes and hope of getting all the chisme on Ana and Esteban.

Ana invited Esteban to come to Marcos's house, but he said no.

"Well, then you explain why to your kids," she demanded.

Esteban took his children to Luby's, where they had their cafeteria-style Thanksgiving with a crowd of families too tired or too inconvenienced to cook. Diego didn't mind. Sonia's father had invited him over for dessert later in the evening (if it was okay with Ana). Carmen was todo mortified, but that did not stop her from telling Ana that it was the best Thanksgiving ever. Ana took her comment in stride, and when the flock of tías y primas joined in ("Yeah, the turkey was kind of dry this year"), Ana didn't have the energy to be annoyed. She went through the day in a daze. Relatives talking behind her back would fall quiet when she entered the room. Pero Ana did not care. Y qué?

At the end of the day, when the food was eaten and

the dishes were washed, and the men had gone to the backyard to watch the dying embers in the grill, and the women gone to the living room, Bianca reminded Ana that they had some quinceañera business to take care of. Ana winced.

"We have to invite the cousins to be on the court."

"So, ask them," she said.

"It's not for me to ask them, Tía."

"So, now you don't want to be in charge of everything?"

Bianca could see that her aunt was not herself. "I'll go find Carmen. We can do it together."

Ana sat on the corner of the couch as Bianca gathered the women together. To Ana's surprise, Carmen joined in. This was her quinceañera, after all. This brought Ana some comfort, and she listened closely as Carmen, with Bianca jumping in, gave out the details as they knew them. When they came to the subject of dresses, Carmen pulled out fabric swatches and passed them out.

"This is the material the damas' dresses will be made from. This is the basic style, and it can be tailored to fit you. So, you'll all have the same dress but still be individual," she said. "That way, everyone can look nice."

La tía con los stenciled eyebrows and the baby-fine hair fry-dyed the color of a cheap wine looked at her daughter hard. The girl was shaped like an apple with four long poles for arms and legs.

"You're going on the Slim-Fast tomorrow!" she barked. Ana bit her lip and patted the girl's knee.

"That color will look real nice on you, mi'ja," she whispered. The apple girl smiled.

"We're all wearing kitten heels like these," Carmen said, pulling out color copies and passing them around.

Buy them in white leather and have them dyed. You can get who you want for your chambelán, but if you don't find someone, Bianca will set you up."

The cousins exchanged looks. They knew it was not best to leave this up to Bianca.

"But what about *your* dress?" one of the cousins asked Carmen.

"You'll see," Bianca said.

Ana was relieved. Carmen had been working on the quinceañera more than she thought. But the fact that she had done the planning without her made her sad también. Afterward, she talked with Bianca to make sure they were within their budget, and the fact that they were brought her more relief.

"Don't worry, Tía. I got your back."

The next day, Beatriz invited Ana over for lunch, and she could see that there was something wrong with her friend.

"How was your Thanksgiving?"

"Fine," Ana said. "Esteban took the kids to Luby's and then told them he was going to see his sick uncle out in West Texas."

"Did he?"

"I don't know." Ana sighed. "Probably. Quién sabe? It was good enough for them. I can't wait till the holidays are over. I want it all to be over."

Beatriz didn't bother asking. She knew the reality of Ana's marriage was setting in, and her pointing out the obvious wasn't going to make it any better.

"You'll never guess who called me over the holiday," Beatriz said. "Mrs. Gruber."

"She called you over Thanksgiving?"

"She called me *on* Thanksgiving. We were just sitting down. I couldn't believe it."

"What did she want?"

"She wanted me to make an appointment for her with the president to discuss Montalvo. She was really impressed with him and wants to do what she can to make him stay. I'm thinking this means some new endowment money is on the way. So, between your office and ours, I think making Montalvo an offer he can't refuse is going to happen. Isn't that great?"

Ana felt as if the clouds were parting.

"We need to do all that we can to make him want to stay here. It would be great for the department and great for the school," Beatriz said. "So, whatever you can do to convince him, I'm telling you, it will be a feather in your sombrero."

Ana couldn't stop smiling.

"What?" Beatriz asked.

Ana wanted to tell Beatriz about her flying with Montalvo. Beatriz was her comadre, pero she wanted to keep something that belonged only to her. And maybe, just maybe, if Montalvo was going to stay longer than his short residency, there was hope of . . . oh, but Ana could not let herself imagine that. That was too big, too incredible. And besides, there was still the business of her marriage, her children. So many things to sort through. Even months after feeling discarded and unnecessary, Ana didn't believe in throwing people away—not Esteban, anyway, even after all he'd done. She wasn't an "eye for an eye" type. It wasn't her.

"What?!" Beatriz asked, puzzled as to why Ana was smiling but not speaking.

"Nothing," Ana said. "I'll do my part."

≋ SEVENTEEN ≋

So, this is the part where you might be thinking: *Ana, throw down your hair! Have some fun already! Jump on that pony and gallop, mujer!* But if you haven't figured it out by now, that's not how Ana, um, rides. Not that she sits all sidesaddle with her blouse buttoned up to her nose and her ankles crossed así. Ay no, hearts are tender things. There's only so many chingazos it can take before it shrinks and crawls off to die.

Before Montalvo came, Ana's heart was shriveling. Oh, she still loved her kids (even though Carmen was being so . . . Carmen!) of course. She still cared for her family (even when they drove her crazy); and yes, she still loved Esteban, even after all the drama he dragged her through. It was that other thing that was dimmed. That feeling when all things seem possible and the drive to live in your skin— really live in it—is something you can't ignore. Before Montalvo came Ana was—how they say?—going through the motions. Running a house. Going to work. Arguing with Carmen. Worrying about Diego. Dealing with her family, shopping, cleaning, working, always doing, doing, doing, and waiting. Waiting for Esteban.

The waiting was the thing that almost did her in, because it's lonesome work; like a porch light turned on for the loved one who never comes home. Keeping a heart on hold for so long does something to it. It puts a limp in its pulse so that before you know it, it makes someone into those cicada shells that collect under the porch at the end of summer: whole and unmarked on the outside but empty inside. It was happening so slowly, Ana didn't even know. Pero, Beatriz knew. She saw from the start as her friend slipped into the hollow version of herself. She knew she had to do something, but she knew with her firm grip there was a chance of crushing Ana, and she didn't want to do that, either. So when Montalvo came—ay, he was the thunder, the spark, the fresh water Ana didn't know she was missing. But Ana was not going to jump into anything because of a few flutters. Okay, it was more like a huge jet engine ready to take off, but Ana was sensible. She wasn't going to throw herself into any foolishness. But she wasn't going to ignore how he made her feel, either.

Being around Montalvo made Ana feel like a flor de peñasco, the rock flower her great-tío Carlos showed her when she was a little girl. The first time she saw it was in the Nativity scene he set up in his living room on Christmas Eve. For her tío Carlos, the Nativity scene was a production, with foot-tall wise men carved from wood, and the porcelain baby Jesus all smooth and shiny, ready for dressing; candles and bloodred poinsettias were everywhere. Ana was told to look, not touch, and she marveled over everything with wide eyes. But when she saw what she thought was a tumbleweed sitting in a dish on the manger, she rushed to tell her uncle someone had disrespected all his work. And the baby Jesus.

"Ay no, mi'ja," her tío told her. "I put that there."

Ana was stumped, so her tío picked up the weed and told her to follow him to the kitchen. He filled the dish with water, put the brown ball in it, and handed it back to her.

"Go put it back where you found it."

Ana did what she was told, thinking maybe her tío was getting the old-timer's disease. But on Christmas morning, he told her to go over and look at the weed. Ana was shocked to see what had happened. The lump had opened. The fronds that were wound into a stingy fist were now uncurled into a moist corsage, caressing the edges of the dish. The plant was—how they say?—verdant and alive.

And *that* was how Ana felt.

After many months of going dead, Ana was lush. And even if nothing happened with her and Carlos Montalvo, she didn't want to let that feeling go away. She thought about that when she placed her own flor de peñasco on the Nativity scene she and the kids set up in the living room. She would keep it watered all through the holidays. but later, after Three Kings Day, when it was time to take down and store all the holiday decorations for next year, Ana would keep the flor de peñasco near her bed as a reminder that she was, yes, still alive.

Nothing had changed. Esteban was still gone, Carmen was still Carmen, Bianca had mostly moved in with her and her kids, and the house—the house had turned into quinceañera central: bolts of cloth, a long sewing table made from an old door, pins and needles, threads, trim, measuring tapes, and even dress forms Bianca made of each dama using duct tape she taped around the girl over a T-shirt (como un mummy), then cut off and stuffed with newspaper, y ya! She had a dress form for each girl (qué clever, no?). Plans and cosas for the quinceañera took up every empty space in the Ruiz house.

Ana lost the battle for a small reception. Beatriz was the one who convinced her:

"You really want all those people tramping through your house? Setting up and cleaning is going to be a nightmare. Larry and I will help."

So a hall was booked for the reception, the food was ordered, the invitations were designed and at the printers. Cynthia and her mariachi were booked. But there were still party favors to be made, and flowers to order, and tables to dress, and on and on and on.

The holiday season made Bianca return to her old ways of trying to make things bigger than they needed to be. Ana decided to allow the girls some decisions as long as she had the final word. But more important, Ana decided that something had to happen, something had to move forward in her life, in her marriage, in her relationship with Carmen. As for Montalvo, well—she couldn't say she was disappointed in what was happening with him. She wasn't with him, not the way Carmen thought after the Montalvo pachanga, but they were definitely getting friendly.

After a couple more lunches Ana met Montalvo at some university events. Nothing as fancy—a lecture, a faculty art exhibit—small, safe events that each of them would have gone to anyway. Montalvo enjoyed her company, and he was happy to have a lovely and intelligent woman to share his thoughts with. Ana was a good listener. She seemed to understand him. And he probably understood Ana more than she knew. Montalvo knew there was nothing worse than going after a woman who was still tied to another man. (Cómo se dice? It's complicated.) Because of her children, Ana would not give in. Montalvo had always gotten what he wanted in the past. He was not used to waiting. Pero, this time he would wait, he told himself. He would enjoy her company. And there was nothing more enjoyable than being around a woman who felt good about herself. Being around Montalvo made Ana feel confident, and the more confident Ana felt, the more attractive she became. After a staff meeting one morning, Cynthia asked Ana if she'd lost weight. As they walked across campus to a meeting, Beatriz asked if she'd changed the color of her hair. Even Mocte couldn't help but ask one afternoon:

"I know this is crazy, miss, but is it possible that you are taller?"

It wasn't the clothes Ana wore, or the color of her lipstick, or the way she styled her hair. It was something else that made even those she had routine contact with wonder what was different about Ana Ruiz. Men at the university who had known Ana for years looked at her a little longer, wondering why they hadn't paid more attention to her in the past. And while things at home were still restless, having an excuse to run into Montalvo made Ana look forward to each new workweek. Still, she wasn't prepared when Montalvo called her to make a bolder move.

"Oye, Ana. They gave me passes to this film festival at the Esperanza Center. You will go with me, yes?"

Ana was holding the phone on her shoulder, balancing a pile of file folders on her lap.

"Un momento, okay?" She put the phone on hold.

"It's Montalvo. He wants me to go with him to a film festival," Ana said to Beatriz, who was eating her lunch in Ana's office.

"The one at the Esperanza? You should go," Beatriz said.

"Why do you think he's asking me?"

"Because . . . he wants you to go with him?"

"No! I mean, *why*?"

"Because he wants to go and doesn't want to go alone? Because he thinks you might enjoy it? Because he enjoys your company and he knows you enjoy his? Take your pick."

It was safe and made sense to see Montalvo on campus, but *off* campus? Ana wasn't so sure.

"What should I do?" Ana whispered.

"Well," Beatriz laughed. "Do you want to go or not?"

Ana was perplexed.

"Híjole! Give me the phone—"

"No!" Ana wrenched the phone away like a four-year-old. "It's just that—it's off campus. That's different from doing stuff around here. You know?"

"Yeah, you'll have to cross the street and everything!"

"You know what I mean," Ana said. "I don't want to give him the wrong idea. I shouldn't go, huh?"

"Okay."

"But if I don't go, would that be . . . I don't know . . ."

"Look, all you talk about is the quinceañera and work and your kids and Esteban. This might be a nice break. Something new."

Ana was still perplexed. She hated this. Hated the excitement and confusion rolled up together. She was still not sure what to do when Beatriz set her salad on Ana's desk and jumped out of her chair.

"Ándale!"

She lunged over Ana's desk, knocking over whatever was in her way, and grabbed the phone from Ana with one hand and pushed the blinking button on the console with the other. Ana pushed herself away from her desk in surprise, spilling the files on her lap onto the floor.

"Señor? Hola! Qué tal? Habla Beatriz Milligan! Bien, bien, gracias! Oye, Ana would love to go with you. Oh, yes, she's here. She had to take another call and I was standing here. We've been having a working lunch. So she says she would love to go and . . . tonight? Sure she can go tonight. Do you need a ride? Oh, good! Then, she'll meet you there. You can find it? Bueno pues, bye-bye!"

Beatriz hung up the phone, plopped back into her chair across from Ana, and went back to her salad. "Ugh! I hate mushy croutons."

"I can't believe you did that," Ana said. She wanted to be angry with Beatriz, but she wasn't. She was thrilled. She took her time picking the files from the floor so Beatriz would not see her. Ana was smiling so hard her face ached.

"I'm sorry. Do you need some help down there?"

"No, no. I got it."

"He's leasing a car now. I told him you would meet him there. So, it's not really a date, okay? And besides, I keep telling you, *everyone* in town is working to keep him here. That's why he's getting invitations and tickets to everything in town. It's no fun going alone. Pretty soon, he's going to stop going, in which case, all of our little elves miss their chance to encourage him to stay and our grand plan is ruined. So, from where I sit, I think it's *your job* to go with him."

"Well, okay Madam Beatriz!" Ana said. She popped back up from under her desk with the files in her arms. She dropped them on her desk and began sorting them.

"It's just hanging out, not hooking up!" Beatriz insisted. "God forbid you might enjoy yourself!"

By the time Beatriz left, she almost had Ana convinced that she was doing her job, going with Montalvo on this not-a-date date. Sort of. No, Ana still felt uneasy when she called Diego's cell phone to leave a message about the evening.

"Hi, mi'jo! It's your mother. I have a meeting tonight after work. It's a last-minute thing. There's some papa in the freezer you can heat up for dinner. Call me at your break and I'll talk you through it."

As soon as Ana hung up the phone she changed her mind.

No, no, no. This is not a good idea, she told herself. *But I want to go.* Ana nearly jumped from her chair when her cell phone rang. It was Beatriz.

"Just go!" her friend bellowed. She knew Ana totalmente.

"Ay, tú! Déjame! Look, I got to go. Mi'jo is calling," Ana said, glad to get away from Beatriz pushing her to the deep end of the pool.

"Hi mi'jo. I forgot. You have band practice tonight, don't you?"

"No. We're eating dinner with 'Apá tonight."

"You are? Oh." Qué coraje! Ana was out of excuses.

"'Amá? I'm going to be late for class."

"Okay, mi'jo. I'll see you later. Tell your sister."

Ana hung up the phone and turned her attention to the papers on her desk, counting the minutes until it was time to see Montalvo.

When Ana got to the Esperanza Center, the small lobby was packed. A banner welcoming the crowd to the Xicana Rites & Rituals Film Festival hung overhead, with a long line beneath it, threading through the lobby and out the door. Ana searched the line for Montalvo. When she didn't see him, she was directed to the place near the stairs where others were waiting for their friends, dates, or companions. Ana cut through to the corner where she would be out of the way. This crowd was different from those at most of the events she and Montalvo had attended. Less gold, silver, and old money; more hemp, inked arms, and message T-shirts:

"Straight but not narrow."

"My other car is a broom."

"Sí, se puede!"

Ana thought the T-shirt a young woman in front of her was wearing had a typo, until a buxom woman found her and gave her a kiss on the mouth. Then the T-shirt made sense:

"Vagitarian."

When the women stopped kissing, they looked at Ana, who was watching them, admiring them, really; touched by their honesty. She smiled meekly, and the women clasped hands and began talking to each other with their foreheads touching.

Esteban would never go for this, Ana thought.

When the rope was finally pulled back to let the ticket holders climb the stairs to the space where the films would be shown, the crowd thinned, leaving Ana and a few others still waiting. *Maybe Montalvo isn't going to show up. Maybe he got caught up in his work and didn't want to stop. Maybe he found something better to do. Maybe he changed his mind.* Ana had gone through all the maybes in her head when she heard a gasp among some of the women. She saw hands fly up to mouths and whispers into the nearest comadre's ears.

When she turned to see what got their attention, there

was Montalvo. He was wearing a crisp, white guayabera over jet-black jeans like he wore the first day she saw him. Because he was so tall and striking, he cut through the crowd como un sail. Women and men looked him up and down as he passed. Those who dared to make eye contact, he nodded at graciously. One woman mouthed the word *wow* to her friend as she fanned herself with her program.

"I would totally do him," a man behind Ana said.

"Me, too," said the woman wearing the "Vagitarian" T-shirt.

"No way!" her girlfriend gasped, grabbing a handful of her girlfriend's nalgas.

"I bet she would!" the man said. "Mr. Yummy has something so totally going on under that 'buelito shirt."

The buxom girlfriend was stricken. "I'd only do it once. And I'd let you watch," the Vagitarian said bien naughty.

"No, no, no—you kitties go braid each other's fur, or whatever it is you all do. He's coming over here for me!" the man said. When Montalvo stopped in front of Ana, las hociconas fell silent, their mouths shaped into airless ahs.

"Ana! Dispénseme, I am late!" Montalvo leaned down to greet Ana with a kiss on the cheek. Now the Vagitarian was watching Ana.

"Why, hello," the man said, cutting between Ana and Montalvo. "You're that artist I keep reading about in the paper, aren't you? Carlos Montalvo, yes?" The man was standing close to Montalvo, his chin drawn to his chest, his hand fondling the opening of his shirt, trying to get—cómo se dice?—a read on Montalvo. Would he be tempted or angry?

"Yes, I am," Montalvo said without hesitation. "And you would be?"

When Montalvo was not rattled or intrigued, the man did not have a backup plan.

"Who, me?" the man stammered. "Oh, I'm nobody! I just came because I heard there was free food!" As soon as the words fell from his mouth, the man felt stupid.

"Well then, con permiso." Montalvo took Ana by the elbow and led her over to get their passes.

"What's wrong with you?" the Vagitarian laughed.

"Oh, shut up!" the man said, dripping with envidia as Montalvo and Ana climbed the stairs and out of sight.

"I'm so glad you came," Montalvo said. "When I get tickets to things like this, they always give me two, and I hate to waste."

"Thanks for inviting me. I've never been here before. I've heard of this place, but this is my first time."

The director of the center rushed over to introduce herself to Montalvo as soon as he reached the top of the stairs. Those who hadn't seen him on the main floor began to chatter about him wildly. The woman who was the featured filmmaker of the night came up to him, and before Ana knew it, she had whisked him off to the bar. Ana didn't know if she should follow him, find a seat, or stand against the wall. She decided the easiest thing to do was to go and freshen up. She looked around for the restroom and slipped in. She wouldn't feel lost in there.

A woman who had already had too much to drink stopped to talk to Ana as she washed her hands.

"Girl, your man is divine!"

"What? Oh, no. We're just friends," Ana quickly explained.

"Jus' friends? Oh, hell. I wish I had a friend like that!"

The woman made Ana uneasy. "He's a visiting artist at the university, where I work. I'm just here keeping him company," she said primly. "We're just—"

"Oh, yeah. I think I heard about him," the woman said, as she swayed from side to side, trying to put on lipstick. "Let me tell you something. Whenever he goes back to heaven, I would follow him! You hear me? You should jump on that angel and fly!" The woman left the restroom with lipstick on her teeth. She knew she shouldn't be, but Ana was pleased. She liked how Montalvo's hand grazed her back as they climbed the stairs, how he leaned in with his whole body to listen to her. She liked the company of his—how they say—arresting male energy. He could be with anyone he wanted, and he chose to be with her. She was flattered, even if nothing would come of it. *Would something come of all this?* she wondered. Ay, no—Ana pushed the idea out of her mind.

When Ana came out of the women's room, Montalvo was waiting with a plastic cup of white wine.

"Perdón, all these people! I'm all yours now."

The director had roped off some VIP seats near the front, but Montalvo asked Ana if she would mind sitting in the back.

"That way," he whispered, "if the films are bad we can leave without anyone noticing." He smiled elegantly at the filmmaker, who was walking across the room to take her seat.

"Isn't she your friend?"

"I know her," he said, still smiling. "But her work is, how the students say: it blows."

The first few films were shorts. The low-budget films had what the people around Ana called "earnest performances and wonky camera angles meant to look arty." The main feature film was about a woman and her daughter. The daughter was going off to college and the mother wondered if she'd prepared her well enough for life ahead. When the mother told the daughter she wanted to buy her a—cómo se dice?—un vibrator, las mujeres in the audience clapped and clapped. *Qué curioso*, Ana thought. She had some kinks it would be good to work out. Pero, when the mother and her daughter went to estor to buy it, she saw it was not the same cosa she was thinking of. Could she do that with Carmen? N'ombre! Nunca! Maybe? She wanted to find out what happened with this woman and her daughter when Montalvo leaned over to her and hissed.

"Híjole! Can you believe this?"

Ana only partially heard him. Montalvo leaned in again.

"Listo?"

"Ready for what?" Ana whispered.

"To leave."

"You want to leave?"

Ana remembered having this conversation with Esteban. She was surprised she was having it with Montalvo. She thought he was different.

"Tengo hambre," he said, rubbing his dark hand over the bright white of his shirt.

"There's a barbecue place across the street, and some other places down the street," Ana whispered. "Pick one and I'll find you later."

When Montalvo didn't move, she turned to him. "I want to watch the rest."

Montalvo stood up, then sat down again.

"How will you know where to find me?"

"I only saw three places. It won't be hard."

Montalvo stood and left, wondering why Ana would want

to watch the rest of the ridiculous movie. In the back of her mind, Ana wondered if letting Montalvo go was a good idea. It's what she did with Esteban when she took him to something where he got bored or overwhelmed. Had she insulted Montalvo? Esteban was always relieved when Ana let him off the hook, and she hoped Montalvo felt the same way.

When the film was finished. Ana stayed for the talk with the filmmaker and two of the actors flown in for the festival. Ana didn't ask any questions—oh, no—but she listened to the women, who talked about sex and pleasure, the mother-daughter story, and how no one had heard a story like that before, especially one with a Latina mother and daughter. When it ended, Ana walked up to the film-maker and told her how much she liked the film and how much it moved her.

"Why, thank you—thank you so much," the filmmaker said. "And what about you, Mr. Hard-ass Critic?" The filmmaker was looking past Ana at the person standing behind her.

"Ay! Qué hermoso! Bien hecho, mujer!"

Ana was surprised to hear the words come from Montalvo. When she turned to look at him, the filmmaker took the chance to reach past her and pull Montalvo close to her.

"No, really. Dime la verdad—you liked it?" the film-maker asked in a low voice.

"Of course!" Montalvo said.

"Let's see what you say after I buy you another drink! Then I can hear what you really think!" The woman looked at Ana. "I bet your friend has to go to work bright and early in the morning, and if I remember correctly, you like to sleep in late." The woman ran her fingertips along the buttons of Montalvo's shirt. He took her hand and patted it in a grandfatherly way.

"But I must get up first thing in the morning, también. I am teaching here."

"Oh, yes," the woman said. "I heard. The teaching gig. You better be careful, mi amor. You climb into the velvet coffin and you might not be able to climb out."

Montalvo chuckled as he released the woman's hand. "Ay, mujer. It's been a long day, and I must prepare for class tomorrow," he said. "Let us have lunch tomorrow, and I'll tell you all you want to know."

"Ay no, mi amor. I fly back to Califas tomorrow! It's tonight or nothing!" the filmmaker said. She wanted Montalvo to know this was his last chance.

"Lástima! Pues, then this is goodbye!"

The filmmaker's face dimmed a little. "Well, we can talk by e-mail, no?"

"Por supuesto!" he said.

Montalvo and the filmmaker exchanged kisses on the cheek before he turned to Ana.

"Listo, ahora?"

"Sure," Ana said. As they were walking Ana started thinking. "Hey, you don't have a computer."

Montalvo looked at her and beamed. "Ándale, before she remembers that."

After several stops along the way, they finally made their way outside the building and walked to the parking lot.

"I hope you didn't think—you didn't have to come back. I would have found you," Ana said, when they reached her car.

"I never left. I was going to, but it did not seem polite to leave you here alone, since I invited you."

"You didn't eat?"

"No. I was not hungry. More like restless. I get very restless and have to move. I was in the back."

"So you saw the whole thing?"

"Yes," he said slowly. "It was better than I thought it was going to be."

"Ah-ha!" Ana said with satisfaction. "So a little patience paid off, eh?"

"Perhaps, but her work is usually—how do you say it?—mixed. Sometimes good, sometimes bad. Most of the time, very, very bad."

"Hijo! You *are* Mr. Hard-ass Critic." Ana laughed. "What did she mean when she said not to climb into the velvet coffin?"

"Oh!" Montalvo scoffed. "She was talking about how it is not good for an artist to join the academy. They stop doing real work and become only someone who can teach."

"But teaching is important," Ana said, remembering her mission.

"Of course it is! But there is always a danger of getting too safe, getting too comfortable. There is something to be said for keeping the edge, and that only happens when an artist is hungry."

"Isn't that starving-artist image overromanticized?" Ana said. "There's nothing wrong with having a roof over your head, a studio, health insurance, travel money, and students to inspire you."

"Yes, yes, all of that is true," Montalvo said. "Stability is attractive, but we fight it, too. Teaching is honorable, but once an artist stops doing their work, the work they were meant to do, it is death."

"So, do you think your friend got lucky, or did she really do the work?"

"She is good at getting people to do her work. She's really very lazy."

"Lazy?"

"The story was lazy. Lazy and unbelievable."

"Unbelievable? What was unbelievable?" Ana pressed.

"What woman would buy her child a sex toy? That was preposterous!"

"She bought it for her adult daughter, not her child," Ana said.

"Would you do that for your daughter?"

"No, probably not. I don't think so. I don't know. Maybe I will when she gets older," Ana said boldly. "I like the idea of a mother teaching her daughter about sexuality in a way that allows her to find pleasure independent of another person."

Who said that? Did I really say that? Ana wondered.

Montalvo felt as if a sword had been drawn and he took a defensive stance.

"Well, if the daughter would have found a real man, instead of that tonto boyfriend she had . . ." Montalvo waved his hand dismissively. "It was ridiculous! It was not realistic to me."

"Not to *you*," Ana said. "But I think it said something to the women in there. It said something to me. And it wasn't all about the sex toy. That was one small part. It was about trying to teach your child to be her own person, the girl to be her own woman."

"I agree!" Montalvo exclaimed. He was slightly annoyed that Ana wouldn't let this go, but excited that she would not back down. "But why did the man have to be so, so . . . always in these women's films, the man is so . . . he was hardly in it!"

"Because it was not his story!" Ana roared.

Before the two of them knew it, they were debating

the film. The story, how it looked, the performances, the script—all of it, taking playful but strong swipes at each other's opinions. Montalvo was dazzled. Challenged, but dazzled. He began to wonder if Ana was this demanding and aggressive . . . elsewhere. And Ana—she took pleasure in meeting each of his serves with a forceful response. No matter what direction he came from, she was able to return. That was exciting enough, but having someone who could do that, who wanted to do that with her—she was thrilled.

"Oye, if we are going to keep talking about this, at least let us do it over tacos. You have made me weak! Vamos!"

"Oh—I can't," Ana said, remembering who she was. "I would love to, but tomorrow is a school day, remember? I have to go to work."

"Lástima," Montalvo said. This time, he said it sadly, as if he did not want the evening to end. Ana's feet were sore from standing for so long. She leaned against the car. Oh! If only Montalvo would lean against her . . .

"This was fun," Montalvo said. "I would like it if we can do this again. After the holiday, yes?" Montalvo leaned on the car next to her, leaving a wide gap between them.

"Of course, maybe during the spring break."

"I will be traveling," he sighed. Then he tried to hold back a yawn, raising his wrist to his mouth. "Híjole! This day is almost over!" he said, looking at his watch. "It's almost midnight!"

"No! Verdad?" Ana said. She looked around the parking lot. They were the only ones in it, their cars parked on either end.

"Buenas noches, Ana. It was a wonderful evening. I think the end of the semester will be busy, but we should have lunch before the break."

"Yes, yes," Ana said, a little frantically. She had turned off her cell phone for the film and forgot all about it. Had her children called? What would they be thinking?

"Of course, but it was nice to see you outside of school," Montalvo said. "Even if your taste in movies is crazy!"

"Ay, qué malo!" Ana laughed. "Do you know how to get home from here? I'm sorry, I didn't know it was this late, and my kids must be wondering where I am."

"Sí. Vaya. Hasta pronto."

Montalvo trotted over to his car as Ana waited for her phone to turn on. He drove up next to her and waved before driving off into the night. Ana was relieved when there were no messages on her phone, and even more relieved when she returned home and found her kids were fast asleep.

≋ EIGHTEEN ≋

The first thing Diego wanted to do after he got his license was to go see Sonia. His tío Marcos had offered to buy the boy a car outright, since Ana was helping so much with Bianca, but Ana said that was too much and that Diego needed to do his part. So Marcos had him doing odd jobs at whatever worksite could use an extra pair of hands. In return, Diego had a few dollars in his pocket and he got to drive the big troca his uncle left behind when he was on the road.

Because Marcos's travel was taking him away for longer and longer periods of time, he suggested they all move into his house, since it was bigger and could easily hold Ana and the kids. But that would mean leaving the house Ana and Esteban built, and Ana could not do that. She just couldn't. Ana and Esteban still met for their household meetings, sometimes in person, sometimes by phone, but the time was coming when they would have that one meeting they wanted to avoid. And it would take both of them by surprise.

Diego got his license during the spring break. Ana could see her son wanted to experience his new freedom.

"Please, 'Amá? *Please?*" Diego pleaded. He wanted to go to band practice and later invite Sonia out for a little drive.

"Ay, mi'jo . . . I know you've been waiting a long time but—"

"Please, 'Amá? I won't get on any freeways. Please, 'Amá? *Please?* I have money for gas—and I'll bring you back a strawberry Slush!"

Ana smiled, a small, crumpled smile. When she and Esteban were first together, he took her to the Sonic for a strawberry Slush and would listen to her talk about her day at school. She remembered telling him how hard it was, and he would listen and nod his head. He didn't ask many questions, but he always offered encouragement. Before every major test, she would fret and worry, and Esteban would tell her she had nothing to worry about. Then, when she passed the test with flying colors, Esteban was the only one who wasn't surprised. He would mark the occasion with a strawberry Slush and a trip to the pet store on Zarzamora. The pet store was a good substitute for the zoo on the other side of town. Ana didn't mind. She liked looking at the animals up close, and if the owner was in a good mood, he would let her hold the small kittens or chatter with the parakeets that ate birdseed from her palm.

The day after she learned about the great Mexican muralists, Ana talked about them nonstop—Rivera, Orozco, and Tamayo were her favorites from the slide show her professor showed the class, but she was bien excited when she learned about some of the women muralists like Celia Calderón and Olga Costa. Esteban didn't know what to say, but he listened to her carefully. The next day, he gave her a box of colored pencils and a pad of newsprint he bought at the grocery store. It was then that Ana knew for sure that she was in love with Esteban Ruiz.

During their first year of marriage, the Slush was a Friday-night ritual. They would pick up their food and drive over to Brackenridge Park or take the long drive down Zarzamora and onto Military Drive, talking about the future. After a few months, Ana began to notice that all those Slushes were expanding her waistline. The evening she suggested they share a Slush something strange happened. She wasn't sure what to think of it, but her favorite drink tasted strange in her mouth. Esteban took a sip but didn't notice anything different. It tasted the same as always to him. Ana took another sip. She couldn't believe he didn't taste the same metallic taste she did. When she started feeling nauseous in the mornings, she knew something was new: She was pregnant with her Diego. The metallic taste went away, and as she got bigger and bigger, she would pat her belly and ask, "Quieres un slushy, mi amor?" She would wait for one of those first, early flutters to tell her yes. Pos, she didn't always feel the flutter, but she liked to believe her little one was in agreement with her.

After the first trimester, the Slushes tasted fantastic to Ana—as long as there was a pickled jalapeño in it! Esteban gagged the first time he saw his wife stirring the bright red drink with the green jalapeño. The way Ana told the story, she asked her belly if it wanted a Slush before every trip. The first time the baby kicked back to say yes, she and Esteban sat in the car for an hour, gently caressing her belly, trying to tell the future about their little one.

It had been a long time since Ana had told her children that story, but Diego never forgot it. Ana knew Diego wanted to spend time with Sonia, and the Sonic drive-in was the place to do it. But Diego was also anxious to go to the place where his parents had been happy. He needed to do this, especially after what he learned on his last job site. His Spanish was not so good, but he understood enough to know what "la otra" meant. When he heard it said along with his father's name, he figured he had enough information to fear the worst, but not enough to really understand what was happening. He didn't know if he wanted to know what was happening. He just wanted to go back to the place where his parents had been happy.

"Really, 'Amá. I'll be careful!"

"I know you'll be careful, but it's the other drivers I worry about." Ana stopped lecturing when she saw how patiently her son was waiting for her to finish. "Be back by six."

Diego was a good driver, even if he was a little timid. He made his way the short mile to Sonia and Rafa's house, happy to not show up all sweaty with a crook in his back from carrying his instruments. Diego didn't want to show off, but he felt bien pleased to be driving up in his uncle's big troca. He didn't care that "De La Torre Construction" was stenciled on the driver-side door. His uncle could have left it locked up in his garage. Diego was thankful.

As soon as he drove up, the boys looked up from what they were doing and came down the drive to check him out. Even Mr. Castañeda came out.

"Nice ride, D," one of the boys said. They all talked about the size of the engine, gas mileage, and what kind of kick it had on the highway. Diego was careful to let everyone know—especially Mr. Castañeda—that he did not drive on the highway and that he was a good driver.

"Well, you must be a good driver if your uncle trusts you with his troca," Mr. Castañeda said. Diego couldn't tell if the man was as impressed as he wanted him to be.

The boys wandered back to the garage. Diego saw Sonia watching them from the window and smiled. She waved and smiled back at him. This gave Diego the courage to ask the question he had been gearing up to ask.

"So, Mr. Castañeda, I was wondering if after we practice, would it be okay if I took Sonia to the Sonic? Just for a little while. I have to be home by six."

El señor stared at Diego hard. He turned to look back at his house, and Diego was relieved to see that Sonia was no longer at the window. Mr. Castañeda turned back to Diego.

"Ask me when you guys are done."

That was the longest hour of Diego's life. El Rey didn't show up that afternoon, and that by itself thrilled Diego. But the unknown answer to his question made Diego todo edgy. He fumbled where he never fumbled before, and the boys didn't get it.

"Dude! Qué tienes?" Rafa asked.

"Nothing, man. I'm hungry, that's all."

"Yeah, me, too," Tomás chimed in.

"I could eat," Rudy said.

"I think we have some chips or something inside," Rafa said. The boys began to pile inside the house when Diego pulled Rafa aside.

"Hey man, I'm going to take off."

"Why? We're going to keep practicing after we eat," Rafa said.

"Yeah, but . . . I got something to do, and—" Before he could finished, Mr. Castañeda was standing at the door with Sonia.

"So, you're ready to go now?" he asked.

"Go where?" Rafa asked.

"They're going to the Sonic, and you're going with them," Mr. Castañeda said. This wasn't what Diego had in mind.

"And take the boys with you," he added. "I don't know where that Rudy puts it." This was definitely not what Diego had in mind, but he didn't know if he'd get another chance.

The kids climbed into the large cab, which had a narrow seat just wide enough for Rudy and Tomás, behind the front seat. When Mr. Castañeda saw that Sonia was going to get in to sit next to Diego, he put his hand on her shoulder and motioned for Rafa to climb in the cab first.

"Ay, 'Ápá!" Rafa whined. Mr. Castañeda didn't have to say a word, and Rafa dutifully climbed in the cab before his sister, giving her the passenger-side window.

"Dude, you so *owe* me!" Rafa said to Diego between his teeth.

"Hey, no holding hands, Rafa," Rudy joked, shoving Rafa's shoulder.

"Yeah? Why don't you take your hand out of Tomás's pants?" Rafa snapped. When Sonia climbed into the cab the boys fell quiet. Diego carefully started the truck and began pulling away. Rudy wouldn't quit.

"Hey, Tomás is touching my knee!"

"Cállate, cabrón!" Tomás said.

Diego took the drive down Zarzamora Street, just like his mother had described from the early days with his father: past the greengrocer, the auto shops, the taquerías, the paleta stands, Laundromats, used furniture stores, video stores (chain, local, and Mexican movie stores), the shoe repair shops, the bakeries, the hairdressers, and all the little places that were the backbone of many families that raised children on their small, hard-won fortunes.

When the kids got to the Sonic at Zarzamora and Buena Vista, Rafa made an—cómo se dice?—executive decision.

"We're going to sit over there," Rafa said, pointing to one of the empty picnic tables in the small courtyard in front of the burger joint. The boys didn't argue. The ride made the backseat seem smaller, and the boys fell out of the cab, stretching their legs and darting over to get a look at the menu. Diego rolled down the windows and ordered for himself and Sonia from the driver-side monitor. When the carhop brought their food, they ate silently, watching the boys at the picnic table flirt with one of the female carhops, turning their attention to their food like vultures when it came, and then, stuffed with french fries, onion rings, burgers, and soda, leaning back with their elbows resting on the table, their backs to Diego and Sonia, to watch the world go by.

"They have good hot dogs here," Diego said. *Why did I say that?* he thought. *Everybody knows they have good hot dogs here, tonto!*

"Yeah, they're good," Sonia chirped. Diego felt better.

"My mom used to love coming here," Sonia said. "She liked their Slushes."

"Yeah, my mom, too," Diego said.

"Oye, when are you going to show me some of your lyrics?"

"Oh, yeah," Diego said. He had forgotten all about his book of words, which he'd kept stored under his bed ever since he found out about his father. "I don't have anything good yet," he said. "I had some stuff, but it all looks really stupid now." Diego had been writing about love, and he believed all the flowery words, even after his parents' split. But after what he thought he found out about his father, the words sounded empty to him. Was all this love stuff a big, fat joke? Could he promise undying love, as he wrote in his secret journals? Or was it a promise he was destined to break? Would he do the same thing as his father one day? He didn't want to believe it, but he didn't want to believe what he had heard about his father, either.

Sonia could see something was bothering Diego and moved closer to him. She slid her hand under his hand, which was resting on the seat. Diego pulled it away.

"What's wrong?" Sonia asked.

"Nothing," Diego said. "I just—I don't ever want to do anything to make you hate me."

Sonia reared back. "Where did *that* come from?" she asked.

"I just—I don't want to be that guy," he said. "I don't want to be that guy who makes promises and then doesn't try and keep them. I don't—I don't know . . ."

The boys burst into loud guffaws, and Diego and Sonia turned to look at them. They had ordered a chocolate sundae during a shift change, and—mira!—there was El Rey bringing their order to them! The boys were floored, seeing Rey in his carhop getup and with his hair stuffed under a Sonic baseball cap. But they were having a little too much fun, Diego thought. He climbed out of the troca and walked over to them.

"Hey man, we ordered this sundae with nuts and *three* spoons," Rudy said a little too loudly. "Take it back, and can we have three cherries?" Rudy and Tomás laughed like hyenas, while Rafa counted the change in his hand.

"Man, I told you we didn't have enough," Rafa said, and then to Rey, "Hey dude, I'm sorry. Can you take this back?"

"No, man. That's not how it works," Rey said.

"I got money! I got money!" Rudy laughed, digging in his pockets but coming up with nothing. "Dang, man, can't you float us?" Rey was getting nervous. His boss was giving him a look from inside the store.

"Be cool, man. I need this job," Rey said.

"You what?" Rudy said. "I didn't hear you."

"Shut up," Diego said, taking the sundae from Rey and shoving it into Rudy's hand. He reached into his pocket for a five and gave it to Rey.

"Thanks, man," Rey said quietly, making change and giving it to Diego, before he turned and walked away.

"What's wrong with you?" Diego said.

"I was just having a little fun with him. No harm, no foul. Chill! Did you see how he looked in that getup?" Rudy scoffed. "Dang!"

"Yeah? And what are you doing with your sorry self? Eat that thing in five minutes or I'm leaving your stupid ass behind," Diego said. Rudy looked to Rafa and Tomás for support, but they decided to side with Diego.

"We'll wait in the truck," Rafa said. As the boys piled in the truck to wait for Rudy, Sonia smiled a soft, knowing smile. Diego wasn't that guy; he was *the* guy.

Ten years later, when Rafa would give the toast at their wedding reception, he would say how if it wasn't for him, the young lovers would have never gotten together.

NINETEEN

Bianca was usually all about the holidays. She loved the tinsel and the wrapping paper, the blinking lights, the music and all the fa-la-la-la-la that went with it. But this year had been different. She told herself it was her father being gone so much and that the orders for her bags had been bien popular, pero a lot of work. That, with the quinceañera, had taken a lot of her time. But no, something else was not right, and Bianca didn't know what it was. N'ombre, she *did* know what it was. But you can't make the horse follow the water, verdad?

It didn't come to Bianca what was missing until she found herself sitting in church with her cousin at the annual Mass of Guadalupe on December 12. This was the Mass held on La Virgen's feast day. Rich or poor, puro Mexicano or Mexicanos Americanos, los famosos or not, it was the day when all good Mexican Catholics showed reverence to La Diosa de las Américas. It was a special Mass where the appearance of La Virgen to Juan Diego was acted out. Carmen, Bianca, and Diego had all done their time acting out the role of La Virgen, Juan Diego, or the Bishop. Bianca still had the costume her mother had made for her, kept in a box wrapped in pale tissue. It was one of the happy memories Bianca had of her mother. The measuring and the fitting, the attention to each cosita, the way her mother made sure the sash fell just so, and how all the gold stars were embroidered on the cerulean-blue mantle made Bianca feel, pos, divine.

Like her Bianca, Teresa de la Torre loved clothes. Bianca liked watching her mother get dressed up for a night out with her father or for one of the many social events they attended. Marcos was ready in no time, waiting in the outer bedroom, reading the paper with Bianca on his lap, the both of them waiting to see Teresa come out from the huge closet looking like a vision. Marcos would complain about all the events and fund-raisers they had to go to since they were the past Charro Queen y el Rey Feo. Pero, whenever he saw his delicate wife appear from the closet, more beautiful than the time before, he got todo wobbly in his knees. To Bianca, her mother looked like a princess—or a fashion model. She was amazed that the woman could walk into the closet wearing nothing more than a robe, her hair tied into a quick knot, and then make her way through the jumble of shoes, belts, and scarves, and come out looking bien fancy.

"Are you a fashion designer, Mami?"

"Oh, no!" Teresa laughed, taking her little girl into her arms. "Maybe one day you will be the designer. I see how you like to draw."

"Really, Mami? I can be a designer?" Bianca asked, looking into her mother's closet and wondering if she would ever be able to work the same magic as her mother.

"You can be anything you want to be, mi'ja."

And Bianca believed her.

. . .

Bianca and Carmen liked to attend the Guadalupe Mass together. Years after they had grown out of participating in the Mass, they still liked to go and see the adorable hombrecitos dressed as mini Juan Diegos as well as the chicas dressed as Guadalupes (who had no idea of what a virgin was but knew being one was good), to the girls who were old enough to have outgrown dressing up for the pantomime play but couldn't give it up because their stage mothers wouldn't let them. Or, maybe they couldn't give up the spotlight. Who would want to give up a starring role as La Diosa de las Américas, even if you were playing it with a herd of girls in look-alike costumes?

This year, they counted twenty Virgens, twenty Juan Diegos, twenty Bishops, and at least that many other characters. They all stood in identical poses, one right after the next, in the front of the church before the congregation. Adults took turns reading the story of La Virgen of Guadalupe making her appearance to Juan Diego at Mount Tepeyac, her instructions to tell the Bishop to build a church on the mount, and how the Bishop did not believe. It took Juan Diego five tries (five!—the Spanish Bishop did not believe the humble indio), but La Virgen gave him strength and urged Juan Diego to go back and try again. On his last try, the humble Juan Diego opened his tilma and fully bloomed red roses, not in season that cold December day, fell to the Bishop's feet. Only then did the Bishop believe. And the rest was, as they say, the start of something big. You can't be a good Mexican and not know who La Lupe is. She is petitioned for everything from relief of common pains to communicating with the departed. She is sought or carried for guidance and solace, which is what Bianca was in serious need of after a month of dreaming of her mother.

She was not happy when Carmen made them get to the Guadalupe Mass late.

"Look, they got a new Lupe!" Carmen whispered to her cousin, as they entered the church. As was tradition at the Guadalupe Mass, the celebrants laid roses at her feet.

Carmen hurried to the front of the church just before the Mass began to make her offering. The new Guadalupe came from Chihuahua, carved from a tree trunk, lovingly buffed by hand, every crease and crevice anointed with mineral oil by a devoted wood carver. The base was three feet wide and still had the shape and appearance of a tree trunk, so La Virgen carved from it was literally emerging from the wood. As Carmen made her way back to her cousin, she looked among the faces for Esteban.

"Tell me if you see my 'apá," Carmen said, when she returned to the spot along the wall where she and Bianca were forced to stand because they were late. "This is one of his favorite Masses. He should be here, somewhere."

"What about your mom?" Bianca asked.

"I don't know. Who knows? You know how she is."

The perfume of roses drifted over them, and Bianca inhaled deeply and closed her eyes.

"Hey, I want to ask you something," Carmen asked, breaking Bianca's peaceful moment. "Will you be the madrina for the tiara?"

"What? Why me?"

"Because you're not in the court, and I want you to be in the quinceañera, too, not just plan it."

"Shouldn't that be for someone older, like your tía Beatriz or your mom? Moms usually bring in the tiara," Bianca said, remembering that that was what was planned for her quinceañera that wasn't.

The music began to play, and the congregation stood

to greet the procession led by the Guadalupanas, the most ancient viejitas in the congregation, whose job it was to keep the memory of La Lupe alive and help plan the Guadalupe Mass. They raised the money to buy the new Guadalupe statue. The three Knights of Columbus who drove to Chihuahua to pick her up and bring her to the church, just in time for the special Mass, followed them.

"But I want you to do it," Carmen whispered.

"Does your mom know?"

"Don't worry about her."

(Ay, qué desgracia!) Bianca knew that Carmen was blinded by the idea that she was a good Catholic girl, but here she was, in church, her two faces side by side—honoring the celestial mother with one, while spitting on her earthly mother with the other. Bianca couldn't stand it.

"Carmen, don't do that," she pleaded.

"Do what?"

"You know!"

"Know what?"

"Don't do her like that. It's mean!"

"She said I could design the ceremony however I want, and that's what I want," Carmen said, just before the priest invited the congregants to consider their sins in silent prayer.

Maybe it was the weight of reverence for La Guadalupe all around her, the perfume of the roses, her stubborn cousin's coldness, or maybe it was because of all of it, but Bianca, like Juan Diego, was struck with a deeply powerful understanding of what she had to do.

The attendant who was betting against Bianca seeing her mother was up fifty dollars. His coworkers were annoyed.

The easy solution would have been to stop betting, but they wanted Bianca to break through her fear, eager for un milagro that would reunite mother and child. In spite of what they had witnessed over and over, they continued betting with the attendant, hoping that Bianca would surprise them. Was that too much to ask, for one small sparkle of hope among so much daily despair? So, when Bianca made her way from her car and into the building at last, the attendants held their breath.

"All right!" the attendant named Marie said, when she saw Bianca walking into the building.

"Oh, hell no," another attendant, Abel, said. "I have plans for my money."

"You're awful," Marie said.

Bianca walked up to the desk qué timid. She carried her esqueche pad, a couple of the bags she'd made, and a pink rose. Bianca wanted to turn back, she wanted to run in the other direction, but just like Juan Diego facing the Bishop, she gathered up all her courage, all her determination, and walked to the main desk and stated her purpose.

"May I see my mother?"

"Of course," Marie said. She didn't have to ask who Bianca's mother was. "Why don't you go to that room over there and we'll bring her out."

The room was much nicer than she remembered. Tall windows let in plenty of light, which in itself was comforting. There were other residents in the room. Some watched her every move, trying to decide if she looked familiar, while others played cards or stared out the window, or dozed upright in wingback chairs. Behind a glass wall, she could see a group of patients doing Tai Chi. The moves looked almost like a dance, and Bianca wondered if her mother, who loved to dance, had ever taken the class.

Bianca's father wanted her to visit her mother, but he didn't want her to go alone. He wanted to be there. But Bianca thought the visits were more difficult when Marcos was around. Bianca thought it was because he was so desperate, but the truth was that she was the one who was desperate. She wanted her mother to come back, to be the woman she grew up with. She wanted her mother to be well again, but more important, Bianca didn't want to be angry anymore. It was too exhausting.

"Here she is," Marie sang, when she brought Bianca's mother into the common room. Teresa de la Torre was tiny and bien flaca, dressed in a powder-blue velour jogging suit. Her eyes were bright, her blond hair combed and held back with a yellow headband. A hint of lip gloss shone on her lips. *It would be like my mother to be the best-dressed crazy person in the joint*, Bianca thought.

Teresa sat in front of Bianca and didn't say a word.

"Look who came to visit you," Marie said. Abel had already bet on how long Bianca would stay and was anxious to make up for the money he'd lost.

"I brought this for you," Bianca said. Teresa looked at the rose, sniffed it, and then showed it to Marie.

"It's pretty," Teresa said. "Isn't it pretty?"

"Oh, yes, very pretty," she said. "Why don't I take that? I have some of that powder you put in the vase to make it last longer. How's that?" Pero, in reality, she wanted to check for thorns on the stems.

"You can do that?" Teresa asked, as if this were some strange magic she'd never heard of.

"Oh yes, don't you worry," Marie said.

"But bring it back."

"Oh, yes, ma'am. I'll bring it back. You visit with this lovely young lady here and I'll take care of it."

Bianca and her mother sat. For once, Bianca had no words—or, it wasn't that she didn't have any. She had too many. Where would she start?

"You still wear your hair that way, eh?" Teresa asked. The question surprised Bianca, and her chongo bobbed from side to side. "Ponytails never go out of style," Teresa said. "Pretty."

"Thank you."

"Just remember, you can't always wear it like that. When you get old, you'll have to wear it down, not like that, not like a teenager."

"I *am* a teenager."

"I know what you are," Teresa snapped. "You look nice."

This mix of sweet and sour had been the first sign that something was wrong with Teresa. It was bien subtle at first. As a little girl, Bianca thought maybe her mother was playing a game she didn't understand the rules to, but when she got older and her mother's moods and words became more extreme, it was clear to everyone that something was horribly wrong with her. Bianca didn't understand why it had taken so long for others to notice, until she realized that somehow her mother had managed to hide her strange behavior from everyone but Bianca. That only lasted a year, pero long enough to make Bianca worry that maybe there was something wrong with her instead of her mother.

"You haven't had sex yet, have you?" Teresa asked.

Bianca was flustered, but she tried not to show it. A less direct version of this conversation was one she would have liked to have with her mother, lying on their stomachs on the big bed Teresa used to share with Marcos, late into the night.

"Don't have sex, and don't do drugs. And don't have kids. They change everything, the way you look, the way you think." She saw Bianca's esqueche pad leaning behind the chair she was sitting in. "What's that?" Teresa asked. Bianca turned to see what her mother was looking at.

"Oh, nothing."

"Let me see."

"Oh, that's okay. It's probably not something you'll like," Bianca said nervously.

"Can I see and decide for myself?" Teresa said. Bianca slowly reached behind her and passed the pad to her mother. Teresa flipped it open and looked at the drawings one after the next. Then closed the pad with a slap.

"These are good," she said.

"Really? You think so?"

"What did I say?"

Bianca smoothed her hair behind her ears.

"I told your father he needed to bring you to see me. What took so long?" Teresa asked.

"I've been busy."

"Busy? Busy with what?"

"School. And this. These are the dresses for Carmen's quinceañera."

"He used to come. Now he just calls."

"He's been traveling," Bianca explained.

"That's what he said," Teresa said suspiciously.

"It's true. He's been gone a lot. Even I don't see much of him."

"You're still my little girl," Teresa said. "You should come see me. More."

"I know, Mami."

"Give me a pencil."

Bianca found a pencil in her bag and gave it to her mother.

"Not this one, a good pencil. Like the ones you use."

Bianca dug in her bag for the pouch of drawing pencils she always carried, and as she was doing that, Teresa
opened the esqueche pad she'd just looked at and began to
tear out the sheets. Bianca lurched toward her mother.

"No! Mami, don't do that!"

"These are good, but didn't we decide on formals for
your quinceañera?" Teresa asked, as she tore page after
page from the pad. "These are for spring. Your birthday is
in the fall, or the winter. When is it?"

"These aren't for my quince," Bianca explained. "Stop
it, okay?"

"When is your birthday?"

"February!"

"And these colors. These are spring colors. You can't
have spring colors at a winter quinceañera. And where
are the muffs? Remember, we talked about muffs instead
of gloves for the girls? Fur muffs, faux fur muffs, dyed to
match the dresses. I don't see any of that here!"

"Mami! These aren't for my quinceañera! Stop! Please
stop!" Bianca finally snatched the pad from her mother,
who looked at her with surprise.

"Why not?" Teresa asked, as if they were having a regular,
everyday talk. "Why aren't these for your quinceañera?"

"Because that was two years ago, remember? I was
going to have one but . . ." Bianca picked up the sheets of
paper before her mother could do any more damage.

"Before I came to this place," Teresa said.

"Yes."

"Why did you bring this?"

"I thought you might like to see what I am doing,"
Bianca said. Her voice was trembling. "And these bags—
see these bags? I made them from my own designs, just
like you told me I could one day. You said I could one day,

and now 'one day' is today. You used to like to see what I drew. You used to like my ideas." Bianca could feel herself falling apart, but something stronger inside fought against her desire to turn and run out.

"Nice," Teresa said. "Where's my flower! That woman stole my flower!"

"I have your flower," Marie said, walking back into the common room, looking at the paper still on the floor. "Don't worry about your flower. It's right here." Marie set the flower on the table next to Teresa. "How are we doing, Mrs. De la Torre? Are you doing okay?" She was looking at Bianca, who was winded from picking up all the paper.

"We're fine," Teresa said. "Except my daughter doesn't want me to help with her quinceañera. What do you think about that?"

"Her what?" Marie asked.

"Her quinceañera! If you knew anything, you would know what that is. How long have you lived in this country?"

"It's like a coming-out party, isn't it?"

"You could say that, and stop talking to me like I'm stupid," Teresa barked. "I'm not stupid. You talk to me like my husband."

"Well, if you say so," Marie said. "Look at the mess you made. I don't think your daughter needs this kind of help."

"I'm not having a quinceañera," Bianca tried to explain. "These are for Carmen, Mami."

"Who?" Teresa asked.

"Carmen."

"Carmen? Ana and Esteban's girl? She's not that old. She can't be that old. If she were that old then that would mean—" Teresa began to remember the quinceañera that wasn't and the years that had passed since then, the years she had lost. She looked at Bianca with sad, wet eyes. "I can fix it. I need to fix it," Teresa said.

"Fix what?" Bianca asked.

"Your dress. Where is it? I can fix it." Teresa stood up and began to look around the room frantically. "I can fix it! I can fix it! Bring it here and I can fix it."

"It's not here," Bianca said. "There's nothing to fix."

"I can fix it! I can fix it!"

Marie was getting ready for the worst.

"Maybe we need to go back to your room now," she said.

"I can fix it! I can fix it!"

"No, Mami. The dress isn't here. It's gone. This quinceañera is for Carmen!" Bianca said as loudly as she could without screaming.

"Oh—I ruined everything, didn't I?"

"It's okay, Mami."

"No, it's not," Teresa said. She only remembered flashes of the quinceañera that wasn't. Most of it was snow, and the rest she wanted to believe hadn't happened at all but was someone else's nightmare.

"I bet you think I'm a bad mother," Teresa said, staring hard at Bianca. "I'm not a bad mother, I do bad things. I don't mean to, but sometimes I do. I'm not bad."

"You're not bad," Bianca said.

"It was nice to see you. I hope you will come back again," Teresa said. "Will you come back again? You should come back again. I like my flower. It's pretty, like you."

Abel, the attendant who had been betting against Bianca, snorted from behind the main desk.

"That's it. She's outta here."

"Shut up!" Marie said. Another attendant took Teresa

back to her room, and when they were alone, Marie turned to Bianca. "Are you okay?"

"Well," Bianca said. "That wasn't so bad."

"So, we'll see you soon?" Marie asked.

"Yes, you'll see me soon."

"Pay up," Marie told Abel, as Bianca left the building.

TWENTY

Wouldn't you know, Carmen was finally getting excited about her quinceañera, but did she share any of that with her mother? And the truth was, it wasn't the quinceañera as much as it was seeing El Rey. She mostly saw him at Diego's band practice, where her brother could feel like he was keeping an eye on her. And she was real careful to make it look like all their meetings were hands off—todo "he's just a friend." And he was a better friend than Carmen knew.

The night he picked her up to take her to the Montalvo pachanga was the night he figured out that the *quince* in *quinceañera* meant fifteen, meaning Carmen was only fourteen. At seventeen, Rey thought that those numbers only added up to trouble. The band didn't seem to be going anywhere, but he liked the boys, he liked—how they say?—hanging out, and he liked having a group he could call his friends, even if they treated him like an outsider, which he was. But he could sure play, and he liked showing off his skills to an appreciative audience. And if Mr. Castañeda was a sample of the fathers he would meet among the girls he met so far, he knew that he better keep his hands to himself for a good, long time. He sure thought Carmen was cute. But even El Rey was not stupid enough to get into a situation that would end his life.

The week before the quinceañera, Ana thought everything was going good. At work, things were going well, too. Everyone was thrilled about the chance of Montalvo joining the faculty. A writer for the weekly newspaper even had something to say about it, printing a long story on Montalvo's work and featuring the handsome artist's photo on the front page. Everything seemed destined to work out.

The Saturday before the quinceañera, Ana was shopping for dresses with Beatriz. She still needed something special for the quinceañera, and she needed some advice.

"I set up the girls at the nail place," Beatriz said. "They're all giggly and happy, drinking their fizzy water out of plastic cups, así." Beatriz posed with her pinky in the air, her eyes staring toward the sky.

"Thanks so much for doing that," Ana said.

"Of course! De nada."

This was the part of the quinceañera Ana loved. Not the dressing up or the primping, the shopping, or the planning, or the booking of this or that. It was finding out who your family was.

"So, did you do all this stuff for your quinceañera?" Ana asked.

"Are you kidding? My mom gave me a ten-dollar perm, my makeup was from the drugstore, and I had press-on nails."

"But it was special? I know you joke about it, but it was special to you and your mom?"

"It was, but it had nothing to do with the ceremony itself," Beatriz said. "I mean, the ceremony *was* special. The Mass was nice, and the few gifts I got were nice, but the best part—the very best part to me—was when it was over, and I sat with my mom and my aunts and my cousins eating leftover cake and talking into the middle of the night. My mom lost one of her shoes and my tiara got bent, but I didn't care. That was the most time I got to spend with her, because you know, she worked so much. If she wasn't working, she was sleeping."

"Yeah, me, too," Ana said.

It had been a long time since Ana had any conversation with Carmen, and she was beginning to think it would never happen again. She had wanted the quinceañera to be a time to bond and become close again. Now, although things seemed to be coming together, it seemed like a way for Carmen to avoid talking to Ana about anything outside the quinceañera; the whole thing was feeling more and more like a giant to-do list.

"All the girls are at the nail salon?" Ana asked, holding up a plain blue sack to her face for Beatriz's response.

Beatriz made a face like she tasted something sour. "Yeah—oh, except Bianca. But they said she was on her way."

"On her way? From where?"

Beatriz shrugged. "I didn't ask. Why?"

"She's been acting a little . . . I'm not sure. Sometimes she vanishes, and I don't know where she is and she doesn't answer her phone. And when I ask her where she's been, she says she was running errands."

"You think it's a boy?" Beatriz asked, holding up a slinky peach dress for Ana to see.

"No," Ana said about the dress. "I want something that says *mom*, not *mamasota*."

"Oh, come on! Just a little mamasota?" Beatriz teased. "Show a little of that juice in the caboose, already! And the girls' dresses? How are they coming?"

"I can't believe it, but I think Bianca is going to deliver," Ana said.

"And she's keeping up with school?"

"Yes, she actually made Carmen's quinceañera the project of her business practices class, with the budget and a production schedule y todo! I was shocked. And she finally got Carmen to give up on that god-awful tiger-stripe print. So, now Carmen is going to be in champagne white and the girls are going to be in pastels."

"Well, then—maybe it's nothing," Beatriz said.

"No, it's something," Ana said, holding up another shapeless dress under her chin.

"Okay, so are you trying to look matronly? At least get something that shows off your figure!" Beatriz said. "So, look, my theory is this: if she's doing well in school and she's still keeping up with all the stuff she's supposed to keep up with, there's probably nothing to worry about."

"That's easy for you to say," Ana said. "You have boys. And how soon we forget, Miss I'm Going to the Library to Study."

"I did go to the library to study—some of the time," Beatriz said.

"Well, I need to get to the bottom of this before her dad gets back this week," Ana said. "If she is doing anything stupid with some boy, I think it will be better for her to deal with me first." Ana continued searching through dresses on the rack before she stopped with a tired huff.

"I can't believe it. I don't see anything I like. Are you ready to go?" Ana turned to look at Beatriz, who was loaded down with clothes.

"Go ahead, I'll wait," Ana said. Beatriz went into a dressing room to try on the outfits. Ana sat on a small padded bench outside the dressing room, facing the three-way mirror in the outer dressing room. A few other women came and went, but they mostly had the dressing room to themselves.

"Maybe I did it all wrong," Ana said.

"Did what all wrong? The quinceañera?"

"No. My life. Maybe all the choices I made were wrong. When Esteban and I got married, I thought it was the most perfect thing. I understood him. I knew what he was about. I recognized him. It all made sense. He was home." Ana sighed.

"What do you mean, 'he was home'?" Beatriz asked from inside the dressing room.

"He was what I knew. You know, a good guy. A good man. Uncomplicated and familiar. Maybe I should have been a painter or an art teacher. Maybe I got married too young. Maybe I should have gone away to school."

Beatriz came out of the dressing room to look at herself in the three-way mirror.

"Why do you assume you are the one who made all the wrong choices? You didn't make Esteban's choices."

"No, but maybe I expected too much."

"Your problem isn't that you expect too much—it's that you expect too little. Don't get me wrong. Esteban is a good man. I've seen how he is. He's a good father. He's got a good heart, but—"

"But what?"

"You always said everyone told you you were lucky to get a man like Esteban. Did it ever occur to you that *he* was the lucky one?"

Never, ever, in Ana Ruiz's married life had that thought

ever come to her. Beatriz went back into her dressing room
to try on another outfit.

"Oye, has Montalvo said anything to you about staying?"

"No. I know he's seriously considering it, though."

"Really? And how do you know that?" Beatriz teased.

"Oh, stop. We're just friends."

"I don't know if Montalvo is the kind of man you can be
just friends with," Beatriz said. "At least I don't know why
you'd want to be," she added under her breath. "Crap!"

"What's the matter?"

"I got the zipper stuck. Can you help me?"

Ana joined Beatriz in the small dressing room, and the
two of them faced the mirror as Ana figured out the best
way to unstick the zipper without tearing the cloth.

"I'll tell you one thing," Beatriz began. "I like how you
are since he's been around."

"Oh? And how's that?"

"Happier, lighter."

Ana lost her grip on the zipper.

"I'm still married," she hissed.

"I know, but you're not dead!" Beatriz hissed back.
"Look, I'm not saying you should do anything you don't
think is right, but just don't—just don't let life pass you by
because you're trying to be noble. I'm serious."

"I know you are. Can we talk about something else?"

"Oye! I've been meaning to tell you," Beatriz spun
around to face Ana. "It's coming down to the wire and
the whole, big honking machine is finally going to produce. I think they're going to offer Prince Charming an
endowed professorship with some travel money, sabbati-
cal time, and, if he's lucky, a housing allowance."

"Really? Where's the funding coming from?"

"Most of it from Gruber. The city is pitching in the first

year, the state arts council the second, and the rest thanks to a deal made through the state legislature—but I don't know how you know that and you didn't hear it from me," Beatriz said in a low voice. "Getting all these people to two-step together in time to the music—híjole! I think the final word is coming down next week."

Ana returned to working on the zipper and smiled to herself.

"So, are you bringing him to the quinceañera?"

"Who? Montalvo? No!"

"Oh, come on! Invite him."

"I could, but it would be weird, with Esteban there."

"But I thought you were just friends?" Beatriz said.

"We are, but . . . I think it would be better if he didn't come. He knows about it. He's busy. Plus, I think he'd rather be working in his studio than stuffed in a tuxedo."

"Ay, but he looks so nice in a tuxedo," Beatriz said dreamily.

"Stop! I told you what Carmen thought about him and me, right? I don't want to replay that drama. And it's *her* day. I don't want anything to make her think otherwise."

What Ana really meant to say was she wanted to keep Montalvo to herself. She made another tug on the zipper, finally loosening the cloth from its teeth, when her cell phone rang.

"Ana, qué onda?" Montalvo said.

"Oh, just shopping. What's going on?"

"I was wondering if you were open for lunch. I have some big news to share."

"News? Really? What?" Ana asked, signaling to Beatriz that she was talking to Montalvo.

"Come over. I need your opinion—and I'm starving. Do you mind bringing tacos from that place I like?"

When Ana told Beatriz what Montalvo wanted, she muffled a shriek.

"Maybe he's decided! Ana! You've got to call me right away, as soon as you know something, okay?"

Ana was singing along with her Stevie Wonder tape as she drove up to Montalvo's studio.

"Isn't she lovely?" Stevie crooned, and Ana had to agree. She felt lovely and happy.

She told herself she was excited her friend was going to stay in San Antonio. She was looking forward to helping him find a permanent home and settling into life in the city.

As she entered the studio, she found Montalvo staring at the piece he'd been working on since the beginning of the school year. It wasn't coming together as he had hoped. Mocte and another student were there, tired and bien haggard, waiting for instructions. Montalvo was walking back and forth in front of it, stopping and thinking. He then turned to the students and told them to go with a rough wave of his hand. They would have run for the door if they weren't half dead.

"Hola, Mocte," Ana said, as he passed her.

"Hola, miss."

"You look like you had a long morning."

"Long night," he said, looking back at Montalvo. "I got to go, miss." The fog around Mocte worried Ana as she continued toward Montalvo.

"What was that about?" she asked.

"They're tired."

"How long have you all been at it?"

"Since ten."

"Well, that's not so—ten o'clock, last night?"

Montalvo nodded. Ana quietly set the food on the table and handed him a soft drink cup. "If you told me, I would have brought food for them, too." Montalvo shrugged, sat at the table, and drank from the cup. She was disappointed in his response but decided to get to what she thought was the root of the issue. "I'm sure if you give it some time—"

"I'm running out of time," he said, pulling the bag of food toward him and digging in. "The semester, the year is almost over, and this is all I have to show for it."

"No one said you had to have the piece or anything finished by the end of the school year. And I'm sure the students, some students, will want to stay involved."

"And then, there's another school year, with more students, and they'll want to start a new project, not continue with this. Why should they? It is a mess! It is going nowhere."

Montalvo threw a partially unwrapped taco onto the table and leaned back in his chair.

"Oye, Ana, tell me: what do you know of Girona?"

"Girona? Where is that? In Spain?"

"Sí, sixty-five miles from Barcelona, más o menos! That's less than from here to Austin!" he said. "Barcelona is one of the great cities of the world. Art, architecture, fashion, the beach—"

"What does that have to do with Girona?" Ana asked.

"I want to go to there."

"To visit?"

"To work."

Ana imagined the look on Beatriz's face, the dean's face, Mrs. Gruber's face, everyone's faces when they found out what she was afraid Montalvo was saying.

"What's in Girona?"

"The Salvador Dalí Museum. Really, it is to the north, but Girona would be a good place to live and still be close to the museum and to Barcelona."

"But I thought you wanted to stay here?"

"I do. I did, but . . . I am not very good at this, Ana," he said, avoiding her eyes. "I'm not a very good teacher."

"What are you talking about? The students love you! Everyone loves you!"

"You are lovely, always so lovely. Have I told you how lovely you are today?" Montalvo smiled, then took a deep breath. "Everyone has been very kind, but I should not be here. The students are wonderful, but the entire time I am with them, I am aware of the work I am not accomplishing. I work best alone. I did not think it would be that way, but . . . Barcelona! Ana, Barcelona! I've always wanted to be in Barcelona. Can you imagine?"

"Just like that?" Ana said.

"Yes! Of course, like that! Barcelona, Ana! Haven't you ever wanted to go?"

"Of course," Ana said.

"Then come with me!"

"What?!"

"Come! You can teach English or get a job in the university there! It's all the same—bureaucrats are the same everywhere in the world. And when you get tired or have spent all your money, you can come back here."

If Montalvo was trying to sweep Ana off her feet, he was doing a bad job.

"But what about my kids?"

"They're old enough to take care of themselves, aren't they? Believe me, they like a little freedom at this age. If I hadn't been stuck with Lili, I would have done this years ago," Montalvo blurted.

Ana's face fell.

"Don't look at me that way," he said. "You know what a burden children—and husbands and wives—can be!"

Ana felt herself closing up like a flor de peñasco.

"I can't just pick up and leave. I have a family here, a life here," she said.

"But I thought you wanted something more?"

"I do," Ana said, "but I don't—I can't . . ." Now it was all becoming clear to her. Except for the time he spent "stuck" raising Lili, he flitted from woman to woman and place to place, leaving whatever headache had been created behind. Even Esteban had not been that cold, that self-centered.

When Ana's phone rang she didn't hear it. She was too busy wondering: *Where did that man I thought was so kind and elegant and exciting go?* Ana felt as if she had been told Montalvo was dead, and this person in front of her was an imposter. But no, this was the real Montalvo after all.

"Ana, your phone," Montalvo said, picking up his drink and walking over to look at the partially assembled sculpture. She flipped open her phone and said hello.

"Ana! Who is this boy?" Esteban asked in an urgent whisper. He was calling from the tuxedo shop, where he and the chambelanes were getting their final fitting.

"Qué, qué, qué?"

"The boy that looks like a rooster! He says he's Carmen's friend. Is that true?"

"I don't know who you're talking about," Ana said.

"The boy with the tattoos and the rings on his face. He says he's her friend. What kind of friend? Why is he trying on a tuxedo like the rest of them?"

"He must be on the court," Ana said, before it dawned on her that she might know who the boy was—the dangerous boy called El Rey that she first saw in the Castañeda garage.

"He is not like the other boys," Esteban said.

"Can we talk about this when I see you later?"

Ana hung up the phone, annoyed and still stunned from where she and Montalvo left off. She turned back to him to find him still staring at the structure. Suddenly, he threw his cup violently. It skidded across the cement floor, ice cubes gliding everywhere.

"What a waste of time! It will have to be destroyed! That's all there is to it," he said.

"You can't do that."

"I can't have my name on it!"

"But the students have their hand in it, too. What will they think when they see it destroyed like it was nothing?"

"They will think that life is unfair. The sooner they learn that, the better," Montalvo said. "I cannot have this remain as my legacy. You understand, don't you, Ana?"

"I . . . no! Thousands of dollars have been spent here, not to mention time and effort, and you just want to destroy it? There must be something to save."

"No, I think it's better to bring the bulldozers in now! Ay, Ana! What was I thinking? I don't belong here. I belong in Barcelona. An invitation was sent to me from the Dalí Museum to make an installation in conjunction with a festival, an anniversary—I don't know the details, but I want to accept it." Ana wondered if this was how Montalvo made his decision to come to San Antonio, because he was tired or frustrated with where he was before.

Montalvo waited for Ana to congratulate him, to cheer for him, to tell him it was all right. When that didn't come, he stood tall and said como el mero big shot, "I am not meant for this place. I am meant for bigger things."

"Well, then. It sounds like you've made up your mind." Ana turned on her heel to leave.

"Ana! Ana!" By the time Montalvo caught up to her, her face was stony.

"Everyone has been working hard to keep you here," she said. "Everyone thought you wanted to be here, make a life here. I thought you wanted to be here. I thought . . I thought you wanted me!"

"I do! I did, I mean—what do *you* mean?" Montalvo asked.

"You know what I mean!"

"I—I wanted a companion, and that's what I got. A very lovely companion and a good friend, I thought. You told me you were married! How long is a man supposed to wait?"

He lunged at Ana, took her in his arms, and lifted her off the floor.

"Ana, Ana, Ana! How long are you going to hang on to this anchor you call your family? Your kids are practically grown! They'll make it the rest of the way on their own!"

Ana was horrified. She pushed herself away from Montalvo and stumbled to the floor. She ran to her car and Montalvo stood there, feeling very worried. It was not like Ana to not support him. But he knew she'd be fine. She had to be fine. She would be fine, wouldn't she? Ana Ruiz, after all, was a strong woman.

By the time Ana got to the taquería where she usually met Esteban, she was in no mood for slanted conversation or any other communication without words. She wanted words. Concrete words to tell her exactly what she needed to know, what she deserved to know. No more of this talking around the truth—she wanted to pull back the cover that hung over it and face it.

How stupid could she be? Her thing with Montalvo, or whatever it was, was all an illusion, all a mirage, all for show, a short movie that ended suddenly and left her sitting in the dark. But with Esteban, no. She couldn't stand it anymore. He could not get away with letting their lives fade away like ink on paper. She needed him to decide. Was he with her or not? Was he going to fight for her or not? Did he want her, or was he just waiting for her to give up? Así no. That was not how it was going to work. Not anymore, Ana decided.

She pulled into the lot at the same time as Esteban and she motioned for him to get in her car. He was surprised but did as she instructed. La 'Onda was always small for him, and he had to fold up his legs to fit inside.

"So, who is that boy?" Esteban asked.

"I don't know."

"Por qué no? I expect you to be in charge of these things!" Esteban said.

"You don't get to be mad about this! You have had all this time to be involved and you've stayed as far away as possible, and now you want to make your grand entrance? Now you have something to say?"

"I thought this was for you and Carmen!"

"I can't do it all!" Ana screamed. "You don't get to check out because it's inconvenient or you're tired or you just don't want to anymore!"

Esteban was uncomfortable, looking out the window, wondering if anyone could hear Ana.

"Lower your voice," he hissed.

"What do you *want*, Esteban?"

"Qué?"

"What do you *want*? What do you want from me that I haven't given you already?"

"No sé qué—"

"You *know* what I'm talking about. I'm not talking about Carmen or the quinceañera. I'm talking about us! What do you *want*?"

Esteban sighed a long, heavy sigh that was part frustration, part embarrassment, part fear, but most of all, a recognition that that huge, thunderous cloud that he knew would find him one day had arrived to rain down on him, hard.

"You, you are the mother of my children," he said.

"But what do you *want*! I am the woman you married, the woman you are still married to. Tell me what you *want*!"

"Ay, Ana. You're a good woman."

"That doesn't tell me what you *want*! All I'm asking is for you to be honest."

Esteban saw that Ana was not going to let this go, and because she was the mother of his children, because he respected her, and because he knew he wanted to do the right thing, he sat up, trying to decide how to answer her. He tried to find the right words, but nothing was coming, and it only made Ana more furious.

"After all this time, can you *please* be honest with me? What do you want? Is that too hard? Let me make it simple for you: Do you love me?"

Because he felt trapped and confused, the only two words that said it all fell from his mouth like a stone:

"I did."

Ana couldn't breathe. She closed her eyes and her face twisted into a sick expression. Esteban reached for her hand, but she didn't respond. She let him hold her hand, and she almost remembered how she felt when they first held hands, but it was a stale memory that faded before it could become bittersweet. Esteban could have been holding the hand of a corpse. The life, the newness, the verdant anticipation Ana had was drying up like the flor de peñasco next to her bed. She decided right then she was going to throw it away as soon as she got home.

"I want to do what's right," Esteban said. "I don't know how to make things right with you, but if you want me to be honest, if that's the only way, all I know is—I wanted to be your man. I wanted to be your man, real, real bad. I knew that when I first saw you. I knew it would be hard, but I tried. I tried, Ana. I wanted your man to be me, but I'm not him."

Ana opened her eyes and was surprised at what she saw. Customers walked in and out of the restaurant. A starling landed on a telephone wire, then flew away. A huge truck rumbled through the parking lot behind them. A dishwasher hauled a bag of trash from the restaurant to the Dumpster under a tree, then stood in the shade to smoke a cigarette. Someone drove by with his car stereo rattling the windows as he cruised down the street. And the sun kept shining. And the sky was still blue. And the clouds didn't explode. And the planets didn't spin out of the galaxy. Gravity continued to work as it always had. The world hadn't collapsed. That this painful, raw moment had no effect on the world was both comforting and stunning to Ana.

"Here," Esteban said, handing Ana a small velvet pouch. "It's from the jeweler." Ana opened the pouch and pulled out a necklace. Muy delicate and lovely.

"It's for Carmen. I told the jeweler to make it from your ring. I thought we should give it to her, you know, for the quince—but I think maybe you should keep it."

So, that's what was taking the jeweler so long. She poured the necklace back in the pouch and dropped it near the gearshift between them. "Shouldn't you be giving that to your woman?" she asked sharply.

Esteban cringed. He picked up the pouch and put it back in his pocket.

"So, that's it?" Ana asked numbly. "You're in love with her now?"

"No," Esteban said. "But I got to do what's right, because, you know."

"No, I *don't* know," Ana said. "Tell me."

"Ella está embarazada," Esteban said. "Pregnant."

"I know what it means," Ana said.

That was about as much honesty as Ana could take for one day.

TWENTY-ONE

Ana did not plan on taking time off before the quinceañera, but after that day with Montalvo and then Esteban, she couldn't make herself go to work on Monday. Tuesday was no better, and by Wednesday she told herself she might as well take the week. Why not? She had plenty of vacation time, and they didn't need her anyway. Beatriz had taken up the damage control over the Montalvo resignation and was too busy to talk to Ana for long.

"We're talking about a counteroffer," Beatriz told Ana over a quick phone call between meetings. "Do you think he'll take it?"

"I don't know," Ana said.

"But it couldn't hurt to ask?"

"It never hurts to ask."

Beatriz was about to hang up the phone when Ana stopped her.

"Hey—I'm sorry."

"There's nothing to be sorry about."

"I thought—I thought . . ."

"Hey, we all thought," Beatriz said. "It's not you. These things happen. I would have liked for it to happen before I took my shot with the lege. There are only so many bites you can take from the apple. But really, Ana, don't take this all on yourself. It's not necessary."

"Okay."

"Everything going okay with the quince?" Beatriz asked.

"For the most part."

"Are you all right?"

"Yes," Ana lied. "Don't worry about me."

The relatives began to arrive on Thursday afternoon, and many of them stayed at Marcos's house. Word had got around that Ana was not up for visitors, and besides, where would she put them? The Ruiz house was overrun with quinceañera supplies. But the relatives may as well have been in Ana's house. With Marcos out of town again and Bianca moving between houses and off to "run errands," the guests always needed something, and they all seemed to have Ana on speed dial.

"Ana, where's the toilet paper?"

"Ana, how do you turn on the AC? It's too hot."

"Ana, where are the blankets? It's too cold."

"You should ask Bianca," Ana told them.

Bianca had been going back and forth between the two houses, and Ana couldn't understand why the relatives kept calling her.

"She's not here and she's not answering her phone," was the answer. Ana knew she had to get to the bottom of Bianca's disappearing act once and for all.

"Do you know where Bianca is?" Ana asked her kids, as they were on their way out to the rehearsal at the reception hall.

"I don't know. I thought she was at her house," Diego said. "She said she was meeting us at the hall."

"She did?" Carmen said. "I thought she was coming back for me."

"I don't think so," Diego said briskly. "Let's go."

"I want to ride with Bianca," Carmen said, as she gathered her things.

"Come with me," Diego said with that look in his eye. "She said something about getting more paper towels and stuff for her house."

"You talked to her?"

"Carmen!" Diego was losing his patience. "Let's go!"

"I'm right behind you," Ana said. "Be careful!" She called Bianca's cell phone, and this time, her voice mailbox was full.

Ana was now very worried about her niece and wanted to find out what was going on. After Carmen and Diego left, Bianca pulled into the drive in a flurry and rushed into the house with several large bags. She was running around, como la loca, getting the things she would need for the quinceañera rehearsal when she ran into Ana, sitting quietly in the living room.

"Ay! Tía! You scared me!" Bianca said, slapping her hand to her chest. "I just wanted to drop off this stuff because it was taking too much room in my car and I—"

"What's going on, Bianca?"

"What do you mean? I'm running around and it's late and we have the rehearsal in a half hour and I'd like to change, but I don't think I have time and—"

"Where have you been?"

"At the store. Look at all this stuff I got. Enough paper products for the whole neighborhood."

"No, Bianca. You might be able to fool everybody else, but not me. Where have you been?"

Bianca's thoughts twisted around in her head before she finally answered. "I was with my mom, at that place."

"Oh," Ana said. "Oh. I didn't know. I thought you were only supposed to go with your dad."

"No one knows," Bianca said. "And I am supposed to go with him, but I don't know—she gets more agitated when he's there. He tries so hard to make everything seem normal, it just makes her worse."

"How long have you been seeing her?"

"I don't know. A few times."

"Well, that's good, Bianca. I'm glad you're visiting her, but why are you sneaking around?"

"I didn't want to tell anyone in case I got scared."

"It's okay to be scared, Bianca. But no one said you had to go alone," Ana said.

"Who else would go with me? You're too busy, and no one else—I don't know anyone else who I trust to see her that way."

"Ay, Bianca, she's still your mother. You have nothing to be ashamed of," Ana said.

"I'm not ashamed, and no, she isn't," Bianca said. She wasn't trying to be mean or even a little dramatic. "She's not the mother I remember, but she wants to be. She tries. I know she wants to get better."

"Well," Ana said, putting her arms around Bianca. "I'm very proud of you."

"You are?"

"Because it would be easier for you to forget her."

"I tried to forget her," Bianca said. "There's still something of her in there. I go to look for that. It's not always there but when it is, it's nice."

"And she doesn't hurt you?" Ana asked, remembering the bright red gash she had treated on her brother's neck.

"No," Bianca said. "She says things, but you know—that's not really her. I've learned how to roll with it. The worst thing about her is that she's still stuck from when she first got sick. I showed her some of the stuff we've been working on for Carmen's quinceañera, and she thinks it's for me. She gets mad when I try to correct her, so I just go along. She keeps saying she wants to make things better."

Ana smiled at her sobrina and suddenly saw how much she had underestimated her. Few adults could do what Bianca was doing.

"How come she won't get better?" Bianca asked. "I miss her."

"I know," Ana said, brushing a piece of Bianca's hair away from her face. "Do me a favor—please let me know when you want to go visit her. Just so I know, okay? I won't tell anyone if you don't want me to. And if you need someone to talk to afterwards, I'm here. Okay?"

"Okay," Bianca said.

"We should go," Ana said. "But I've been meaning to ask you something for a while," Ana said. "I was wondering if you would be the Madrina de la tiara."

"Me? No, Tía, that should be for you!" Bianca said. "I think that's for the mothers to do."

"Well, it's for whoever we want to do it," Ana said sadly. "And I think you should do it."

"But why?" Bianca asked.

"Because you're the closest to Carmen. I think she would prefer it."

"Did you ask her?"

"I don't need to ask her."

"I'll do whatever you want, Tía. But if you change your mind, tell me. I won't mind," Bianca said. "We should go. We're going to be late!"

As they were leaving, Ana's cell phone rang. She took the call and said a few words before she snapped her phone shut, threw her phone in her purse, and shook her head.

"What? Did they run out of toilet paper again?" Bianca asked, thinking it was one of the relatives staying at her house.

"No," Ana sighed. "It was your uncle Esteban calling to say he was going to be late."

"But he's still coming, right?" Bianca said.

"Quién sabe?"

When Esteban had asked Carmen about the strange boy at the tuxedo shop, she was put off guard.

"Who, 'Apá?"

"That boy with his face and ears poked like a fish. He said he was your friend."

"You mean Rey?"

"How many boys do you know like that?"

"Where—how . . . ?"

When Esteban explained that he met El Rey at the tuxedo shop, Carmen had a dumb realization. She liked the idea of upsetting her mother, but she forgot all about her 'apá. Qué Carmensa!

"I don't believe you," Diego said to his sister, as he was driving them to the reception hall. The court was meeting after school for the dreaded dance lesson with Bianca. "You play like this and you get what you deserve. So, *now* what are you going to do?"

"I dunno. Tell him not to come?"

"You can't do that!"

"Can *you*?"

"Oh, hell, no!"

"It's not like he paid for anything! Tío Marcos is paying for the tuxedo rentals."

"That's not the point! You invited him! Híjole, Carmen! You're so lame!"

"I didn't think he'd do it after—"

"After what?"

Carmen was thinking of the night she called El Rey and got him to come over and drive her to the Montalvo pachanga. She remembered how he leaned in close to her, brushed her forearm lightly with his index finger, making her giggle, and how, when they got to the subject of the quinceañera, his body language changed.

"Hey, you know, you're cool and all and, you know. I'll come and all, but let's be cool," Rey had said before he dumped her on the corner like a bundle of newspapers.

"After what?" Diego repeated.

"Nothing. Can't 'Amá uninvite him?"

"No, Carmensa! Don't bother her with your crazy shit! She's upset enough as it is."

"About what?"

"What do you care? All you do is try and make her miserable. And she's going to tell you the same thing I am. You can't invite someone and then tell them not to come. How would you like it if someone did that to you?"

"But 'Apá. . ."

"But 'Apá, but 'Apá," Diego mocked. "Why don't you think about 'Amá for once?"

Diego was percolating with anger, not because he was afraid Rey's feelings would be hurt, or because taking back the invitation would show his sister's bad manners, or even because he was worried what anyone would say. He was upset because he could see that something had changed. His mother's mood was darker, her spirit gone dull. He thought maybe it was all the work leading up the quinceañera, but he wasn't sure. Maybe his mother found out about "la otra." Maybe she already knew. He didn't know. All he knew was that someone needed to be on her side. She was the strong one. That is what the family said, but he knew she needed help, even if he didn't know what he should do.

"You need to tell 'Apá you invited him and you lied to 'Amá about it and deal with it!" Diego barked at his sister.

"I can't do that!"

"Yes, you can! You talk to him better than anyone. What's he going to do, disown you?"

"D!"

"I don't know why 'Amá hasn't by now! You're a mess! Go with him, if you want! You deserve each other!"

Carmen had no idea why her brother was so angry. She sat sulking in the far side of the cab. She was not used to her brother talking to her this way.

"You're mean," Carmen said.

"Yeah? Well, that's the only way you hear."

When they arrived at the reception hall, everyone was waiting outside. Carmen was relieved Esteban wasn't there, but not so much when Ana told her that he called and said something had come up and he would be late.

"What do you mean, something came up?" Carmen asked.

"You'll need to ask him," Ana snapped.

Once they got inside the hall, Bianca took charge. She made the pairings as they planned with Carmen's circle of friends, pausing when she looked at the primas. The girl shaped like an apple brought an ecstatic young man, happy to be invited to the party. He was dressed in body-hugging jeans, Roper boots, a belt buckle the size of an ashtray, and a Longhorn orange polo shirt with the collar flipped up. The other couples were cousins who agreed to be paired with each other in order to spend a long weekend in San Antonio. Bianca tried to pull a fast one by pairing Carmen with the male cousin.

"Hey, what's up?" El Rey asked. They all looked at Bianca, who looked at Carmen, who looked at Ana.

"Well?" Ana said while on hold with the caterer. Carmen turned to El Rey.

"You're with me."

El Rey smiled and in his flattened Spanish exclaimed, "Órale!"

Bianca taught them the dance they would do at the reception. It was really nothing more than walking with the music, but she made it interesting, with the couples lacing through each other, hands clasped and arms turned into arches for the couples to walk under and around, couple by couple. The cousin shaped like an apple was bien agile, and her partner clapped when he got to twirl her. The other couples managed to hold their own, going through the steps following Bianca's orders. She knew the dance from her own quinceañera that wasn't, but no one remembered.

Ana was running down her to-do list as she wrote a check and listened to the caterer on the phone go over the final details. The waltz music was playing in the background and Ana was soothed by it until she came across something on her list that struck her as odd. She finished her call and called to Bianca over the music.

"Don't stop!" Bianca ordered.

"Bianca, what did the photographer say about the deposit?"

"What deposit?"

"The deposit. Didn't he want a deposit?"

Bianca looked at Ana blankly.

"I don't know, Tía. I wasn't in charge of the photographer." Qué coraje! Ana quickly called the photographer and when she heard a message saying he was taking the month off and wouldn't be taking appointments until next month, she couldn't stand it. How had this huge detail been overlooked?

"Don't worry, Tía. We'll just put disposable cameras on the tables and let everyone take pictures."

"But what about at the church?" Ana said. "Crap. . ."

Ideas to fix the situation were racing through their heads when the two of them were startled by a squeal and a thud. They both turned to look at where the noise had come from.

"Dang!" Rafa said. The girls were frozen. El Rey was standing with his arms apart, standing over Rafa, who was rolling on the floor, a bright pop mark blooming under his eye. "Dang!" Rafa said again and again. "Dang!"

"What the hell is going on?" Ana asked, as she bent down to look at Rafa. "Mi'jo, are you all right?"

"Dang!"

"Are you all right?"

"Yes, ma'am."

Ana stood up.

"What happened?"

"I was aiming for him!" the apple-shaped girl sputtered, pointing at El Rey before she ran off, shaking the smart from her hand.

Her partner tried to explain. "She's really hungry," he said with a *tsk*.

"Dang!" Rafa said. "Give her a freaking taco or something!"

"And this gabacho was saying pendejadas about—I don't *even* know what—and her mom?" the boy said, tossing his hand in the direction the apple-shaped girl ran off. "She is too much, you know, with the dieting? And when we got to that part in the dance where we make the bridge, así?" (He demonstrated.) "I really like that part, by the way. Anyway. I think this one might of, accidentally on purpose—I don't know, I'm just saying—I think he touched one of her girls, and you know, she went off."

Everyone was stunned, trying to decide what was more crazy: the fact that this boy was the apple-shaped girl's best ally, that she had a mean right cross, or that Rafa got popped good. The boy kneeled down to talk into Rafa's face.

"She's really a doll, once you get to know her."

The kids burst out laughing.

When Ana's phone rang she answered it quickly. "You better be on your way," she said, thinking it was Esteban.

"Ana Ruiz?" Ana didn't recognize the voice on the other end of the phone. "I am calling from St. Ignatius Hospital. Mr. Carlos Montalvo is here, and you are listed as his emergency contact." The color drained from Ana's face.

"Was there an accident?"

The kids helped Rafa to his feet and were loudly discussing how bright his shiner might be, but they fell silent when they heard Ana's serious tone.

"I'm sorry. I can't share that information with you on the phone. If you could get here as quickly and safely as possible, I can fill you in."

"St. Ignatius Hospital, you said? I'm on my way."

Ana's heart was pounding. She talked to the kids as quickly and calmly as possible.

"We have this hall for another hour. Does everyone have a ride home? Good. Rafa? Are you sure you're all right? Tell me now!"

"I'm okay," he said.

"'Amá?" Carmen asked.

"What happened?" Diego said over her.

"This doesn't involve you."

"'Amá?" Diego pressed.

"I've got to go now!" Ana said. "After this, you all go straight home. You hear me? Straight home!"

She left the building, forgetting that her children would assume the worst: that their construction worker father had been injured on the job.

"Why else wouldn't he be here?" Carmen asked her brother, as they jumped into the truck. "Something must have happened. Something bad."

"Don't go there. You don't know. You don't know anything," Diego said.

"It's just like her to not tell us anything, like we're stupid or something."

"What are you talking about?"

"Like when she kicked 'Apá out? There was no warning; she just opened the door and ya, he was gone!"

"Stop it, Carmen. You always go back to that, like that explains it all!"

"That's how she is. He could be dead and she wouldn't tell us until it was time to go to the funeral!"

"Shut up, Carmen! You don't know anything!"

"I know what I saw! I saw how it happened! That's how she does everything!"

"Yeah? Well what about him ditching you at Mass that one time? Did she do that to you, too?"

"He told me he had a flat tire!"

"And you believed him?"

"Why not?"

Diego bit his tongue.

"Why not?" Carmen repeated. When her brother would not answer she leaned in and pulled on his arm, scaring him and making him almost hit the car in front of him. He slammed on the brakes and the truck made a long screech on the street, the back end of the truck swaying out and nearly hitting another car. When the truck came to a full stop, the drivers around them honked and yelled curses out their windows.

"Shit, Carmen! Stop talking and let me drive!"

Carmen's mind began to race. If her father said he had a flat tire, he had a flat tire, didn't he? Why would he lie to her? It was beyond her ability to believe that he could *ever* lie to her. He wouldn't lie to her. He couldn't. What would he lie about?

The light turned green and traffic started moving again. Diego leaned forward into the large steering wheel, putting all his attention on the traffic around him. He felt bad. His anger toward his father had been churning since he heard of "la otra." He was tormented with thoughts of how he wished he could stand up to him and tell him to his face what he thought about him, tell him what he thought about what he'd done to his mother and to their family. For a brief moment, he even thought of what it would feel like to pop his father in the face, like his apple-shaped cousin did to pobre Rafa, only he wouldn't do it by accident. His blow would be deliberate, his fist carrying all of his anger.

But all of that evaporated like a puff of smoke when the thought of his father being hurt or worse became real. Suddenly, all the unspoken words of affection and pride came to him. There's something about thinking you've lost a person you love that makes all the stupid things they've done fall by the wayside, especially if that person is the one you most want to please but have no idea of how to do it. Diego wouldn't find out until he was well into middle age how honored Esteban was to have a son like him. And he would be shocked to find out when Esteban was most proud of his son.

At the intersection where Diego should have turned toward their house, he turned in the opposite direction.

"Where are we going?" Carmen asked.

"To the hospital."

When Ana arrived at the hospital, she was ready for the worst. She marched through the emergency room doors as they parted and walked toward the main desk. Then she saw Montalvo through the glass wall of an exam room, sitting on a gurney. His left arm was tightly wrapped to his bare torso. A young nurse was smiling as she helped pull a hospital gown over his shoulders. Montalvo was all smiles, and even in his painful condition, he managed to be charming. Ana walked into the exam room as the nurse at the main desk called to her.

"Ma'am! Ma'am! May I help you?"

Ana ignored her.

"Ma'am!"

When Montalvo saw Ana, he was embarrassed, relieved, and—how they say?—a little loopy.

"Ana! You are here! I was afraid you would not come! Please, meet my lovely nurses. They have treated me so well. I feel like a new man. I know I feel like a younger man." He winked at the young nurse, who whinnied like a pony. An older nurse stood in the corner of the small room, scribbling notes in a chart. Montalvo's way did not amuse her.

"Are you his next of kin?" the older nurse asked.

"That is my Ana!" Montalvo cheered.

"Has he been drinking?" Ana asked.

"No, it's the painkiller we gave him."

"I mean, she is my girl, friend, my friend who happens to be a girl," Montalvo said. "Pero, look at her! She is more than a girl, verdad?! But you, *you* can be my new novia, no?" he said to the younger nurse.

"Ay, tú," the older nurse said plainly. "You, go back to the nurses' station," she said to the young nurse. "Romeo, you wait here while I talk to your friend."

The older nurse helped Montalvo lay back onto the gurney and he closed his eyes, a todo dopey grin still on his face.

"What's wrong with him?" Ana asked, as the older nurse led her to the main desk.

"He wrenched his arm good and tore his rotator cuff. We thought there might be some nerve damage, but I think he's clear on that. The doctor can explain more when he comes back." The nurse at the main desk handed Ana a clipboard with several forms to fill out.

"You can go in and keep him company," the older nurse

said. "He's not making much sense. When we asked him what happened, he said he hurt himself flying."

Ana explained who Montalvo was and the work he did.

"Oh. Well, then I guess it wasn't the painkillers talking. But he won't be doing that for a while," the older nurse said.

When Ana walked back into the examination room, she thought Montalvo was sleeping. She sat down and began to fill out the forms the best she could.

"I'm sorry," he said with his eyes still closed. "I thought about what you said about me leaving and the students being disappointed and I tried to go back to work. I pushed when I should have pulled, or I pulled when I should have—I do not know. I began to fall and I thought I could stop myself but, well, here I am."

The pen Ana was using scratched the paper until it ran dry. She set the clipboard on the edge of his gurney.

"Someone else will have to fill this out for you. I have to go back."

"I'm sorry."

"You told me."

"No. I did not tell you enough. I did not tell you I wanted there to be more. I did not tell you that your husband is a fool for leaving you, but I . . . I know how to get women, but I do not know how to keep them. And you are a woman who deserves to be kept."

"I don't think that's what you mean to say, but thank you," Ana said. "Oye, I have to get back. There's the small disaster of not having hired a photographer and the quinceañera is Saturday."

"Ay! Perdóneme!" Montalvo said. "What a nuisance I am! Perdóneme!"

"No te preocupes. I'll call the dean. I'm sure he can help you."

"Ana, I want to help."

"Help with what?"

"I . . . I thought I might make a portrait of your daughter in her quince dress. I am very good with pen and ink. I had wanted to tell you that before the offer from the Dalí Museum came, but after that, I . . ." Montalvo's voice trailed off.

"You were going to do that for me?"

"I wanted to. I wanted to do something to help with your celebration without being in the way."

Ana suddenly felt bad that she had not invited Montalvo to the quinceañera.

"I'm sorry, I have to go. I really have to go, but I'll call the dean for you." Ana patted Montalvo's free arm, then hesitated and leaned over to give Montalvo a kiss on the cheek. "You don't know what you've done for me already," she said. He took her hand with his free hand and kissed it tenderly.

"I've got to go," Ana said. When she turned to leave, she saw Esteban through the glass, staring at her with a pained expression. (Híjole! Could this day get any stranger?) His hands were shoved into his pockets and he wasn't wearing his cowboy hat. Everything about him was off. When she reached him, his eyes were red and full with tears.

"Quién es?" he asked, pointing to Montalvo with his chin.

Ana wasn't sure if he was asking or interrogating. "Someone from work," she said.

"You act like that with everyone from work?"

"He's a friend. He's a visiting artist I helped bring in—" Before she could finish, Esteban began to weep. Ana pulled him by the arm to the wall. She wanted to believe his tears were for her, but she knew they were not.

"How—how did you know I was here?" she asked.

"I didn't," Esteban said, wiping his nose with a kerchief he pulled from his back pocket. "I'm here because the baby—the baby might die. There was blood everywhere." Esteban pulled himself together, but his eyes were swollen with anguish. "At first, I didn't believe she was pregnant. I didn't want to believe it. I told her I didn't want the baby. God help me, I even thought of giving her money to get rid of it. But she didn't, and now . . ."

"'Apá!" Carmen yelled from the door, relieved to see her father standing upright.

Qué horror! Ana thought when she saw Carmen and then Diego walk through the door.

"I can't," Esteban said, turning his back to his children and pleading with Ana. "I can't. Ana, por favor?" He stomped off as Carmen and Diego reached their mother.

"What's going on?" Carmen asked. "Is he okay? What happened?"

"I told you to go home. How come you didn't go home?" Ana asked.

"We thought something had happened to 'Apá," Diego explained. Something *had* happened to their father, but not what they had imagined. They looked to Ana for answers.

"Did one of the men at his worksite get hurt?" Carmen asked.

"No, it's not from work," Diego said. He didn't know what had happened, but he knew it had nothing to do with work. If that were the case, more of the men would be there keeping vigil, the way men who watch each other's backs in the course of a workday do, because when one goes down, they all go down.

"How do you know?" Carmen asked her brother. When he didn't answer, she turned to see a doctor approach Esteban and take him by the arm down the hall and out of sight. Carmen followed and Ana called for her. Carmen pushed by anyone who was in her way. It was like he disappeared into the air, and Carmen panicked.

When she finally found him, he was in a small room, sitting on the edge of a chair, one knee on the floor. The doctor was bent over Esteban with his hand on his shoulder.

"I'm sorry for your loss," he said. The words tripped something in Esteban that made him let loose a sound that didn't make sense coming from him—a cry that was ugly and frail.

Ana and Diego reached Carmen and the three of them saw Esteban. The doctor tried to help Esteban to his feet, but he waved him away as if he couldn't stand to be touched. The doctor decided to give Esteban his privacy. As he left the small room, he saw Ana and her children.

"Are you with him?"

Diego nodded for the three of them.

"Give him a moment."

Carmen and Diego had never seen their father cry. When their father left, they felt as if the house had collapsed on top of them, but this—this was far worse. They could see that their father was in misery, and that in itself made their heated anger and confusion seem puny. Neither of them knew what to do. They looked to Ana, again, for guidance. She had no idea of what to say or do, but she knew she had to try.

"He lost someone. Someone he loved very much," she said. "That's all I can tell you right now."

"Who?" Carmen asked.

"Let's go home," Ana said.

"Who?!" Carmen demanded.

"Nobody we know," Diego said. Ana looked at her son and felt sick. Ay, qué desgracia! He knew more than she thought he knew. That knowledge brought her some relief, but mostly heartache, knowing that her son carried burning disappointment. That hurt her more than anything Esteban had done to her.

"Carmen, please—let's go home," Ana said.

"I want to stay with him," Carmen said, as she moved toward her father.

"Carmen!" Diego pleaded.

"'Apá?" Carmen said gently. Her face was bright and expectant, like a little girl's. Ana's heart twinged. Her girl had no idea what she was approaching, the howl of grief that Esteban must be feeling. Carmen wanted to make it better, and no matter how hard she tried, Ana knew it would never happen.

Esteban stared down at the floor. He was now standing on both knees, seated on his haunches, his hands gripping his thighs. He refused to look at his daughter. His cry was now reduced to snorts and pants.

"Go home," he barked.

"I want to stay with you," Carmen said tenderly.

"Go home!"

"'Apá . . ."

"Go home with your mother where you belong."

TWENTY-TWO

Ana wasn't surprised when Carmen refused to go to school the next day. She told Diego he could stay home, too, but he didn't want to.

"Unless you need me here," he said to his mother, as he was going out the door.

"No, mi'jito. I think we'll be fine."

Carmen wasn't talking. She did not come out of her room most of the day, playing her power punk and pop CDs, the Sweethearts, Girl in a Coma, Piñata Protest, before moving on to los oldies, Blondie, Joan Jett, and the Go-Gos. Around noon, she turned to the hard stuff borrowed from her brother's room: the Ramones, Black Flag, and some other raw nerve music that finally made Ana ask her daughter to listen with her headphones on. Carmen didn't argue, but as soon as the music went silent, Ana worried about what was going through her daughter's head. Maybe distance was best for now.

Ana kept trying to track down a photographer and deal with all the last-minute details of the quinceañera. As planned, the girls showed up after school with their mothers carrying baskets and bins of hair rollers, brushes, lotions, and sprays.

"Bianca told us to come here for the final fitting," Alicia, or Mari, or Patti said.

Ana sent them to Carmen's room and tried to make small talk, offering the mothers iced tea, but they could all tell something was wrong. They were asking a thousand questions Ana didn't care about: Panty hose or bare legs? Lipstick or lip gloss? Would the girls get to ride in the limo to the reception? Who would drive them back to their cars? Ana was relieved when Bianca showed up, and, just like always, she was happy to take charge.

"Siéntate, Tía," Bianca instructed. Ana sat on the couch with the other mothers. The girls came out, one after another, each more adorable than the previous. Even the cousin shaped like an apple looked sweet, a flounce at the hip helping to give her a waistline. Her fry-dyed mother clasped her hands to her heart. ("Ay! Qué chula!") Bianca pulled out a pair of lacey, fingerless gloves for the apple-shaped girl, who was relieved that her swollen knuckles would be covered.

"I got gloves for all of you, so you can match. If you want," Bianca said.

The girls looked at each other and decided they should all match. Bianca went about checking hems and bodices and clipping loose threads, after which the girls went off, each feeling confident that she looked as lovely as she felt. They were returning to Carmen's room to change and get ready for the final rehearsal when a soft "ahh" came from Carmen's room. When Ana finally saw her little girl she was astonished. What had happened to her baby girl? Unlike the others, Carmen's dress was floor length but strapless, in a gleaming satin with a small shrug trimmed with a wide ruffle, which framed her face like a bud. When Ana got a good look at the dress, she noticed that the shrug was also white but was patterned with white-on-white tiger stripes!

"Bianca! Where did you find this material?!" Ana gasped.

"It wasn't easy," Bianca said. She began to corral the girls into cars so they could head to church and then to the reception hall for the final run-through. Diego had just shown up when the girls were being herded out.

"Diego! Don't be late for rehearsal!" Bianca called over the chatter. When the girls and their mothers and Bianca were all gone, it was just Diego, his sister, and Ana. The house was weirdly quiet. He set down his books and sat.

"You look nice," he said to his sister, who was looking at herself in the mirror they'd moved to the living area. She looked at him and smiled meekly.

"Thanks."

"Carmen, let me make you a quick something before we go."

"Okay," she said, and they all went into the kitchen. Ana began spreading some peanut butter and jelly on bread when the doorbell rang.

Diego went to answer it, and when he returned to the kitchen Esteban was behind him. He was carrying his cowboy hat with a large plastic bag inside.

"Buenas," he said to Ana and Carmen, as if he were a guest in the house. Carmen's mood brightened. She offered her father a seat at the table and asked if he wanted half of her sandwich.

"Ay, mi'ja. Let me get a look at you."

Carmen twirled in her dress and Esteban was amazed at how lovely his little girl was. He looked at Ana, and for a brief moment of grace, they were on the same wavelength. They were both proud of their girl, while at the same time sad that she was no longer their baby but, soon enough, a young woman ready to go into the world.

"I came by to give you this," he said. Ana thought he

was going to give her the necklace he showed her before, but he surprised her by pulling the plastic bag from his hat and handing it to his daughter. The bag was filled with water and three goldfish, happily swirling around.

"I remembered you told me, so . . . I know this isn't the time, but I wanted you to have them for your pond."

"Thank you, 'Apá," Carmen said. She took the bag from him and set it on the table. "They're cute, 'Apá!" Carmen could see that her father had something else to say. She took his rough hand and held it like she did when she was a little girl.

"I wanted to do something because, I know the fish don't have anything to do with the quinceañera, pero, I—I don't think I can make it," Esteban finally said.

"Why not?" Diego said. He looked at his sister, expecting to see her break into tears or one of her tantrums, but she looked at her father dearly, as if there was nothing, *nothing,* that he could say that would turn her heart. "Why not?" he demanded again.

"Shut up, D," Carmen said. "'Apá, is there something else?"

Esteban didn't answer.

"Why can't you come?" Diego asked again. Esteban looked up at his son and then back down to the floor. "Well, then, will you tell us what happened yesterday?"

"Diego, that's enough," Ana said.

"We want to know," Diego said.

"I don't have to explain myself to you, mi'jo," Esteban said tightly.

"We wish you would," Diego said.

Ana looked at Esteban.

"Dígales," Ana said. "Tell them something, if that's what you came here for."

Esteban felt as if he were caked up to his neck in cement. He looked into his children's faces, then out the window.

"I am not proud . . . I'm not proud . . . some things I've done I am not proud of, but I am proud of you. You will always be my children but I . . ." He put on his cowboy hat and pulled it down near his eyes. Somehow, that made him better able to speak. Carmen sat down so she could look up into her father's face. She looked like an angel, Ana thought. Her love for her father was still delicate and pure and unmarked.

"It's okay, 'Apá."

"Your mother is a good woman, and I want you to always respect her," he continued. "Yesterday . . ." Esteban cleared his throat again and shifted his weight to the other leg. Inside he was screaming. He wanted to leave. It would have been easier to storm out, shouting obscenities, as if he had been wronged. That would have been easier. But he had decided it was right to stay and face his children.

"I lost a baby. A girl. She wasn't that far along. Maybe four months. There was trouble from the beginning."

Carmen stood up, looking as if her youth had been drained from her face. Esteban thought about going to her, but the idea of her pushing him away—ay, no!—he couldn't take it. He continued talking, as Carmen moved to the window and stared out into the pond.

"Besides you, I have another little girl named Carmela. She's three." Carmen felt as if she had been kicked in the stomach. Her face was lifeless. Ana was afraid she'd stopped breathing. Esteban took a deep breath and continued: "But the baby—the new one—we lost her yesterday."

"'We'?" Carmen asked. "What do you mean 'we'?"

Esteban didn't want to cry again. He couldn't. He bit his lip and scratched his chin.

"So, it's not just us?" Carmen asked.

Esteban shook his head and shifted to the other leg.

"Why?" she asked.

Why? *Why?* There is no real answer to that question, but Carmen wanted to know. For the rest of her life, she would always want to know.

"Why, 'Apá?" she asked louder. "Why?"

"Perdóname, mi'jita. Perdóname, pero I have to go get ready to bury my baby girl."

Esteban turned to leave. There was no other sound in the house except for the dull thump of his boots striking the wood floor as he walked into the dining area, through the living area, and out the front door. Ana searched Carmen's face for some sign of what was next. Carmen's barren expression worried her. She went to her daughter and tentatively put her arms around her, and when Carmen sank into her arms, Ana felt a bittersweet pang. She wanted to spare her children this most bitter disappointment in someone they loved, but she had failed.

"Mi'ja?" Ana whispered. "If you don't want to have the quinceañera, we can cancel it."

"We can do it," she said.

"We don't have to," Ana said.

"Yes, we do," Carmen said. "Everybody is here, and Bianca and everybody went to a lot of trouble. It's okay. Only I don't want him there. I don't ever want to see him again." Carmen went to her room to change. Diego stood silently, and Ana turned to him.

"Mi'jo?" She put her hand on his shoulder, but he turned away angrily and headed for the door.

"Diego! Where are you going?" Ana asked frantically.

But Diego didn't answer her. She felt a knot forming in her temple. She wondered if she should have said more, or cried, or screamed, or tore at Esteban. She didn't know anything, but when Carmen returned to the kitchen ready to leave, she knew she wanted to try and make the best of this very strange situation. She didn't want Carmen to remember her fifteenth birthday for this. How she was going to make that happen, she didn't know.

Ana went through the quinceañera rehearsal in a daze, and she took no "I told you so" pleasure in telling her brother, Marcos, that he had been elevated from Padrino de vestidos to the father figure who would escort her daughter down the aisle of the church.

For once, a sad "Ay, Esteban" was the most he could say, and that was good enough for Ana. She was too worried about where Diego had gone to argue with her brother. She wondered if continuing with the quinceañera was a good idea, if going through with it was right for Carmen, and if there was something she could have done to avoid the whole situation altogether.

When they got home, Ana called everyone she could think of to see if they had seen Diego, including Sonia and her father—whom of course, she had already asked several times at the rehearsal. Sonia promised Ana that she would call her if she heard from him. Calls to Esteban and Diego went unanswered, and worry was beginning to choke her.

It was midnight when Ana thought she should call the police. Thankfully, Diego called her first.

"Where are you, mi'jo?" Ana asked, too relieved to be angry.

"I drove around, and then I, um, I went and talked with 'Apá."

Ana didn't bother asking what they talked about. She assumed it was one of those conversations that only men understand—with few words about the real reason pulling them together but bringing them to a place where they can at least respect one another. With fathers and sons, Ana decided, that strange, still dance had its own, special tempo, its own frequency that she could never hope to fully hear. Sometimes there are no words to substitute for the simple, healing act of sharing space.

"You could have called me!" Ana said. "I've been freaking out!"

"I know. I'm sorry."

"When are you coming home?"

"I'm leaving now," Diego said.

When Ana hung up the phone she heard Carmen get up and go into the bathroom. The sound of her daughter vomiting made her rush in.

"Mi'ja! Ay, mi'ja!" Ana cried. Carmen's face was red and swollen from crying. Her daughter was going to be the reigning princess of the day, but she still cried like a little girl, swallowing phlegm until it made her sick.

"Really, Carmen, *really*. We don't have to do it if you are not up to it." Ana felt guilty. It had been her idea to have the quinceañera. Carmen didn't want to do it, but Ana kept pushing for it. Bianca kept pushing for it. Carmen may have agreed out of her own sneaky reasons, but the idea of making her daughter go through with the quinceañera now made Ana feel like the worst mother on earth.

"Carmen, I would understand if you don't want to go through with it," Ana said, her voice cracking. "Really, mi'ja. This day was supposed to be for you, and now it's all . . ."

Carmen finished spitting up and Ana rubbed her back and ran a shower for her as Carmen brushed her teeth. Ana made up her bed with fresh sheets. As Carmen showered, Ana wondered how loudly the tías y primas would howl when she called them first thing in the morning to tell them the quinceañera was off.

When Carmen returned to her room wearing fresh pajamas and her hair wrapped in a towel, she sat on her bed next to her mother.

"It's okay, Carmen," Ana said. "We don't have to do it."

"I can do it. I have to do it."

"No, you don't," Ana said.

"Yes, I do," Carmen said. "I was trying to figure out why you didn't say anything about all this before, why you let me think you had kicked 'Apá out, and how mean I was to you. I was so mean to you, 'Amá. I was *so* mean! All the things I said and did. I couldn't figure out why you didn't say anything." Carmen looked at her mother, realizing the million little deaths Ana had suffered because of her. "You deserve a better daughter. I need to try. I need to be as good a daughter as you've been a mother."

Ana burst into tears. Diego had just come home, and when he saw the two of them sitting on Carmen's bed, Ana crying and Carmen sitting there, he couldn't believe it.

"Damn it, Carmensa! What did you do? Why do you always need to be so—"

"Leave her alone!" Ana cried, taking Carmen in her arms and Carmen embracing her back. "Leave her alone! Leave her alone! She didn't do anything wrong!"

Diego was perplexed. "Then, why are you crying?"

Carmen was now in tears, too. She looked at her mother

and they both exploded into laughter, sniffling and wiping their eyes, crying and laughing at the same time. Diego began to wonder if he should have stayed at his father's house.

"No, really," he said, trying to be very serious. "What did you do?" His question only made them cry and laugh harder. Diego gave up.

"I'm going to bed," he said, leaving his mother and sister to continue whatever it was they were doing. He was exhausted. His mother and sister were punch-drunk, finally unburdened of the jagged emotions that had bent their spirits, twisted their smiles, and made them talk to each other with sharp words all these months. It took an hour for them to finally settle down and for the Ruiz house to finally fall into a peaceful silence.

Diego left the house when the girls started showing up for their primping. He stayed long enough to see how pretty his Sonia was and asked Ana to take a picture of the two of them.

"Let's make sure to get another one from Mocte!" Ana said. She woke up in the middle of the night, thinking that Mocte might be able to help her with her photographer problem. She called him as soon as the sun came up.

"I know this is ridiculously short notice, but do you know anyone who can help me?" Ana had asked.

"Yes, miss. Me," Mocte said. "'Member how I got those pictures ready for the Montalvo reception? If that's good enough for you, I can do this for you."

Ana was drunk with relief. "Mocte, you *rawk*!"

A crack baby, a ward of the state, a foster child, a huffer, a onetime street hustler, a born-again Christian, a Chicano activist, and a telemarketer. Now Moctezuma Valdez could add photographer to his biography. In a few short years, when he would have the first exhibit of his large-format photographs, Ana Ruiz would be the first he would thank for helping him discover what he was meant to do with his life.

Ana turned to look at the houseful of girls and their mothers preparing for the quinceañera. Beatriz came over with pan dulce, made coffee and juice, helped with traffic control, and was ready for any last-minute errands. When Ana told her what had happened with Esteban, she couldn't believe it.

"Wow," Beatriz said. "Wow. Are you okay?"

"I'm not the one who lost a child," Ana said. "Carmen said she doesn't want to see him ever again, but I don't think that will last."

"So, what's the status with the two of you?"

"I think I've done all I can do," Ana said. The two friends quietly drank their coffee as they watched the girls and their mothers get ready for the quinceañera. Ana knew most of the girls since they were children, and there was something thrilling and sad about watching them get ready. Ana's fondest memories of Carmen and Bianca were when they were girls. If only they knew how much they would be giving up when they whined to her about how they couldn't wait to grow up. There were good things about being a woman, but being a woman wasn't about wearing high heels or getting to wear lipstick, or staying up past midnight, though that's what she suspected most of these girls thought it meant. And it wasn't just about the body changing and going through that transformation.

"So, what do you think our ancestors were thinking when they started this ritual? What are we commemorating here?" Beatriz asked, as if reading her comadre's mind. "The death of a girl or the birth of a woman?"

"I don't know about them, but I'm celebrating survival," Ana said.

"Tía?"

Ana turned to see Bianca fully dressed and ready to go.

"Ay, mi'ja! You look so pretty!"

"Do you think you can handle things here? I want to go show my mom how I look."

"Of course," Ana said. "But watch the time, eh? We're not going to start without you."

When Bianca got to the facility where her mother was staying, Teresa was already dressed and waiting for her daughter near the window in the common room.

"She's here!" she called out, when she saw Bianca's pink Bug pull onto the grounds. "She's here!"

All the nurses and attendants gathered around to see what all the excitement was about. By the time Bianca got to the building, the main corridor was lined on both sides with attendants, patients, and visitors, curious to see who the lovely young woman was who'd entered the building.

"You look real nice," Abel, the attendant who had bet against Bianca, said. "Doesn't she look pretty?"

"She sure does," Marie said.

"Let's go over here in the light," Teresa said to her daughter. Teresa asked Abel to take a picture of her and her daughter, and she smiled brightly as they stood together.

"I have something for you," Teresa said. She pulled out a crumpled paper bag and gave it to Bianca. "Here. I'm

not supposed to have it, and it belongs to you anyway."
Bianca dug into the sack carefully and was shocked to find
a tiara—her tiara from the quinceañera that wasn't.

"How did you get this?" Bianca asked. "I thought—I
didn't know where it went. I thought it was lost forever."

"Now, you have something pretty to wear today."

"No, Mami—it's not my quinceañera. It's Carmen's.
I'm going to be the Madrina de la tiara. So, I can't wear
this," Bianca explained. "Only the quince gets to wear the
tiara. Remember?"

"I don't want to remember that day the way it was. I
want to remember it the way it should have been," Teresa
said. "Please, just put it on for me to see."

Bianca wasn't sure if it was a good idea, but she did as
her mother asked, and it made Teresa ecstatic.

"Oh!" Teresa said. "I want to make it better."

"There's nothing to make better," Bianca said. "I have
to go, Mami. I can't be late." She started to take off the
tiara, and Teresa began to whimper.

"No! Leave it! Leave it! You should wear it!"

"I'm not going to my quinceañera, Mami."

"Well then, keep it. It belongs to you. But I have something else." She shoved her hands into her other pocket
and pulled out a small velvet-covered box and handed it
to her daughter. Bianca was shocked when she saw what
was inside.

"Those are my favorite earrings," Teresa said. "I
bought them specifically for your quinceañera. They might
be too grown-up for you, but if you're old enough to be a
madrina, I think you're old enough for a good pair of diamond earrings."

Bianca noticed how hard her mother was working to
be clear and focused, and she decided she should ask the

question she'd been wondering about since she began visiting her mother.

"Mami, do you—do you want to come?"

Teresa was tempted, but her fear was larger.

"Oh no. Oh no. Oh no. I can't leave here. I can't," Teresa said.

"Okay, okay," Bianca said, patting her mother's hand. "I'm sorry. I didn't mean to upset you. I just wanted you to know, you're invited," Bianca said. Teresa immediately calmed down.

"I have nothing to wear. I have nothing to wear, and my hair. No, I can't go. Not today. Not yet."

Bianca tried on the earrings and Teresa was pleased.

"Oh—you're almost all grown up," Teresa said forlornly. "Promise me something."

"Mande."

"Promise to bring me back a piece of cake and to take lots of pictures. And . . ."

"What else, Mami?"

"Don't forget me in here. I'm going to come and visit you one day. Out there. Not today, but soon. I will," Teresa said. "But not today."

Bianca wasn't sure her mother would be able to keep her promise, but it didn't matter. It was the idea that she wanted to try that mattered most to her. Bianca would be surprised and most touched when she organized her first trunk show and Teresa de la Torre was there, looking todo fabulous on her proud husband's arm.

Ay, the way people talk! The chismosas were in high gear when it came time to start Carmen's quinceañera. There's something about drama—especially when it's someone else's drama—to get the mouths blabbing. Everyone likes to watch a fire, but the chismosas really love to fan it, starting rumors about this and that, making people wonder what's going to happen next. So, let me tell you how it *really* happened before the truth gets burnt.

The day was a blur until Ana found herself standing on the steps of the church, her feet throbbing, and her hair wilting, but she didn't care. She didn't even care when the cake was late. And who said the mariachi didn't come? No, they were late, too, driving around in circles, which is easy to do porque San Antonio is laid out on a wagon wheel. No joke. Cynthia finally called and Ana set them straight. The tiara? The quince doesn't get the tiara until she's up there at the front of the church! Híjole! Everyone knows that! And since Bianca was the Madrina de la tiara, you know for sure that that thing was going to be right where it was supposed to be, when it was supposed to be. Bianca tearing her dress? Pura mentira. Rafa ignored Bianca's offer to give him a touch-up for his black eye, and the boy poked aquí and ollá, that was just El Rey trying to be helpful. And it was a good thing, too, because when the cake almost fell, who do you think was there to save it? Even the apple-shaped girl who almost popped him the day before had to give him props for that. The only time Ana worried, really worried, was when she could not find Diego and she didn't know where he was. When he showed up with Esteban, she was afraid there was going to be trouble, so all of them went to the room where Carmen was waiting for the ceremony to begin. When the door snapped shut and it was just the four of them—Diego, Esteban, Ana, and Carmen—Diego turned to his sister.

"He should be here," he said to his sister. "I know

what you said and I know this is your deal, but he should be here."

Carmen said she never wanted to see him again, and if Ana were to be truthful, she would have loved to have kept Carmen and this day all to herself, but she knew that was not right.

"Mi'ja, he's your father," Ana said into Carmen's ear. "I know what you said, and I know you meant it, but trust me—this will be one of those times you will always regret if you do it the wrong way."

The woman who worked for the church knocked on the door. The ceremony had to begin.

"I want you to walk me in," Carmen said.

"You mean, me and your tío Marcos?" Ana asked.

"No, just you and me."

Ana wasn't sure if that was the right thing to do.

"'Apá can dance with me at the reception," Carmen said. They hadn't practiced the fancy dance Bianca had choreographed for the reception, but Esteban would do his very best. He would try. And Ana was right. Many years later, when Carmen looked back at her quinceañera, she would agree that she was glad Esteban was there after all, porque that first waltz was the first step on the long climb to forgiveness.

"Thank you," Esteban said to Ana. "Thank you." He was still in shock and mourning. He lost one daughter, he was going to do all he could not to lose another. Later, when he was old, and living alone with his thoughts, his garden, his tools, and his TV, he would look forward to the days when his two girls, one a young mother and the other visiting from out of town, would come as sisters and friends, to check on their old 'apá.

This would not be the end of drama in Ana's long life. Ay, no, but at least it was the kind she was looking for. She lost her luggage in Rome. She broke a tooth in Ireland. In Paris, she thought she lost her wallet but was relieved when a handsome stranger returned it to her. She invited him for coffee afterward and spent the next morning eating cheese and apples in his bed. She spent one New Year's Eve in Mexico City and another in New Zealand with Beatriz. Ana would not marry again, but she would never be alone.

As Cynthia played "Las Mañanitas" on her harp, and the court filed in, Carmen and Ana stood in the back of the church, the last of the pairs to walk down the aisle. As they started walking, Carmen looked at her mother, clasped her hand, and promised herself she would never, ever let her go.

READING GROUP GUIDE

1. Did you have a quinceañera, a sweet sixteen, or a bat mitzvah? What did it mean to you? To your loved ones?

2. Traditional quinceañeras have deep ties to Catholicism. How is religion treated in this novel? In your opinion, is it a good thing that traditionally religious celebrations (like the quinceañera) are becoming increasingly secular? Why?

3. There are several stereotypes that this novel plays with and ultimately diffuses. For example, Mocte describes Cynthia as "the white girl from Kansas." However, she is probably more familiar with Mexican folk music than any of the other characters in the novel, as she is in the mariachi band. Can you name some other stereotypes this novel entertains and then turns on their heads?

4. When Ana first meets Montalvo, she is obviously struck by his physical presence. Although she senses his interest in her, she does not allow herself to enter a relationship with him. What do you think of her reaction? Is it noble? Should Ana have been more responsive to his advances?

5. Do the young adults in the novel see the quinceañera as merely an opportunity to have a party, or do they attach greater significance to it?

6. What happened to Esteban and Ana's marriage? Was it just the indiscretion that drove them apart?

7. What do you think of Montalvo's self-absorption? Do you see it as a manifestation of the artist maintaining his autonomy, or a selfish and immature approach to life?

8. There are early clues that Montalvo may not be as wonderful as he seems. Can you name some of them? Were you surprised by his behavior when he revealed his ultimate plans to Ana?

9. Near the end of the novel, Beatriz asks Ana if the quinceañera is commemorating "the death of a girl or the birth of a woman." What is your opinion?

10. Ana protected her children by not telling them the truth about their father. Her children continued to look up to Esteban and blamed Ana for the separation, and yet she still didn't tell them about Esteban's affair. Why do you think she did this?

1. ¿Tuvo usted una quinceañera, una Sweet Sixteen, o una bat mitzvah? ¿Qué le significó? ¿Y a su familia?

2. Las quinceañeras tradicionales tienen lazos profundos con el catolicismo. ¿Cómo se trata la religión en esta novela? En su opinión, ¿es una buena cosa que las celebraciones tradicionalmente religiosas (como la quinceañera) están llegando a ser cada vez más seculares? ¿Por qué?

3. Hay varios estereotipos con los cuales esta novela juega y difunde al final. Por ejemplo, Mocte describe a Cynthia como "la muchacha blanca de Kansas". Sin embargo, ella probablemente sabe más sobre la música tradicional mexicana que algunos de los otros caracteres en la novela, porque ella está en el mariachi. ¿Puede usted nombrar algunos otros estereotipos que esta novela entretiene y como los gira?

4. Al principio, cuando Ana conoce a Montalvo, ella nota su presencia física. Aunque ella detecta su interés en ella, ella no se permite que incorpore una relación con él. ¿Qué piensa usted de su reacción?

¿Es noble? ¿Debe Ana haber sido más receptiva a sus avances cuidadosos?

5. ¿Cómo ven la quinceañera los jóvenes en la novela: como simplemente una oportunidad de tener una fiesta, o hay un significado más grande para ellos?

6. ¿Qué pasó con el matrimonio de Esteban y de Ana? ¿Fue solo la indiscreción que los separó?

7. ¿Qué piensa usted en el ensimismamiento de Montalvo? ¿Cree usted que es una manifestación del artista que mantiene su autonomía, o un acercamiento egoísta, y no maduro a la vida?

8. Hay pistas tempranas que indican que Montalvo no es tan maravilloso como él se parece. ¿Puede usted nombrar algunas de ellas? ¿Le sorprendió su comportamiento cuando él reveló sus últimos planes a Ana?

9. Cerca del fin de la novela, Beatriz le pregunta a Ana si la quinceañera está conmemorando "la muerte de una muchacha o el nacimiento de una mujer." ¿Cuál es su opinión?

10. Ana le protegió a su marido, quien la traicionó, por no decirle a los niños la verdad. Sus niños continuaron admirar a Esteban y le echaron a Ana todo la culpa por la separación, pero Ana todavía no les dijo nada sobre el asunto de Esteban. ¿Por qué piensa usted que Ana hizo esto?

**TURN THE PAGE
FOR A SNEAK PEEK
AT THE NEXT
≫ QUINCEAÑERA CLUB ≪
NOVEL:**

*Sisters, Strangers, and
Starting Over*

Beatriz was floating near the edge of sleep, where memories, dreams, and secrets seeped into the seen world. She was still tired from the day before and wasn't ready to wake up yet, happily sunk in the lazy sensations of her dreams: the sun on her naked back, bare feet in cool water, the smell of a newborn, first kisses, and laughter. It was the laughter that stirred her—wild and uncinched, the way children laugh. At first, she thought she was dreaming of her boys when they were little, wrestling like puppies in the backyard. But the laughter wasn't from her boys, it was from one child—a girl, her laughter tinkling like a bell that Beatriz remembered but had spent so much of her waking life trying to forget, she almost didn't recognize it. Just as Beatriz was about to realize whose laughter she was hearing, she felt a slump, as if someone had sat down hard on the edge of the bed near her feet. The sensation snatched her from her dream and she snapped her head up to see who was there. But there was no one.

The sun was just pulling itself into the sky, so Beatriz didn't need to turn on the lamp to see the outline of her husband, Larry, sleeping like a stone on his side of the bed. Her heart was racing, but she was relieved, taking in the familiar jut of her husband's jaw and the arc of his cheekbones. It wasn't light enough to see, but she knew a moss of reddish-brown hair flecked with gray, was sprouting around his mouth, over his jaw, and down his sinewy neck. Longer locks of that same-colored hair fell over his forehead and into the corner of one eye. Beatriz leaned over and swept the hair away with her fingertip and then laid her head on top of her hands to watch him sleep. One deep breath cleared the strangeness she felt earlier—it was just a weird dream, wasn't it? It didn't mean anything. It didn't even make sense. She steered her thoughts toward the long list of things to do before their anniversary party later in the day, even though she didn't want to get caught up in all that yet. What she wanted was to enjoy the stillness, when it was just her and Larry, alone in bed. She wanted to sway in the waves of his breath, sink into the luscious comfort of their bed, and enjoy the tantalizing closeness of his bare skin near hers.

When Beatriz saw Larry sleeping, she saw the boy she fell in love with twenty years ago. Twenty years already! It amazed her. She'd seen what her comadre Ana went through when her marriage crumbled—a painfully grinding breakup that almost turned her to dust. Since witnessing that, Beatriz began to wonder if long-term marriages were a thing of the past. But here she was, in bed with the man she loved and still loved more than she thought possible. Larry Milligan was the father of her children, two strong boys that had given them many days of joy and aggravation, sometimes at once.

And Beatriz couldn't think of a better companion to have gone through those days with. Larry was there for all of it, from the joyous moments to the let-me-crawl-under-the-bed blues. Beatriz felt a sudden twang of affection for her husband and wanted to kiss him, but she didn't want to wake him. It was going to be a long day and they needed all the rest they could get. But when she rolled over and closed her eyes, it was too late. The long list of things to do had already started filling her head, one popping into her head after the next, crowding each other and flowing over until she was staring wide-eyed at the ceiling. Beatriz sighed. Ana and some of the last-minute deliveries would show up early. She decided to get up and make sure everything they set up the night before was still as they left it.

Beatriz wrapped herself in the silky, emerald robe Larry had given her as an early anniversary present. He loved how the green fabric gleamed against her caramel-colored skin, how her hair cascaded over her shoulders, her curls crazy in contrast to the quiet smoothness of the cloth. He could barely contain himself when she modeled it for him, opening it to reveal the matching slip of a gown and exposing the voluptuous hips he adored. When she had crawled into bed the night before, Larry pulled Beatriz toward him ravenously. Unfortunately, they had been working on the house all day and into the evening, getting ready for their big pachanga. Both of them were hungry for some intimacy, but the comfort of their bed was more seductive, and they began to doze off.

"I'm sorry, mi amor," Larry slurred before he finally drifted off to sleep. A moment later, Beatriz was also sleeping, her arms wrapped around her husband's neck, her head nestled under his chin, Larry's hand cupping the fullest part of her rump, another one of his favorite parts of his wife's curvy body.

Beatriz cinched the robe around her waist and padded out of their room. As she made a cup of tea, she looked into the backyard. The extra tables and chairs they'd rented for the party were there, gleaming bright white against the adobe fence she and the boys had painted a warm pumpkin. The small tent set up next to the house for the bar area was still standing, as was the tent near the grill, opposite and away in the far corner of the yard. The long tables that would be covered with yards of slick Mexican oilcloth in bright reds and yellows that Beatriz bought at Fiesta on Main were standing end to end, ready for the food she had prepared the day before, and more to come from friends and loved ones. They could have catered their anniversary party, or reserved a nice restaurant, but Beatriz was tired of formal events. She had enough of that at work. She wanted a party where parents would feel comfortable bringing their kids, where guests could kick off their shoes and los viejos could sit in peace but not be ignored.

Beatriz stirred a drop of milk into her tea then walked out into the yard. The sweet magnolias from her neighbor's tree greeted her, and she inhaled deeply. She could see everything was in place from the night before. So why did she feel like something was not quite right? She walked around the entire yard, admiring the greenery Ana and her daughter, Carmen, had helped Beatriz plant along the fence last weekend. She took one of the wooden chairs stacked against the fence, opened it with a snap, and sat, resting her cup on one knee, which she crossed over the other. The basics were covered, Beatriz thought. So what was the problem? She closed her eyes. Maybe she dozed a little (or maybe she didn't), but when she felt a hand on her shoulder she lurched as if one of the legs of her chair had given way, making her tip her cup. The tea sloshed over her knee and down her leg.

"Ay, Dios!"

She turned to see who had snuck up on her, but there was no one. The sun was blinking through the branches of the jacaranda and the birds were chirping like crazy. Maybe they saw who touched her.

"Quién es?" Beatriz called out. "Who's there?" She stood up, wiping the tea from her knee and shaking the liquid from her hand, as she turned around. She could see she was alone, but she couldn't stop herself from asking, "Hello?"

This was not the first time this had happened to her. In bed, she could say it was just a dream, but when the weirdness began to happen when she was awake, she started to wonder.

One time she felt the hand on her shoulder when she was alone in her office. Another time, she was reading e-mail on her laptop at a coffee shop and was convinced the woman next to her was playing tricks on her. When the woman moved to another table to avoid Beatriz's darting glances, Beatriz decided the woman was probably innocent. Probably. No, this was not the only time Beatriz felt the strange sensation. The first time it happened, she was a little girl. Her baby sister, Perla, loved to sneak up on Beatriz and make her jump out of her skin. Beatriz didn't know how she did it, but every time, no matter how on guard Beatriz thought she was, somehow her sister found her and scared the living molé out of Beatriz so bad she would get angry and chase the little girl, who would run off, laughing devilishly.

"Chiflada! You gave me un susto!" Beatriz would scream. "Why can't you leave me alone?"

Perla was the baby of the family—that last surprise and

the only other girl after Beatriz and four brothers. The little girl adored Beatriz, who was twelve years older than her, and was the new light of their very tired daddy's dimming eyes.

"Leave me alone!" Beatriz would yell angrily, still horrified that her elderly parents had managed to, well, you know, produce this spit of a little girl whose only value seemed to be to make Beatriz's teenage years miserable.

Perla only laughed before running off to play with the other kids. One of Beatriz's last memories of Perla was not as a young woman but as that mischievous little girl with the gummy grin, the long, knobby-kneed legs, and skin as dark as molasses from playing in the sun.

Ay Perla, Beatriz thought. *Ay, Perla.*

Larry was coming out of the shower when Beatriz walked back into their bedroom. She shut the door behind her and walked over to the window that looked out into the backyard. Larry was humming to himself and drying his hair with a towel as he walked into the main part of their bedroom and saw Beatriz.

"Why, hello, señorita," he said in a pronounced Texas drawl. "May I say, you shore are the purtiest woman to walk into this room." He walked over to his wife and kissed her.

"Here's your coffee," Beatriz said.

Larry gently took the cup and placed it on the nightstand near them and took Beatriz in his arms.

"Happy anniversary, mi corazón." He pulled Beatriz up toward him and kissed her again, a long, lingering kiss that was fueled with all the pent-up passion he wasn't able to spend the night before. "And thank you for being the prettiest woman to walk into my life."

"Oh, my!" Beatriz said, suddenly feeling the hardness of her husband kneading her belly.

"I think we have some unfinished business," he murmured into her ear.

Beatriz smiled. "I think we do, too."

Larry hoisted his wife up off the floor and she wrapped her legs around his hips. They fell onto their unmade bed, and he continued to kiss Beatriz on her face and neck, pushing her up so he could cover her breasts with kisses. Beatriz was liking this. She was liking this a whole lot. The dream, the weirdness in the backyard, it all burst like a bubble. So, when the doorbell rang just as Larry had circled his tongue around Beatriz's nipple, she gasped.

Ana. Beatriz had forgotten she'd asked Ana to come early.

Reluctantly, knowing the moment was lost, Larry reached for his pants. "I'll get the door, mi amor. You get dressed to meet your comadre." Pulling his shirt over his head, he added with a wink, "And then I'll see you back here later."

By the time Ana came upstairs, Beatriz was already showered, towel-drying her hair while standing in front of the closet, deciding what to wear—the eggplant-colored dress that was comfortable, or the white, form-fitting dress that she knew would drive her husband wild?

"Hola!" Ana said, as she tapped on the door and poked her head inside the room. "Can I come in?"

"Sure. How are you?" Beatriz exchanged kisses on the cheek with Ana.

"How am I? How are you? What a big day! Do you need help with anything?"

Beatriz held up both dresses for Ana to see. "What do you think?"

"I like the white one," Ana said.

Beatriz frowned.

"Okay, I like the purple one. Wear whatever you'll be most comfortable in," Ana said.

Beatriz laid both dresses on the bed and began to shape her hair with her fingers.

"And don't worry about anything. I'll take care of those annoying details that come up at the last minute. Oh! That reminds me—I got the new guayabera for Larry. The one you asked me to pick up?"

"Uh-huh," Beatriz said, looking at her face in the mirror, trying to decide how much makeup to put on.

"Okay, then. Well—maybe I should leave you alone," Ana said, unsure of what was going through Beatriz's mind. "Are you okay?" she asked, as she reached the door.

"What? Sure!" Beatriz said. "I'm just—I don't know. I'm kind of out of it, I guess."

"Did you and Larry have a fight or something?"

"Oh, no," Beatriz smiled, imagining what their morning could have been like had they not had the party to deal with. "It's just—I wish everybody could be here, you know?"

"Ah, sí," Ana said, closing the door and leaning against it. "You mean your parents?"

"Yeah. I really miss them at times like this, you know?"

"Sure, sure," Ana said. "They would have loved this. When I walked in the house, something smelled so good, I thought your mother was cooking. But at least your brothers and their families are coming, right?"

"Yeah," Beatriz said faintly. "It'll be nice to have us all together again."

But that wasn't true. Sure, all the Sánchez brothers were coming in with their wives and children, but there was one sibling who would not be there: Perla. Beatriz wondered if any of them would dare bring up her name.

The guests began to arrive around eleven o'clock. The first wave was colleagues from work who dropped by to offer well wishes and intended to stay for only a couple of hours. But some of those guests were still lingering by the time the relatives began to show up around noon, their voices and laughter bubbling from the house and into the yard. Beatriz had forgotten all the weirdness from the morning, too busy greeting people, accepting dishes of food, giving directions, and, finally, enjoying all the activity. It wasn't until her oldest brother, Erasmo, showed up, that Beatriz was reminded of the earlier strangeness. Erasmo was the brother who looked most like their father, and as he got older the resemblance only became stronger. She hugged her big brother at the door, welcoming his family into her house. Her eyes were tightly closed as she hugged him close.

"Qué pasó?" Erasmo asked, when he could feel she was holding on to him a little longer than normal.

"Nothing, it's just that you look so much like 'Apá."

"Yeah," he said. "I get that a lot. But we're here, so they're here, too." He patted his sister's shoulder as he edged his way past her to get a look at their baby brother and his new wife, pregnant with their first child. Beatriz smiled a sad smile, thinking of what her brother said. He was right, she thought, as she closed the door to join the crowd. But as she looked out the door, she saw something that made her pause. A little girl was standing on the curb near her brother's truck, standing and waiting. Beatriz recognized the dress the little girl wore, and she blinked her eyes against the sun to try and see the girl's face. When the little girl smiled a gummy smile that Beatriz instantly recognized, a jolt of adrenaline shot through her.

"Erasmo! Erasmo!"

But Erasmo was lost in the loud bellows of hellos and laughter that come from too much time passing between seeing relatives and friends.

"Erasmo!"

"Mande!"

"Come here!" Her heart was racing now. If she was seeing what she thought she was seeing, she wanted Erasmo as a witness. He was the one they would believe.

"Erasmo!" she said, yelling into the house so she would be heard.

"Sí, sí, sí. Qué pasó?" he said, marching to the door as soon as he saw his sister's shocked expression.

"Did you bring that little girl?"

"Who?"

"Over there, the little girl standing by your truck."

When Erasmo looked out the door he reared back a little. He looked at her and shook his head.

"Little girl? That's *my* girl Angie, and her friend Lidia," he said. "No problema, eh? The more the better, verdad?" he asked, looking into his sister's anxious face. But the girl he was referring to wasn't the girl Beatriz saw, but a young woman walking up with Angie. Both were a year younger than her Carlos, who had just turned twenty.

"Hola, Tía," Angie said obediently, giving her aunt a kiss on the cheek. "This is my friend Lidia. 'Apá said you wouldn't mind if she came."

Beatriz looked over the young women's heads back where she thought she saw the little girl, but there was no one. It was a long moment before she realized that the two young women were still standing before her expectantly. Lidia glanced at Angie nervously.

"I hope it's okay I came," Lidia said.

The embarrassment in the girl's voice brought Beatriz back to the present.

"Discúlpeme! Of course! Of course, you're welcome! Please forgive me, I have a million things on my mind. Any friend of Angie's is a friend of mine. Pásale, mi'ja. Pásale." The girls slipped past Beatriz into the house and sought out the other young people in the crowd. Beatriz scanned the street for the little girl.

I saw her! Beatriz thought. *I saw her.*

But of course, that wouldn't be possible. Perla wouldn't be a little girl anymore; she would be a full-grown woman by now. *But it was her,* Beatriz thought. She knew it.

When Larry came behind his wife and slipped his arm around her waist, Beatriz shrieked.

"Jesus! Larry!"

"I'm sorry, love. My uncle James is asking for you. He's over by the bar," Larry said. Then, he noticed the stricken look on his wife's face. "Baby, what's wrong? You look like you saw a ghost!"

"I did—I mean, I thought—it's nothing. It's okay. I think I need to eat something."

"Well, then—you came to the right place," Larry said, swooping his wife back into the house.

ABOUT THE AUTHOR

BELINDA ACOSTA has written and published plays, short stories, and essays. As a journalist, her work has appeared in the *Austin-American Statesman*, the *Austin Chronicle*, the *San Antonio Express-News*, the *San Antonio Current*, *AlterNet*, *Poets & Writers,* and on National Public Radio's *Latino USA—the Radio Journal of News and Culture.*

Belinda received a master's of fine arts in writing from the University of Texas in 1997.

She lives in Austin, Texas, and is the TV columnist for the *Austin Chronicle.*